MORA TORI UM

MORA
TORI
UM

12-19-23
For Tony —
Thanks for your
help —
Holiday
Greetings
— Gary

SHORT STORY COLLECTION

GARY PERCESEPE

atmosphere press

Published by Atmosphere Press

Cover design by Senhor Tocas

atmospherepress.com

Praise for GARY PERCESEPE and *MORATORIUM*

"Powerful, deeply engaging stories that live in their history as if the past were the present. Percesepe has the gift of recreating time and place in the way of Philip Roth and Roddy Doyle, replete with telling detail and characters we can all recognize." ~ **T.C. Boyle**

"However he did it, these stories are simultaneously crisp and gentle, and, repeatedly, Gary Percesepe seems to have found the right viewing distance. The language and sentence cadences sometimes nod to Hemingway, by way of Carver. The stepping stones thrown down are literary, with a nod to (among others) Irwin Shaw, as well as to Patrick Modiano. These stories are surprisingly, refreshingly direct, involving, and very convincing. Really wonderful." ~ **Ann Beattie**

"Gary Percesepe's new collection is a jewel, a marvel, a remarkable find. These stories are tasty, tight, bitter, angry, deeply sad, occasionally relieved, and always about both teaching and learning. Moratorium is a gritty performative work that shakes the bones inside the closets where we hide all of our skeletons." ~ **Frederick Barthelme**

"Gary Percesepe is an American treasure, a master of short-form fiction whose signature minimalist style veers sharply between earthy naturalism, wry humor, and transcendent spiritual insight that blazes like sudden light on a window-pane. It's impossible to stop reading this powerful collection of stories of men and women fumbling toward acceptance and redemption as they emerge from states of emotional limbo created by the inevitable losses that life presents. Percesepe's characters are by turns dark, sexy, comical, and often maddeningly flawed, but are always depicted with a revivifying sense of wonder that renders them both deeply human, and unforgettable." ~ **Andrea Lee**

"There is a certain grace that permeates the air just north of Manhattan in the stories of Gary Percesepe's *Moratorium*. Percesepe's characters are haunted, lolling through long-simmering crises that began in childhood—the deaths or disappearances of siblings and friends, or the old burn of a high school romance, when the narrator memorized a young woman's gestures like a prayer, the question of his faith never fully answered. But the real magic occurs when Percesepe reveals humanity in all its dimensions, like when an eager student watches his famous novelist-teacher dance with a chair as his partner, a stand-in for Fitzgerald's Daisy Buchanan. These days are gone for Percesepe, but, lucky us—their generous revelations persist." ~ **Maureen Pilkington**

"The characters in *Moratorium* talk to each other a lot, but they are continually aware of the terrible things that are left unsaid. "I was striving for a kind of cool, remote distance from my body," one of them says, and this striving repeats in many of the stories, an escape from the exigencies of the flesh that the characters never achieve for long. These stories display the admirable flatness of reportage, but with an undertone of sorrow and bewilderment. The title story, like many of those that follow, is immediately gripping, a tale of family trauma that is linked inextricably to the national drama of war and civil unrest. In another, "Missionary," the characters struggle with religion and morality (which pull them in different directions). Marriage with all its delights and horrors—the territory of Cheever and Updike—takes a central place: many of the stories focus on divorce and infidelity, never more cleverly and almost tenderly than in "In Telluride," which features a revealing conversation on a plane among strangers who almost understand each other. This struggle to know and be known happens over and over in *Moratorium*, each time served up fresh to the reader with a wealth of well-chosen detail, compulsively readable and insinuatingly unforgettable." ~ **Mary Grimm**

"*Moratorium* is a gift of a collection: thirty-eight of Gary Percesepe's best stories from as far back as 1995, originally published in such places as *Story Quarterly, Mississippi Review,* and *Short Story American.* This is a writer who knows the human heart, renders lives and relationships with compassion and candor. These stories, run through as they are with love and sex and tenderness, missed connections and loss, never fail to leave a mark. How lucky we are to have them published together for the first time. My advice: Keep this book close, read from it often, allow yourself the pleasure of experiencing the world anew through Percesepe's inimitable voice and vision." ~ **Kathy Fish**

"These are stories of longing, love, and tragedy, where characters earn their downfall—or their redemption. Observant, witty, revealing, and always entertaining." ~ **Joelle Fraser**

"In this exquisite wonder seat, we learn to leave things out, and make as if we would go further." ~ **Ruth Margraff**

"The short stories in Gary Percesepe's *Moratorium* are funny and sad, messy and sexy and always wise. This collection is a wonder." ~ **Marcy Dermansky**

Resea Resea Resea Resea

TABLE OF CONTENTS

MORATORIUM

I haven't seen my sister in twenty years. She left home in September of her senior year. She didn't go far, just over to the next development, where she bunkered in with her history teacher, Judy Bennett, and waited for college. She came home occasionally for books or her mail, but otherwise we didn't see her much.

I was a sophomore that Fall, with a cheerleader girlfriend and a promising high school basketball career.

This was in 1969.

My coach was a West Point man who thought that I was lazy. He approached basketball with a sense of high moral purpose. Loose balls must be dived on, mistakes atoned. He was offended that I didn't sweat like the other players. When I took a charge or got knocked off a pick I always stayed on the floor a second longer than necessary, enjoying the change of perspective, the new view of those musky, twisted, competing bodies. I hated contact, and did my best not to present angles to be hit. I was rarely squared away on the court, angling sideways, elusive, never long in one place. Watchful, always in motion, hard to hit, I was striving for a kind of cool, remote distance from my body.

When Joan left things got ugly. My little brother Charles, drawn by the screaming, came downstairs and asked what was wrong. My father panicked and called the New York State Troopers. He slammed the phone down and cradled his head in his hands. Joan countered by calling the ACLU. Somehow she was put through to an attorney. In a calm voice she described the beatings she'd received, how our father tied her up and lashed her to the banister, how his sick Republican values had led him and Nixon and the country to this violent moment.

Then she added, And he murdered my brother Johnny.

My father roared his denials into the phone from behind my sister's ear. His large hands rose and fell in frantic gestures, chopping the turbulent air around her white throat. Joan's voice rose into the phone, "You hear him, he's mad! He's a lunatic, I told you. He wants to kill me. This is his fucking war come home, it's in his goddamn fucking living room now and he can't stand it, he still doesn't get it. Did you write down the address? I've got to get out of here. He's fucking crazy, I told you!" Charles bit his lip and looked pleadingly at me. Our mother whimpered in a corner, clutching her Bible to her chest and imploring God not to let the children see. Don't let them remember this, Dear Jesus, she kept repeating. And for twenty years I didn't. I had the scene on mental tape, but never played it. Until now.

By the time the Troopers arrived we had the living room equivalent of what Walter Cronkite on the CBS evening news might have called a demilitarized zone. Rooted to the ground, immobile, as if witnesses to a train wreck we stood there, mute with shock. Tall men with large gray hats and holstered guns, the State Troopers asked questions: What had happened? Nothing. Why had they been called? Silence. They looked at my father and pointedly asked: What do you want us to do? It was clear that my father had not thought about this question. Finally, he gestured to Joan's luggage, piled by the door, and asked them to give him a hand. They looked at him, then at Joan, who was crunched in the space between the kitchen and the hall, still holding the phone receiver in her left hand, staring into space. No one said anything. The dog circled and sat by the kitchen door. Finally, the Troopers helped Joan out the front door and when she left she didn't look back, not even to acknowledge our mother's pleas for a goodbye hug.

I see these things so clearly now. My mind, I knew then, was a camera. But it was as if I held the camera facing outward, it never focused on me. There was no interior footage, no camera for that. I was never in the picture. So much wound up on the cutting room floor.

I want it back.

*

Here is what I know so far:

My name is Joseph DeMarco

I am thirty-eight years old.

I am tired of lying.

My life is not working.

I am in Paris, on leave of absence from CBS, where I am regarded as a bright and ambitious technology reporter, with highly placed sources in Seattle and the Silicon Valley.

I have come to Paris to destroy what my life has become.

I know that I want to start over. And that I'm frightened. My wife and daughter wept when I told them I was leaving, but did not try to stop me. The flight I booked has an open return date. No one accompanied me to the airport.

I know that I prefer the company of women to that of men, though I don't know what to make of that.

I have been unfaithful to Liz, more times than I can remember, since before Abbey was born. I feel dispersed, like I'm out there, everywhere, and when I see a certain type of woman, with lyric beauty and tragic eyes, I feel that I've come back, I feel that I'll live forever. In her arms, things come into focus, temporarily. I want her. We set up a hotel civilization, the two of us, founded on lies, built from bits of borrowed time. It generally ends badly; I don't want to want her. Then the search begins again.

No one at work tried to stop me from going, no one pled with me to reconsider. No other family members were notified. My parents are dead, as are my brothers. Charles was killed while climbing Mont Blanc with some fraternity brothers. This was years ago. His fall, I am told, was spectacular. His grave, like Johnny's, is unmarked.

My sister ran away from Miss Bennett's house, on the night of the Moratorium against the Vietnam war. She never came back. Miss Bennett's story was believed generally, by the public: She didn't know anything, Joan just disappeared. She hasn't seen her. Some years ago, I met up with Judy Bennett at a party in New York. She had quit teaching the year after Joan's disappearance–she got the Peekskill job right out of college–and was a fund raiser for an environmental group that worked on cleaning up the Hudson. We had an affair. I still see her occasionally, though we haven't slept together in years. She is rumored to have contacts with radical ecology groups. She tells me she thinks of me as her brother. She holds to her story.

Joan is thought to be alive and active in the underground left. She is wanted by the F.B.I., who still search for her in connection with car bombings in several states on Christmas, 1972. These bombings were of black Buicks wrapped in white Christmas paper, with embossed red crosses and "Henry Kissenger, War Criminal," written in blood on the hoods. They occurred promptly and simultaneously at midnight, on wide boulevards in Midwestern states crucial to Nixon, with no fatalities but one famous maiming: An eight year old boy who had run from his parents after exiting a movie and tried to unwrap a Buick. There is a file photo of a woman in black running from the stricken boy, eyes wide apart, mouth open in a silent scream, dark hair flying. The Bureau believes this to be Joan.

Charles is buried at Mount Hope in Yonkers. My mother was eight months pregnant with him when Johnny died.

"Born to sorrow," my mother used to say. At the funeral, there was still no word from Joan, she was still lost to us, still at large. Standing beside my parents at the grave, I realized that Joan and I were shades of death. We were fading. We lived in a place halfway between the living and the dead. We hadn't much time.

After the graveside service I asked one of my uncles, a man reputed to have mafia connections, where my older brother was buried. No one seemed to know. Thirty feet away, my parents were helped into a waiting limousine. Asking them was out of the question. A buried child is a difficult thing to talk about under any circumstances. My uncle Ron lit a cigarette and shook his head, remembering. "Geez, Joe," he said. He ran his manicured fingernails through his curly hair, gestured vaguely over his shoulder and said, "Over that hill, on top, that way. It came so sudden, none of the family had any plots out here yet, we just looked in the yellow pages and found this place. Mount Hope. Your mother liked the sound of that. She was glad for the hill, too, she liked that, but there was no one around him at the time we buried him, no strangers." We stood silent for a while, standing up to the blasts of frigid air coming out of the north, looking up at the hill. He tugged at the collar of his topcoat, turned and faced me. "That was a tough one, that one. Not that this here is any picnic, you understand, but that one, well shit, we were all so young. We hadn't seen so much. No one could have seen it coming. It hit us all hard. You stayed with us. You don't remember that, do you?" He looked at me. I shook my head. "I thought so. How could you, you were what, three? Four?" He dropped his cigarette to the ground and crushed it with a patent leather shoe. "No," he said, "You wouldn't remember. Your father, though. I thought he was going to throw himself into the fucking grave with your brother. My sister—" He broke off, putting another cigarette to his mouth, and dabbing his eyes with his cuff. "Your mother—It was awful, trust me,

Joey. The worst."

*

I look out the window of my hotel at the cafes and art galleries of the narrow rue Jacob, on the left bank of the Seine. From here I can see the waiters in their short black vests, carrying their small trays, performing their timeless duties with an economy of movement, walking between the small crowded tables with quick, sudden steps. The brightly colored cars and trucks on the street seem to pass right through me. I have neither slept not eaten since I arrived two days ago. Hours ago, I went outside, thinking I was hungry. In the Sixth Arrondissement, entering a cathedral bathed in early morning light, I stood before the southern wall which holds the body of a dead philosopher famous for his meditations, interred upright.

I visit the streets of my childhood memory, in Yonkers, and try to call back the pieces of myself, back from wherever it is that they have gone. I vow to call true what comes back, in whatever way it appears, whether in dream or waking life. I want to swear off the sustaining lies of my middle age, and with them all of the strategies of self-evasion that have brought me to this moment.

My last affair ended last week. A girl named Wendy who worked in a video store, who snapped gum as she dusted the shelved movies and laughed the long, cleansing laugh of the young. The pattern of these affairs has finally become clear to me. Here, in a hotel room. The irony of this. I now can identify beginnings, middles, endings. As the structure of the affairs comes into focus the women themselves blur, become indistinct and interchangeable, then fade completely. Gone, too, the remembered rush of spontaneity that had accompanied the onset of a new affair, the feeling of newness I'd depended upon, that made the truth seem tired, dull, and irrelevant by comparison.

On the third day I let myself be lifted out of ordinary time, drawn into the draft of what was, of what has been. I sit in my room at the Hotel d'Angleterre, close my eyes, and wait for the jolt. Deprived of sleep, I can feel my consciousness thinning out, becoming translucent. Waiting here, in Paris, I see the tenses of my life hover and float, chaotically mix and separate, disappear. No past escapes imperfection, no future has been ruled out for possibility. The one thing that never could have happened, has. All is present at once, the way a god might remember, or a ghost with infinite capacity for substitutions. At last there is a sense of destiny, and with it the terrible things that are left unsaid.

I have spoken with Judy Bennett. A meeting is arranged. Tomorrow.

In the days after Joan's departure, my father withdrew. We didn't see him, though surely he was in the house somewhere, perhaps in the basement. He didn't sleep in my mother's bed. Lying beside her in the evenings, she confided in me: He wasn't a spiritual leader in the home. He was a man, the head of the house, but he wasn't fulfilling his God-given responsibilities, and if he didn't, what could she do, a wife? She had talked to Pastor about this. He was losing his family, my father. He was a gentle man, my father, you didn't know him then, she said. Her hot tears fell on the flowered sheets of the bed, dropped onto the pages of her open bible, blurring the black ink of Saint Paul's epistles. I cried with her. I was an oldest son. There was no talk of Johnny, her firstborn.

My father stopped talking to me. He was absent at my games that season, and the next. I had my career to myself. We all did.

Sometime in October my parents despaired of her ever returning, and I was assigned her old room. Entering her second floor bedroom, I felt like a trespasser, that this was a form of criminal behavior that would someday be prosecuted. I piled my stuff in the middle of her room like a tourist in a hotel. Face down on her bed I looked around the room and tried to connect things to Joan. It was hard. There wasn't much left. The bedsheets held a faint trace of her spicey scented bath splash. Her white dresser had three diamond shaped openings in each of the six drawers. It came equipped with colored placards three deep in each opening. You could alter the color according to your mood: blue, yellow, pink. Joan's were blue, but I found no great meaning here. The furniture, I now realized, had been my mother's idea. What I saw was a mother's idea of what her only daughter's room should look like. The telephone on the small night stand was white, the walls blue, the throw rugs on the polished hardwood floor, gray. The mirror I could see from my vantage point on the bed held an image, but not Joan's.

I wondered in that moment what it had been like for Joan in the mornings before school, what that mirror had shown her day by day. I thought about her putting on makeup. I tried to puzzle out the movements she might use, the delicate line of her arm raised, fingers touching face, the way her hands played over her skin. I raised my arms and waved them slowly, shifting positions on the bed until I saw them magically enter the mirror's memory. I looked at my hands, the visible part of my brain. So many things hands do, things they can remember, gestures that are learned in childhood: tie your shoes in kindergarten, mimic your father's strong, quick movements. Smile his smile back to him, inhale his pride, his manly smell, untie his knots. The hands in Joan's mirror had done this, by the banister, late at night, when her gentle weeping called me like a lover. I untied her hands, I read my father's knots.

In my Paris room, I sleep. The waters of childhood memory carry me back to Yonkers. I dream of angels and great swooping birds with faces like humans. I see a duck the size of a house peer in my window, wanting in. He taps lightly on the casement window, he shows me how to crank the lever, his white wings are hairy and hand-like, with leathery knuckles. I refuse. Astonished, he disappears. I awaken.

One Saturday, shortly after I inherited Joan's room, I visited her at Miss Bennett's house. I stopped on the way to pick up my friend Jeremy. The two of us walked down the Aqueduct that ran behind our development, connecting it to Waterbury Manor. We talked trash the whole way— which girls were hot, who'd gotten laid and who hadn't and who wasn't likely to. We stopped for a minute to harass three junior high kids who were throwing rocks at the pump house windows. Jeremy scowled and asked what the hell they thought they were doing, throwing rocks like that. This was community property, didn't they know that? What if everybody decided they could throw rocks at their houses? Where were their mothers, anyway?

Jeremy's feathery voice got higher with each question, and the brats kept throwing rocks. One of them finally hit a window. We heard the eerie sound of crashing glass falling on the concrete floor inside the empty pump house. Something turned over in me when I heard that shattering glass, some early scene of childhood disorder was jumping in my memory: another mess, another clean-up. Jeremy turned to look at me. A thin line of perspiration had formed above his upper lip. He looked pathetic, like a teammate frozen with embarrassment after throwing the ball out of bounds. I frowned and walked up to the biggest kid. Placing my hands on his shoulders, I turned him around so that he was facing his friends, then said, "I know who you are. All of you. I know your fathers." They ran off.

The pump house sat like a medieval castle at the top of a forty foot embankment. The mechanical heart of the New York water system, it pumped the precious fluid through clay arteries throughout the state. I'd looked at that pump house for years without seeing it. It was constructed of red brick and mortar. The four side windows were barred. There were dirt paths leading up to it on four sides. We climbed up one of those paths and put our faces to the north window, which was caked with grime, and peered between the black bars. Nothing. Jeremy walked to the door and took out his pocketknife. He picked the lock. We swung the heavy metal doors open. Inside, it was dark as night. Mutely we stood there, waiting. Expectant. And then we saw the pipes, gleaming. I touched one of them and felt the moisture beading on my finger. There was a low incessant rumbling that came up through the soles of our feet and made every move we made seem more important. There was an urgency in that building. I felt connected finally, to whatever it was, at the darkened source of all that mattered in this world.

I heard a sharp sudden intake of breath. It was Jeremy, beside me now, cussing. He had stepped on the glass the kids had broken. I helped him kick it away from the pipes to the side wall, our sneakers sliding sideways on the smooth cold floor. We didn't talk. It was silent as a church in that pumphouse. When we finished we walked to the doors and pulled them closed, taking care to see that the lock clicked.

Ten minutes later we were at Miss Bennett's house.

A tall guy with boozy breath answered the door. He said his name was Dan or Dave, I forget which. He invited us in when I told him my name. "Yeah," he said, "I know your sister." I glared at him until his eyes focused again and then said, "I'd like to see her." He shrugged and walked off down the hallway. Jeremy and I stood there by the door looking at the beer cans scattered on the floor, and the cheese dip spilled on the coffee table. I was wondering to myself how Miss Bennett fit in here when Dan or Dave came back in the room offering us drinks. Jeremy started to ask for a beer but I cut him off and said, "No thanks." The guy did this thing with his shoulders that was meant to be another shrug, you could see that was what he was after, but his timing was off this time, or maybe his muscles weren't up to it, and it came off looking like a bizarre kind of stretching maneuver, a bad imitation of that guy Jack Lalanne on TV. I looked at Jeremy and started to laugh, then checked myself when I heard loud screams coming from another part of the house.

The guy looked worried. He left us standing there, again. The screaming escalated into a full throated roar, then suddenly subsided. This was followed by a woman's mournful sobbing. Another woman's voice could be heard now, calm and soothing. Then a quiet whimpering.

Jeremy looked confused. I wasn't talking.

Minutes later, Joan came in. She was wearing a faded blue smock with hand painted daisies on it, and jeans with the knees and butt ripped out. On the smock, over her left breast, was a black and white button showing suburban Cape Cod houses, four in a row, and factories belching smoke. At the top you could make out some kind of luxury car, maybe a Lincoln Mark IV or a Cadillac, and at the bottom six businessmen with briefcases, each with a hat and topcoat, each going off in the morning to build America, to make her great. In the middle of the button, in the space that should have been the infrastructure of the houses and factories, it said "Middle Class."

Joan was always the political one in the family, the only one with the will, Christmas Day, 1968, to pull the World Book Encyclopedia from the dusty shelf, looking past the inscription to dead Johnny. "To Joan Marie, Joseph Allen and Charles Franklin," our mother had written in her shaky hand, "In memory of their brother Johnny, who had a thirst for knowledge." It was Joan who found Volume 9 and looked up Indochina and showed us maps at the Christmas dinner table. The war, though it came later, in the decade following Johnny's death, was nevertheless connected to it in some delayed, yet powerful way.

It was hard, in 1969, to see this. No one knew who to believe. Kids had learned to question the stories of their fathers and mothers, to find the loose thread in the family fabric and the courage to pull it. Nothing seemed to add up. There was not even agreement on so basic a question as whose war it was. It was easy to say that it was our parents' war and to let the fact escape us that it had become *our* war, the evidence for this mounting each week with the body counts. What was happening was violent. The war provoked violent emotions and we learned to be violent with each other, ruthless.

As far back as I can remember, Joan was teaching us. There were questions she thought couldn't be ignored. I guess, at the time, we thought ignoring them was okay. This annoyed her. She needed to know. If we couldn't tell her, she'd go elsewhere to find out. Joan was a female King of Thebes, relentless for the truth, even if it meant her own destruction.

She'd do anything, sacrifice anything, pay any price, but she was going to know. If she felt knowledge was being withheld, or that she was being lied to, she'd become enraged. Then she'd attack. She could be ferocious.

My sister, as a young girl, had liked to sit in my father's lap and look at maps. He used to tell us war stories, and Joan, as a child, listened closely. She was two years older than me. She went over the maps with my father, seated in his lap, while I played with toy soldiers and marbles in a corner of the living room, less anxious than Joan to enter history. Together, the two of them traced the dotted supply lines, the ragged lines of battle. But like most men of his generation when speaking of his war, he'd clam up if you asked him about what he'd seen, about the killing. He'd fought it, it was over, he thought. He wanted to rest now. But there seemed to be something inside that he wasn't facing, stories that he not only hadn't told us, but hadn't told to his wife, or even to himself. As she got older Joan sensed this, and she stirred something inside him. She brought it out in the open; he found what he needed to respond, then, riding her raw energy, and the result could be frightening. And now there was this other war. But no one had a good reason for why we were fighting it, or at least one that satisfied Joan. Once, my father screamed at her, "Why is it so damned important to you, Joan! Why can't you just accept it? Why can't you just live like the rest of us!" And Joan walked to the shelf, pulled down the World Book with its inscription to Johnny, and handed it to him.

Her sense of drama. The way she held us all spellbound, there in that living room, was intoxicating.

We were, I think, all a little bit in love with her. I know I was. She was an older sister.

*

Staring at her button there at Miss Bennett's I wanted to ask Joan if we were still a close family, ask her to give us all insight into what was happening to us, to shed light on family life now that it seemed like we were at the end of the world, adrift in a leaky ship, like those old world maps cartographers made that showed monsters and sea-demons at the edges of the known world. I wanted her to navigate us past them. But more than that I wanted to ask her when she was coming home, how she liked it there at Miss Bennett's, if there was anything I could get her, anything I could do for her.

Instead, what came out was, "Hey Joan. Great button."

She stared at me, disbelieving. Her brown eyes were puffy from crying and her hands looked swollen and pale. She glared at Jeremy until he looked at his shoes. Just then, Miss Bennett entered the room. She was tall and fair, and walked with a slight limp. She bent over the sink, and ran water over some dishes. When she saw that no one was talking she went to Joan and stood behind her, waiting. And then Joan said to me, "Is that it? That's all you got? Is that what you came here for, hotshot? Did they send you? That's it, isn't it? Boy wonder, with his pal Timmy, come over to rescue errant sister. Where's Lassie, boys?"

I got angry and denied it, No, no, no! No one had sent me, I told her.

Then why are you here? she asked.

It was a simple question, and it shouldn't have, but it did: It stumped me. A voice buried deep inside was prompting, *the pump house, you fool, tell her you want to show her the pump house,* but listening to it, and seeing Joan standing there before me, I was incoherent. I muttered something about just walking around with Jeremy in the neighborhood and she rolled her eyes and said, "Bullshit. You're a shitty liar, you know that? You're worse than them."

She put a flier in my hands. Her voiced was changed. She was talking to two children. "Look," she said, "Have you heard about the Moratorium? It's this Saturday. We're meeting at midnight at the school flagpole, in the parking lot, and we want you there. It's important for your class to be represented. Joe? Did you hear what I just said?"

And then I did it. I lost her. That she would think I would have gone all the way over there as a child spy for my parents, that she would have thought about me merely as someone to organize—it angered me. I momentarily flashed on my father's deep sadness, felt instinctively what remained unspeakable in him. Willingly in that moment I accepted the role of the good son, felt the anguish of the middle child, the eldest one still living. I didn't want any part of her movement, her protest. I began to have the sense that I have had ever since, that I didn't want to belong to anything, that I was not a joiner.

And what did I say to her in that moment?

"Mom and Dad are right. You're out of your mind."

Miss Bennett frowned. Joan spit on the dirty linoleum floor. Dan or Dave hustled out of the room, spilling his beer. I ripped the flyer in half, threw it to the floor, and steered Jeremy out the back door, slamming the screen door closed behind us.

That was the last time I saw my sister.

In my hotel: Insomnia.

The meeting is set for tomorrow, 10 A.M. At midnight I walk the Boulevard St. Michel, heading for the Bibliothèque Nationale, where I used to spend a great deal of time in my other life. Cars hiss by, and carriages carrying tourists. Horses hooves strike the pavement like a hundred angry hammers. A slender man, dressed completely in black, uses both his hands to turn down his overcoat collar, which keeps standing up in an annoying way. The way he walks is amusing, one foot on the curb and one on the black street. Then he gives a short hop, stops short, reaches for his collar again. I follow him. The restlessness of his walk has now moved to his shoulders. He draws them up, twice, and lets them fall. He does this six or seven times in rapid succession. Then he takes his umbrella and hooks the handle to the back of his coat collar. Vertical, it parts his back between the protruding shoulder blades. It seems to support him, he walks confidently now, striding, but the umbrella slips sideways, as if activated by demons, and the man's convulsive hands, shaking wildly, struggle to steady it against his spine, as though they want to make it part of his hopeless body.

I turn aside and cross the street. It feels impossibly wide, I have never seen it so wide. The far sidewalk appears like a shoreline that never quite comes into focus from the shaking sea. I stand for a while leaning against a bridge railing. My knees quake. I feel used up, as if this man's fear had been accepted and transferred to me. I have become him. I want his umbrella.

In bed: I dream that I am in my parents' house, seated at the kitchen table, when the phone rings. The caller's voice is Italian. He appears to ask for Joan, but there is a bad connection and the static on the line distorts his voice so that he sounds as though he is singing a strange Puccini aria. He has found work for her, he says, I must contact her. He gives an address and phone number for me to relay to Joan, and I want to, because I know she needs the money, but I have no pencil and he is talking too fast. Frantic, I call out to my parents, who come at a run and start speaking at once, then bark directions at me, so that I cannot hear the man on the phone. There are three voices speaking at once and it annoys me so that I scream also and as I do the line goes dead.

*

Morning. I sit in my room and try to remember what Joan looked like. She was short, our mother's height, maybe five foot two. Her hair was long and dark brown. When I was twelve, at the dinner table, I made the mistake of calling it black. She went into a rage, saying that no one of European descent had black hair, that this was known scientifically! She treated us to a learned disquisition on the hair color of the world's peoples, delivering it in a blistering stream of rabid words that were as molten lava creeping across the narrowing space between her mobile mouth and our astonished eyes. Couldn't we see, didn't we have eyes? Grabbing the ends, she thrust her hair out in front of our faces, holding it with both hands for our inspection. Then she flipped over a bowl of peas and stormed off to her room. The peas rolled across the table like tiny green marbles onto the floor. She was a furnace of contempt for anyone too stupid to know the difference between brown and black hair.

I find it odd that I cannot remember what my father or mother looked like when I was a child. After my father's death my mother didn't last long. She had a stroke, a major one, then a series of aftershocks that seemed momentarily to electrify her eyes, her blood popping in a series of invisible explosions. When she died last month I wanted to lay my head on the velvet pillow beneath her head in the casket, to feel the coolness of her cheek, to know the secret of her final end, a peace that passes all understanding.

Speak. Come, memory.

*

My earliest memory is of my sister.

I am standing on the balcony of my grandparents' home. It is Christmas. In my hands I hold Joan's new talking doll, her Christmas doll. She is below me, on the ground floor, calling, pleading with me. I throw the doll off the balcony. It crashes to the floor. Joan screams.

I am four. Joan is six. We have had to leave the big house where we lived, grandfather's house, because he has moved to Florida. We are at play in our apartment, in Yonkers, on Stanley Avenue. It is not a large apartment, and we are underfoot. It is morning. We step lightly over the vacuum cleaner with the easy grace of children. Our mother laughs as Joan draws pictures of snowflakes on the windows, wet with winter's condensation. Mother is baking apple pie for dinner, our favorite. The air smells inside the apartment is fruity and warm. The exhaust fan on the stove hums. Outside, I see it is snowing madly. Joan and I watch at the window together as our father shovels out the car. He is dressed, our father, in a heavy coat and black gloves. Beside him stands nine year old Johnny, our brother. The car's engine idles roughly, its windshield beaded with melting snow. It is a heavy February snow, and my father grows weary. Johnny takes the shovel manfully, and flails away at the snow. But he tires quickly, there is no end to the snow, and now he is cold. My father opens the rear door to the car on the passenger side, and Johnny climbs in to warm himself.

It happens with the quickness that terror comes upon you, with the suddenness that alters lives forever.

Our father appears at the door, Johnny's beautiful body limp in his arms. They fill the doorway of our apartment, blocking the light. On our father's face is a look that I have not seen before. My mother looks at his face, then at the silent form in his arms, and shrieks. We feel her spirit leave her body and carom off the walls, the cabinets, appliances, hurtling itself into the world of uncaring things until it crashes into my father, and me and Joan, then lies wailing on the tiled kitchen floor. After this, I remember, she had difficulty forming sentences. The parts of speech which she offered could not easily be formed into a whole. And my father began his long, slow journey to a place where he would never arrive, a place not on any map, where he sought to amend his misliving.

There are men in the room now, tall men with hats who stoop to the floor and place their heads near my brother's face. Johnny's face is blue. A tall tank appears, with clear tubing attached. The hatted men speak to each other but to no one else: Fumes, yes, odorless, doesn't take long, just backs up, carbon monoxide, we've seen this before, yes. Yes. One of them begins to beat on my brother's chest, hitting him harder and harder, shaking his hatted head. I scream. I tell him not to hit my brother. As they deliver their blows my brother's face turns bluer. I cry and ask my parents to tell this man to stop hitting Johnny. Can't they stop him from hitting?

I am sent upstairs to a neighbor. She is an old woman who smells of stale beer. She has no toys. Joan is not with me. I do not know where she is. I have taken my dog, a dachshund that Johnny won on a TV game show, and the dog's ball. I roll the ball and Sergeant gives chase, placing his long snout under the water heater to retrieve it. The old woman's hands are shaky as she answers the clanging phone. A horrible smell drifts up from the apartment beneath us. Acrid smoke curls upward from the floor register. My my, the old woman says, someone is burning something in this building.

I don't tell her what I know, that it's my mother's pie burning.

We meet in the church of the dead philosopher. She walks straight towards me and buries her head in my chest. In seconds we are rocking violently, wracked with sobs, so that I fear we will tip over backwards onto the stone floor. There are teary jokes about the dead philosopher, and remarks on each other's looks. Her olive skin is unlined and smooth, and she looks dangerously thin. As I press her to my chest again, now, she flutters like a small wounded bird.

"Were you followed?" she asks

"No, I don't think so."

"Good."

She slips a scrap of paper in my hand. "We can't stay long at any one place. Meet me at this address tonight at six. Goodbye, Joe."

Père Lachaise. Away from the camera clicking tourists, the beer caps and flowers strewn on Jim Morrison's grave, we walk to a far green place, in a corner near a fence. Joan walks ahead, her small hand in mine, tugging slightly. We sit.

"I come here a lot. This is the first place I found in Paris that I called mine."

"How long have you been in Paris?" I ask.

"Ten years, off and on. The party found it useful that I spoke French. I was useful for a long time. I'm not so useful anymore. They didn't like that I kept in contact with Judy. They figured she'd tell you, eventually."

"She didn't want to."

Joan is wearing a wig, shoulder length bleached blonde. I play with the ends, then say, "A girl with great blonde hair like this, why does she want to go and dye the roots black."

She laughs, then punches me and says, "Brown, asshole."

Her face clouds over. She looks up and says, "Bobby Turnmire."

"What?"

"Bobby Turnmire. The kid we hurt on Christmas. Did you know he's a systems analyst now with Hitachi? He works on Westchester Avenue in White Plains, down the road from where Dad used to work. He's got a wife and two kids and lives in Somers. He's okay."

"The embossing on the wrapping paper was a nice touch, I always thought."

"Yeah, well, that was my idea. All those art classes in high school."

She drops her head into her hands. She is sobbing now, shaking convulsively.

"It was awful, you know. The blood, Joey. I couldn't stop it. His arm was just gone. I didn't know where it was. I couldn’t find it. He just laid there bleeding out in the street and crying, and I freaked. I ran."

I try to hold her. "We run, Joan. That's what we do."

She looks up. She takes off the wig. Her hair is short and spiky, lighter than I remembered, the color of her eyes.

"Not anymore," she says.

We sit there on the damp grass, our legs crossed, Indian style, talking it out.

Before we leave, she takes out a homemade cross from her bag, just two straight twigs, really, lashed together with twine, the kind of thing you'd make at summer camp. She moves things around in the bag, then takes out another one, identical. Then two more. She sticks these crosses in the ground, twisting them in the soft earth until they stand by themselves, facing each other, about a foot high. Then she reaches in once more and pulls out the Book of Common Prayer.

It takes us about an hour, I'd say.

Later, we sit with our feet in the water at the fountain outside the Église de Saint Eustache. It's getting dark, a warm summer night. Joan rests her head on my shoulder. In her hands she holds a white and black tube of chapstick. Beside us, an elderly woman reaches into a picnic basket and pulls out a turtle. The turtle walks slowly towards us, pausing every few seconds to lift his head. His lidless eyes are small and unblinking.

"Joan, did you know that I went to live with Uncle Ron after Johnny died?"

"I didn't know where they had taken you," Joan says. "The last time I saw you Uncle Ron was carrying you through the snow to a car. I cried and called for you, but they wouldn't tell me where we were going. I remember I didn't go to school for a long time. I don't know how long it was. Mom cried the whole time, every day. Why do you think they separated us?"

"I don't know. At Charles' funeral I asked Uncle Ron what happened. It took awhile, but I finally got out of him that Mom had a breakdown after Johnny's death. They gave her electroshock, the whole fifties treatment, and put her away for a few months. I guess they thought it would be easier for Dad and Grandma to take care of just one."

The turtle is staring up at Joan, inches away from her bare knee. She reaches down and strokes the painted shell, from back to front, with the index finger of her left hand.

"I'm turning myself in, Joe. I was going to contact you to tell you last week, after Judy called to tell me about Mom."

I lift her head from my shoulder and turn her face toward me. She wears no make-up and her lips are chapped and broken. I reach over and take the chap stick from her hands and apply it gently to her lips, from the center outward, to the edges. She opens her mouth to make it easier, then purses them together.

"I called Judy, asked her to set it up. The Green Party, the press, Hoover's boys, the whole sorry spectacle. She's coming in tomorrow."

"Who's your lawyer?"

"William Kuntsler."

I nod, assured. "He's the best," I say.

"It's all set, Joe. I'll be okay."

I nod. "I know. I know you will. It's just that I'm getting used to having you around."

"Hey! I'm not going to be that easy to get rid of, you know."

Joan gets up and carries the turtle back to the woman. She comes back and stands behind me. With one hand she covers my eyes, with the other slips something into my hand. "Guess," she says. I use up my three guesses. I look. It's her middle class button, dented in the middle.

"You always liked this, so I figured, it's yours."

We laugh.

"So what about you? What are you going to do, Joey?"

"Quit. At your press conference. Devote myself to your defense. "

"And after?"

"After what? You're high maintenance, it's a full time job."

"With your reporting skills, Joe, and your profile, I mean, think about it, we could set you up with Noam Chomsky and—"

I take her hand and bite it gently, then flip her over and pin her shoulders to the grass. Then I take the button and pin it to her shirt.

"I want to see my wife and daughter. That's it."

"That sounds like a plan," Joan says.

"So where do we do this spectacle of yours," I ask.

"At the Pantheon," she says. "Between Rousseau and Voltaire."

I laugh. "You're kidding, right?"

She looks at me, squinting into the setting sun. Then she gets up, pulls me to my feet.

"No sense thinking small," she says.

Joan spends the night in my room at the hotel. She sleeps with her mouth open, her knees curled into her chest, her left hand lying limp over the side of the bed. She barely seems to take up any space at all on the king- sized bed, and a few times, when I look over at her from the couch, I'm afraid she's gone.

I get up to use the bathroom. I part the curtains and see the spire of the old church, looming. I go to Joan, take her arm and place it back on the bed. She moans, then turns her head into the pillow. I wait. She is still.

I sleep.

In the dream, I take the keys from their place on the credenza and back my parents' car out of the garage. I steer the station wagon through black space in the direction of Peekskill High School, eight miles away. The moon appears like a white hole at the top of the sky. I see school buses, row after row of yellow, silent monsters, with delicate black lettering that looks like lines of carefully applied mascara. In the student parking lot, I wait. A crowd gathers, carrying torches, bright in the November night. They meet at the flagpole. I see an American flag, dipped in blood, lit by fireflies, a thousand specks of striped light rising to the top of the pole. A small figure approaches, carrying a candle. I cut the engine. A hooded sweatshirt shadows the face. She stands there, outside, peering in the glassy windshield, the candle lighting her face now, her head tilted at an odd angle. Her head pivots, then dissolves into the blackened hood.

SUMMER: 1972

In the summer of 1972 I was a camp counselor in the Adirondack mountains of New York. The camp was fastened to one end of a heavily wooded island in the middle of Schroon Lake, not far from where a friend of mine had been killed. Three of us signed up to work that summer, but in December Mr. Contenti mistook his son Tony for a deer and blasted him in the gut with a Remington pump thirty-ought-six at forty feet. Tony fell like a Christmas tree, his Peekskill letter jacket splattered with blood. So then there was me and Angela Hard.

Angela's surname was difficult one for teenage boys to deal with *("Hey baby, I'm hard too! How hard could it be? If you're easy, I'm hard!")*, but she was a good sport. Her no nonsense demeanor won her grudging respect at school. That, and her dying mother. I might have liked her. But my mother took care of that when she announced one day at dinner that Angela was the girl I would marry. I was thirteen years old.

Angela's mother was a sympathetic figure in our church, where she attended without her wayward husband. Ed Hard was a shadowy presence even in his own house. There were rumors of drinking and abuse. We were a small clan of Italian-American Baptists whose life centered on the church. In those days it was unheard of to be an Italian Baptist, especially in New York where we were surrounded by Irish, Italian, and Polish Catholics. Even the name, *Roman* Catholic, should have included us, since my family came from the Umbrian hills north of Rome. It was embarrassing. If we couldn't even get our religion right, what else were we screwing up?

The Irish and the Italians had "a thing" in New York. There was still talk of "neighborhood integrity." Not long after my mother confessed that she was praying for me to marry Angela, my dad sat me down and filled me in. We rarely talked. This was short. "Never marry an Irish woman, Tom. They can't cook, they don't keep house, and they drink."

I found myself drawn toward the Irish Catholic girls in school.

My mother intensified her efforts to steer me in the direction of the girls in the Calvary Baptist youth group. It gave her pleasure to think about me with Angela, and the beautiful children we would have, with Angie's soft curls and full lips and my wavy hair and deep set eyes.

I saw Angela frequently at church. Later, she and Sarah sang with me in high school chorus. Sarah was a year younger. At seventeen, she was a real looker, with lovely pale skin and copper green eyes. My mother never said a word to me about Angela's younger sister.

*

Vincent Contenti was a beefy divorced man of forty who owned Vinny's Meats on Division Street. He stuck his hand into Tony's guts and applied pressure, managing to slow the bleeding while someone ran to call an ambulance. A Roman Catholic priest was summoned, arriving as the ambulance reached the hospital, but Tony refused last rites. He was a strong kid, the starting left tackle on the Peekskill football team. The funeral was held at our Baptist church with our pastor and a Catholic priest attending, as a concession to Tony's mother, a pitiable figure in black who sat silent and hunched on the first pew of our little brick church. I stood with Angela, her sister Sarah and the other kids from Peekskill High

School. We held hands, we sobbed. We shook. We prayed. And we left, in separate cars.

*

The camp was located on a heavily wooded isle of stately pines and ramshackle old buildings. It was owned by an ex-New York City bandleader who exchanged his trombone and nightclub patter for full-throated hellfire and brimstone that scared the hell out of the kids.

I was a bust as a camp counselor. Unsure of what I believed myself, I felt uncomfortable telling others what to think. I requested a transfer and accepted a job working long hours in the kitchen as a line cook, where I flirted with the salad girls and barked at the waitresses. I didn't give a tinker's damn about cooking, or the camp, for that matter. But the girls in their summer dresses and bare legs, the heat of the kitchen, and the joking camaraderie, kept me in a state of perpetual arousal.

At water's edge was the boathouse, where counselors awaited new campers each Saturday. Campers and their parents hiked a long hill lined with Norway spruce up to a sprawling three-story building that served as camp headquarters. Behind this dilapidated building sat the cafeteria, craft shop, and ball fields. Brilliant sunlight raked the tall pines, passing between the high clouds. In addition to the virgin spruce, which reached well over a hundred feet, the island was dense with sugar maples, American beech, white and yellow birch, and white pine. Midway down the steep hill was the meeting hall. The lake was a mile wide, and nine miles long. A ferry floated the campers across from the mainland, while ski boats whisked the staff back and forth. Captaining the boats was a plum job, reserved for the relatives of the camp's owners, who were bent on taking America for Christ and protecting campers from godless atheists, homosexuals, hippies and drug addicts.

Angela had a disarming way with the kids, not preachy, always willing to listen. Many of them were up from the city and in "the country" for the first time. They confided in her. Sarah lied about her age and got a summer job as a shot girl in a short skirt and heels at a Peekskill watering hole across from the train station, on the Hudson. Tony was dead. The others worked around town, doing retail or fast food, whatever they could find.

One evening I ran into Angela in the mail room. I hadn't seen much of her that summer since I'd moved to the kitchen. Her face was flushed. In her hands she held a letter. The sun was setting. Its slow descent streaked the sky with gold, lemon yellow, and then plum and rose. She grabbed my arm and asked me to walk with her. The dying sunlight struck our tense hands as we walked through the woods down to the lake, past the summer cabins, and down the rickety steps to the beach. Three campers splashed in the water, which rippled from the wake of a passing speedboat. A bored lifeguard bent to gather his gear. He whistled to the kids, who reluctantly waded into shore, their cutoffs dripping. We sat down on the cold sand of the beach.

"I heard from Dad," Angela said. "I have to go home."

I nodded. Looking out on the lake, I could see the white barrels rise and fall on the water, marking off the swimming area, and the wet rope between them. Small wavelets curled and collapsed, exhausted, into the dirty brown sand. A dead smallmouth bass lay stinking in the water, its bloated body eddied back and forth. The sky was darkening, and the wind was picking up. A lone egret picked at a wrapper at the edge of the lake, its spindly legs partly submerged in the water. Crickets played their haunting hymn. Across the lake was a long pier where fishermen would cast for hours in the twilight. Beyond the pier was the camp parking lot, and above it, Route 9. A steady line of cars were cruising up to Canada for the weekend. I saw all of this, and wondered when it was that I had really seen or heard anything. The kitchen was getting to be a drag. I wanted to go home. It was already August.

"She's going to have another round of chemotherapy," Angela said.

She added: "My mother. Things are a mess. Sarah is taking it hard."

I looked at her, surprised. Suddenly she laughed, a lovely laugh centered low in her throat.

"The hard way," I said.

"You remember when you used to tease me about my name, constantly? You and Tony and the rest of your crew?"

"We were jerks," I said.

Angela gazed out at the lake, at the crooked tree shadows dancing on the lake. The dead bass had finally made the shore where it would continue to rot until the lifeguard found it and removed it on his rounds tomorrow morning.

"I didn't mind," she said. "It bothered me at first, but then I realized I was happy for the attention. It made me feel less plain."

There were two small silver rings at the top of her ear. Her dark hair was pulled tight against her scalp in a ponytail, held by a rubber band. Several strands had escaped and were blowing in the light breeze. She had a strong jaw and a slight overbite.

"That was sad about Tony," I managed.

Angela frowned. She looked at me a long moment. "Yeah, well. I don't know," she said. "It *was* sad, sure. I'll give you that. But think about this, Tom. Maybe he had it easy. I don't mean to make light of his death. But he was fully alive, you know? At least that's the way I remember him. He had a lot of friends, he made us all laugh, and then he died and people came to his funeral and cried and said what a great guy he was. What I mean is, he only had a short time, which sucks, sure, but he also didn't have time to screw things up? He was just here for a while and then he was gone. Who knows what would've happened to him if he had lived? He might've become a serial killer or a rapist or a perv, a frickin' pedophile. Stay with me on this, okay? I'm just saying. Maybe that's where he was headed, how would any of us know? Who knows the future, Tom? Maybe he tears up his knee in college, gets frustrated and drunk, runs a light in his truck, hops a curb and kills a bunch of children playing on a sidewalk."

I couldn't feature that, but didn't object. "I guess I never thought of that," I said.

"Of course not. No one does," Angela said. "But things like that happen all the time. And I've had a lot of time to think. And I don't know about any of this, these are just thoughts that come to me, okay? But at least death ends things. It's final. For us, it's harder. We get to cope with it all but for them it's over. They don't have to *become* anything, they just are. Their work is over. They can't disappoint any longer, and that's something, isn't it? That's not nothing. I'm saying Tony had it easy, compared to the rest of us. I don't mean to be cruel, but it's true."

"Is this what you tell your campers," I asked. I was surprised that I said this, and immediately regretted it. Who knows why we say things?

Her eyes narrowed. "Sure, I tell them that and a lot of other things too. Stuff I think up myself. Stuff that's not in the camper's manual. This shit we're serving up here is not real, Tom, can't you see that? Or do you enjoy being locked up in the kitchen with those idiot salad girls and getting pale while the owners of this place pay us our ten dollars a week and laugh all the way to the bank?"

"What are you saying?"

"I'm saying grow up, Tom. In another month you're going off to college and so am I. Or at least I was, before today. We're going to be exposed to people and ideas that don't match up to what we've been force fed all our lives at church, and we're going to have to make some choices. So we may as well get ready for it. Camp is over."

We sat there for a few minutes in stunned silence. Two things occurred to me: that I had never heard anyone talk like this, and that it was possible to be harmed by something as simple as human speech. I realized then that I didn't know the first thing about Angela, and I had known her all my life. I hadn't ever really listened to her. Who else had I failed to hear?

I hadn't thought about Tony for weeks, hadn't given him a solitary thought, and what she said disturbed me. Worse, it seemed to make sense. But it only made the dead more mysterious. What is it that the dead know? What is dead in us? What is the living part in them? Had Tony been calling to me all along, and I hadn't heard? This seemed preposterous. I wondered what Tony thought about in the minutes before he was shot– if he had been thinking how hungry he was, say, or whether enough sandwiches had been packed by his dad at Vinny's Meats, or whether he could find a cream soda at the store in town– before his flesh was in ribbons and his body placed in a black plastic bag, his big toe tagged. Angie dug her sneaker into the wet sand. I traveled my own private orbit.

I stared off into the middle distance, afraid of what might happen next. The slow swells of the lake continued to break and disappear. The bass stayed put.

Finally, I said, "I'm sorry about your mother."

And Angela said, "It's my father I'm worried about. It's not death that's difficult, Tom, it's dying. Death loves us. Death is easy. It's getting there that's hard."

We stood to leave. It seemed as though we were rehearsing

to leave. Walking beside her, I felt terribly self-conscious. Darkness lapped at the boathouse door. We walked up the hill to her lighted cabin. I had rehearsed a goodnight hug in my mind, but she surprised me by reaching up to kiss me lightly on the lips. This was illegal according to camp rules, and grounds for dismissal. I tried to kiss her back, but she pulled away from me and ran up the steps and into her cabin.

The next day, her father picked her up at the boat landing on the mainland. They set out south on Route 9. I remained in the kitchen until the end of the season.

The day Angela left I thought about our high school graduation. Midway through the program the Chorus got up to perform. The auditorium was stifling hot. As we walked to the stage our paths crossed. Angela smiled at me. As she walked she pretended to faint from the heat, using her mortarboard to fan herself, drawing a few chuckles from the crowd, then caught my eye, pointed a finger at her head and mouthed the word "Pow!" I laughed at that and almost tripped as I approached the stage, where she split off to join the altos. I climbed the risers to the tenor section.

I listened for her voice, concentrating, but as our eighteen year old voices blended, perfectly for once, we sounded like one living organism, like those aspen trees in Colorado that are the world's largest living thing, a creature with many parts but one breathing heart. I imagined her voice, low and supportive, underneath the melody, next to mine, together at last. Two weeks later, we were at camp.

Returning home that summer, I thought about calling Angela,

but inexplicably waited until the night before I was to leave for college to ask her out. It was Labor Day weekend. She sounded subdued on the phone, but said, sure, why not. We went to a movie in Manhattan. Driving home on the Saw Mill River Parkway, we stopped for pizza in Yonkers.

The movie was a disappointment. After talking about our school plans for awhile—I was going away to New England, she planned to enroll in a community college nearby so she could live at home—the conversation stalled. Her mother had stopped her chemo treatments. The cancer had metastasized and was taking her organs.

Angela picked at her pizza. She rearranged the salt and pepper. She fiddled with her paper napkin, tearing it into tiny strips. I tried to engage her about school (dinky Pace, in White Plains), about what she wanted to study (business), or who she was going to hang out with (she didn't know). I asked her about Sarah. She said that Sarah was dating a guy from Ossining named Frankie Blunt, a total loser, and that she expected her to turn up pregnant before the end of the year. I didn't have a response for that. The silences were awkward, but we couldn't find any words to dispel it. It was as though we had conspired to murder speech. With the drive into the city, and then the movie and pizza, we had been gone a long time. Finally, she asked me to take her home, and I did.

I turned onto her street. We were not far from the Hudson River. With the windows open, I could hear the throbbing of a ship's motor sounding clear from the river, its screw deepening as she chugged steadily upriver. Someone was frying fish in the neighborhood.

Angela sat stiffly beside me on the bench seat of the car. We pulled up to her house, a white Cape Cod with brown shutters in an Italian neighborhood just off Division Street, not far from the church. Cars were parked crazily all over the front yard. A crowd milled about on the lawn, and around the side of the house to the back yard. I started to ask Angela what was going on, but she had her hands to her face, covering her eyes. She was quivering.

"Maybe it's just some people come over for a cookout," I said, lamely.

"No," she said. "It's here."

"What's here," I asked.

She uncovered her eyes and looked at me. "She's dead, you freak," she said. "My mother is dead. Oh, God! She's dead."

I turned off the radio and gripped the steering wheel. She waited for me to say something. My hands remained fastened to the wheel. I did nothing to disturb the silence. In this too, I was mistaken.

Angela bolted the car and ran into the night. She was soon engulfed by some people I didn't know, kin from out of town, I guessed. They put their arms around her slumping body and steered her to the back yard. A man approached, and she leaned into his open arms. Was this Ed Hard? I couldn't make him out in the gloaming. I turned the ignition, forgetting that the motor was already running. The car shook like a wounded animal. The grinding of the starter's gears shook my hands off the steering wheel. Without looking I pulled into the street and hit the gas too hard. The car rocketed into a pickup truck that was turning the bend in the narrow street. There was a sickening sound of crashing glass. I panicked and jumped on the brake with both feet. My head hit the windshield, and snapped back. Everything went black.

When I came to, some guy was screaming and gesticulating wildly. It was the pickup driver. His truck was wrapped around a tree. Glass covered the dashboard of my car, glittering with a blue edged hue. I picked two pieces of glass out of my neck, and felt warm liquid leak into my shirt collar. My blood smelled metallic. Pain shot through my left shoulder. I heard a loud pop, like a birthday balloon popping. Then there was shrieking from the backyard, a wall of shattered sound. In that instant the world seemed perfectly past repair.

I fell out of the car. Getting to my feet, I saw the driver of the truck coming for me. He was a big man with angry cropped hair, and fat knuckles on his ham sized hands. He lunged at me, and I smelled beer on his breath. I ducked, eluding him. My left knee buckled, and I dropped to the pavement. He came at me again. I screamed at him "My wife!" and limped off toward the crowd of people in Angela's back yard, trying to find Ed Hard, figuring it was time to introduce myself.

But it was too late. Edward Hard lay face down in the wet grass, the fingers of his right hand wrapped tightly around his service revolver. Crumpled in a heap beside him, wearing a halter top and jeans, her dark hair matted to her lovely, ruined face, was Angela, clinging to her younger sister, whose shrieks pierced the night.

I never saw Angela again. She married a guy from high school I knew only by reputation, the lead singer of a cover band called Ritchie Rich. I heard that he knocked her around, but who knows what to believe. They got mixed up in some bad loans at a business they started together, and left town. They lived for a while in Lake George, Glens Falls, then Troy, and after that one small town or another. Occasionally word would get back to me about her, but after a time there was less news, and then no news at all.

I remember that summer as one of violent and erotic dreams: thunderclouds over the mountains, a dead volcano. A rolling green lawn with a carpet of white flowers. The woods filled with violets and the broken spines of small animals. The air smelt of decay, as wind passed through the pines, and in the distance a castle with purple and gold lancet windows. Before the castle an iron gate, a pool of rain. I dreamed I saw a summoning bell grinning in the sun with broken teeth, and in the lancet window, a face.

I miss again and again the fact that I am not young and that these places of my dreams are places for young lovers.

I remained in the city of my university, where, more suspicious of words than ever, I became a professor of English. I specialized in the poetry of Yeats.

Years later I would marry a cool, cerebral Irishwoman, a blonde, who would often say of me, "When I met him the troubles of my life began."

LULU IN THE YEAR OF GATSBY

At fifteen I loved a girl.

There was no one to talk to. My older brother was dead before he turned ten. My sister Joan had moved out of the house. She fought with my father over the latest American war raging overseas. There were pitched battles during the CBS news with Walter Cronkite. For her troubles he beat her senseless. I agreed with Joan about Vietnam but didn't know how I could stop it when I couldn't stop the war in our living room.

But this girl. Her name was Lulu. I hadn't looked for her, but she found me.

We met at a ninth grade dance on the freshly waxed floor of our high school gymnasium. I was hanging out with my basketball buddies. Lulu came up and asked me to dance.

It happened like this: I had held hands with Lulu's best friend and next door neighbor, Melanie King. I knew Melanie from Chorus. On the night of our big concert she was on crutches with a broken leg. We stood next to each other, soprano and tenor. She asked if she could hold onto my hand during the performance. For support. Sure, I said.

This was new. I couldn't remember the words to any of the songs. We exchanged glances throughout the performance, between bursts of applause from the audience. Her touch as we interlaced fingers made me sweat, then shiver, but Melanie already had a boyfriend, my basketball teammate Danny (whose brother would die in Vietnam six months later). Melanie turned me over to her neighbor after that evening of hand holding, in some kind of womanly transaction (I never got the details), and the next thing I knew, Lulu was in my arms on the floor of the gym, and at fifteen, I was plunged into the mystery of girlhood.

Love is a brawler. My father and Joan fought constantly, terrible rows that would begin at dinner and last long into the night, ending only when he would try to stop her screams by grabbing her and holding on. He was not a violent man, though he had crawled up Omaha Beach in June, 1944, watching his mates cut to ribbons by machine gun fire. The suburbs of Westchester must have seemed like his leafy reward when he came home from the war and fathered his first two children. But now his first born was dead and his only daughter was calling him a murderer. His third child was me, watching.

When Joan resisted his hugs he shook her. Then hit her with an open hand, and finally pounded her into a puddle of submission on the living room carpet. I got to watch all this.

Things would be quiet for an hour or so, and then she would start up again (she was fearless), going into new territory, from Vietnam to the Nixon bombing of Cambodia, with accusations that bundled Kissinger, the CIA, the State Department, and the local New York State police—*how was it that my brother died, father?* Enraged, he would resume beating her while our mother cringed in the corner, waving the New Testament.

One night he went out to the garage and came back with a length of rope. He lashed Joan to the banister for the night. Not long after that she moved out and went to live with her history teacher. (She later disappeared for twenty years, having joined the student underground antiwar movement.) This was the same high school where Lulu approached me that night, in ninth grade, in the gymnasium. The same high school where T.C. Boyle (now an acclaimed novelist) would try to teach his English students to write, the place where I read *The Great Gatsby* for the first time, and mourned poor James Gatz from North Dakota in the story, who deserved better. The same gymnasium where my parents would go to watch Lulu and I get our diplomas, though by then we barely knew one another.

Breaking up had not been my idea. It happened in the breezeway of Lulu's house, seated on the chintz sofa. I had parked my parents' station wagon in the long blacktopped driveway. We had talked earlier that evening. I called her every day (I was a good boyfriend).

There was something in her voice. I asked, was she okay? She thought a minute, then said maybe you better come over?

The breezeway was the same room where she often spoke to me on the telephone while watching TV or painting her nails. She had hair the color of Catherine Deneuve's, shoulder length, parted in the middle. I had seen Deneuve for the first time that year, in a movie called *April's Fool.* The film starred Jack Lemmon as a hard working stock broker whose wife is so busy as an interior decorator that they barely see each other. Enter Deneuve, the boss's stunning wife. They meet at a party of Beautiful People and fall madly in love. Will Jack Lemmon throw it all over and follow Deneuve to Paris? Sitting next to her in the spacious Paramount Theatre in Peekskill, I looked at Deneuve on the giant screen and then back to Lulu's hair, and then back to the screen. Lulu caught me looking and frowned. She rested her hands in her lap. Her skin was fresh and clean. She smelled like Ivory soap. I thought Lemmon a fool if he didn't go to Paris.

Lulu's parents greeted me in the breezeway, then excused themselves. Lulu patted the sofa where she intended for me to sit. I took my time getting there. The TV was off. Her chemistry book lay open on the coffee table. The cat fled the room.

Lulu said it'd been a good year and a half. A good run, she called it. She said she'd cheer for me when I made varsity. She said some other stuff about what a good boyfriend I'd been, how I was always there for her, how I was reliable, steady. She'd learned a lot about herself by being with me, she said. I used to steal other girls' boyfriends, just to be mean, she said. Just because I could. You didn't know that, did you? (Actually, I had heard that, had heard too that she was a good kisser, and more; Lulu had not been a subtle person.) But you, she said. You never thought the worst of me, even though you could have, and you didn't bother to track down rumors. And because you believed in me, I worked to make myself into a better person. She dabbed at her eyes. She didn't deserve me, she said. I can't give you all that you want, and you deserve the world. She hoped I got what I wanted out of this life. She'd always be my personal cheerleader. I still can't remember the best things she said.

That night. She was saying we shouldn't see each other anymore. I asked her why.

Lulu sighed. She sat on her hands and bit her lower lip. She wasn't wearing makeup. A faint line of freckles bridged her nose. Her pink fingernails were bitten to the quick.

Joe, you're just too serious for me, she said, finally. I'm not a serious person, okay? Listen to me! Don't turn away! She pulled me by the shoulders and made me look at her. You might not like this but you need to hear it. I can't stay this good, Joey. And you're going off to college to some fancy school. We're kids, for chrissake. Did you think we'd stay together forever? It would never work. You've got to let me go.

We sat there a while in the breezeway. I asked if there was someone else and she said there wasn't. I believed her. I said what was I going to do without her, and she said I'd go on, we both would. She said that was a lousy thing to say at this time, maybe, but it was still true. Then I got up to leave. She tried to pull me into a hug but I jerked away from her and fingered my keys. I walked quickly to my car.

That was the year we studied *The Great Gatsby*. I wasn't a reader. But Mr. Boyle (he later asked us to call him Tom) made Fitzgerald's life sound magical. He had the girls in the class from the start, with his long reddish hair and Irish good looks, tall and lean. But he made a special effort to lure the guys in the class into the story. He was a seductive teacher. We learned about Zelda and her illness, about Gerald and Sara Murphy, the models for *Tender is the Night*. A born performer, Boyle would read passages of *Gatsby* to us out loud, doing all the characters. He made Daisy breathy and sexy and impossible to resist (though a bit whiney). Her voice *was* the voice of money. Tom Buchanan he made sound like a Chicago asshole. Nick Carroway sounded mysterious to me, and indirect, like someone I wouldn't trust. As for Jay Gatsby, I was immediately drawn to him. I could see the soldier in his handsome uniform, holding himself erect, dancing with Daisy. The roomful of collarless shirts in his crazy mansion, shirts of every hue! Tom Boyle closed his eyes and danced an imaginary Daisy around the classroom, using a chair as a prop and stroking it tenderly. We all laughed. I knew that Gatsby was doomed.

But it was Jordan Baker who captivated me. Mr. Boyle called her a minor character, but she fascinated me. She was from Louisville. I had never been to Kentucky, in fact had never left metropolitan New York except for brief trips through New Jersey to Philadelphia. And Jordan was an athlete, a professional golfer. This appealed to me. A woman who made her own way in the world, who didn't need a man. There was a lot to like in that. I saw her as slim, athletic, youthful. A Gibson Girl, Mr. Boyle said, and then he brought to class flapper dresses from the era. Some of the girls in the class tried the dresses on in the girls room, walking back into the classroom to much oohing and ahhing. Mr. Boyle spun a record on a turntable. Some of the students got up and did a fox trot.

Lulu was one of the girls who wore a flapper dress that day. As she danced, her short dress shimmered green and gold. The dress had a low slung waist, its shapeless silhouette emphasizing the angularity and verticality of her proportions. She was sleek as a skyscraper, free, and dangerous. She was Jordan Baker, a bad girl who cheated at golf and took what she wanted, because she was pretty, and because she could. She was reckless and careless, and I wanted her. She had been my girlfriend. Her dance was intoxicating.

*

As Lulu danced around the room my eyes were drawn to her slippered feet. I allowed myself the sweeping look up the line of her figure (no one was watching me). I didn't understand how women could be so beautiful. I wanted to know: How did that they do that? How girls moved was a kind of prayer, a different kind of power from anything I'd known. I was learning to resent it. Just the way she moved could bring me to tears. Lulu finished the fox trot and ran back to the girls room to change back into her cheerleader outfit, and as she left she looked at one of the other boys in the class, whom I wouldn't have suspected, and then she caught me looking. She lowered her eyes, releasing my gaze. She bit her lower lip and ran out the door in Mr. Boyle's flapper dress.

I steered the car home and laid down on my bed. The room had been my sister's, but she was in Wisconsin for her first year of college. I hadn't moved any of Joan's stuff out of the room. We hadn't been close for a long time, but I missed her. I began to suspect that missing was something essential to life, and that because Joan and I had lost a brother to an early death (there were missing pieces to the story, and neither of our parents were talking), things would always be this way.

I missed Lulu and I missed Joan. I missed my brother. There in my room, I began to weep for all the things I didn't have and for all the things I could not fix. Two years after the Summer of Love, Martin Luther King and Bobby Kennedy were dead. I wasn't eighteen and already I had seen so much violence and destruction; the war in southeast Asia had claimed my own family, though we didn't appear on any statistics sheet. In class Mr. Boyle said that before he was thirty years old he had already glimpsed the most compassionate leaders our nation could produce, and they had all been assassinated. And from this time forward, he told us, things would only get worse: our best political leaders were part of memory now, not hope. They could only be satirized, or sanitized, not saved. The world was in ruins and I was seventeen.

Lying on that bed I thought about old LBJ, sitting in the White House selecting bombing targets, pulling on his long Texas chin. And now Nixon, the new president, whose hero was George S. Patton, a man who had slapped a soldier silly in a VA hospital for crying. I thought of Danny Amato's brother, whose funeral we all attended, and then I thought of Melanie, and then I thought of Lulu, and then the pain started over again.

Tom Boyle was writing his way out of our high school. He was going to find a way to make a career as a novelist. I wondered if that were possible.

I pulled *Gatsby* from my sister's bookshelf and thumbed the pages until I found Jordan Baker. It was Jordan who had introduced Nick Carroway to Gatsby, Jordan who had been the liaison between Daisy and Gatsby and Tom and Nick. She was a bad driver. More than ever, it seemed, Jordan Baker was essential to the story.

Weeks passed into months. I swore off love, pledging that I would not fall in love in college or after, that I would love no woman after Lulu, and thus only Lulu. She was my first love, and she would remain my first and only love. If I couldn't have her, then I didn't want anyone else.

I had some money saved up from working summer construction, and worked part time with the campus maintenance crew. In a New York City phone book, in the Yellow Pages, I found the number of an escort service. A woman answered the phone. I described what I wanted. She gave me an address on the west side and told me to be there in sixty minutes.

The girl was tall, with boyish hips and a tight smile. She looked as young as me. I handed her a beaded flapper dress and told her to strip. She took it from me as if she accepted dresses in hotel rooms every day of her life. Stepping out of her clothes, leaving them piled on the ugly shag carpet, she entered the bathroom, pulling the door closed behind her. The cheap lock clicked. I checked the labels of her clothes, wondering who had bought them, then folded them and laid them on a chair. Taking off my own clothes, I laid on the bed and waited. I had never done this before with anyone but Lulu.

The girl came out of the bathroom and I handed her the money. She modeled the dress. I described how to do the fox trot. She frowned and looked around the room, looking like a bored teenager.

Her name was Sonya. I asked her not to talk. Then I removed the dress and positioned her on the bed. She knelt with her ass in the air, supported by her arms and knees. I told her to touch herself while I watched. She didn't look all that much like Lulu and I decided that was okay. I told her to lick her fingers and she did. Then I told her to make her red fingernails disappear inside herself. She did, taking her time with it, rocking her small hips. She looked up at me, twisting her head around to find my eyes, then she placed her fingers in her mouth and licked them one at a time, which is what I told her to do.

Later, I asked her to spend the night. She phoned and got permission, quoting me the rate. Again, I asked for her name. This time she said her name was Ingrid.

She was from Minnesota. I said that's a long way from home and she nodded. She asked, "What's your name?" I told her again my name was Joe and that I hadn't lied to her yet. Joey, I said. It's okay for you to call me that, if you're going to spend the night.

She had high shoulders and they were so white. Some light freckles clustered together, there on her shoulders, but she was white as the sheets.

I was thinking about how slowly time moved, how the hours of the night had Latin names that the monks had assigned but no one remembered. I wanted Ingrid to hold me long into the night and I would teach her the right way to hold me, the way Lulu had showed me in the breezeway on the couch when her parents were away, till the long hands of the clock had spun over and the night terror had deadened and I could sleep.

Then she wanted to know how old I was, and I told her I was almost eighteen. She asked how I had managed to get fake ID, and I explained that I was tall for my age and knew the right people.

Ingrid said, So Joey, it's your nickel, what do you want to do now? I reached into my book bag and said, Have you ever read *The Great Gatsby?*

She shook her head no. Her shoulders were bare but she had the sheet pulled around her, bunched at the waist. She said, what is it about? I told her it was about impossible love and she laughed and said that's the only kind.

She didn't look eighteen. I asked what did she know about love, and she said she didn't know anything and neither did I. Sure I do, I said. Then I told her about Lulu.

I'm not dumb, Ingrid said.

What? Her eyes were dark and hooded and her mascara was bleeding.

You look at me like you think I'm dumb, she said.

What if I do?

I held the book in my hands but I didn't want to read it. It had a stupid cover. I wondered why I hated things that Lulu and I had shared, how even the memory of them now made me feel hateful and small. She had given me a gold cross for my birthday. After we broke up I had taken it off and placed it with my sister's jewelry. A polo shirt she gave me lay soiled on the bottom of my closet.

I don't think you're dumb, I said..

Lulu isn't dumb either, you know.

Shut up. You don't know her. You don't know anything, do you? I never said she was.

I know she gave you up like a bad habit. And she was right

to do it.

What do you know about it? I screamed. I yanked the covers off her and she pulled them back. I wanted to see her bare legs again, but figured that could wait.

Well, you're here with me, right? You think you're still all in love with her, but you're here with me. Maybe she knew something.

I'm here with you because I can't be with her. You have no right to talk about her, anyway. Who asked you?

She looked at me, unblinking. Then she lit a cigarette and ashed it in the tray on the nightstand beside the cheap bed. Her nails were chipped and her hands looked defeated.

The telephone rang. Someone was asking for Edward. I said there was no Edward and slammed the phone down. The girl looked at me hard. I sat on the bed and cradled my head.

What, she said.

My sister thinks my father killed our older brother, I said.

So, did he?

My sister is full of shit, I said. And so are you.

She said, I'll tell you what's bullshit. Your teary Lulu story. You're here with me because you chose it. You're here with me for one reason, to fuck.

What if I am?

So you don't love her. So what, she said, it's okay.

I lifted my arm, then dropped it. She flinched when I did that.

I didn't say that. Don't put words in my mouth. I told you not to talk.

I took the cigarette from her hand. She let me. I took a long draw, then coughed. Her eyes followed my hand but I didn't like that. I didn't like her looking at me when she didn't know me. But I needed her to spend the night.

Then why are you here?

Because Lulu turned me loose, I said.

That stopped her.

Outside, it was raining, and the cheap curtains were gray sails lifting and we could hear the splash of the rain in the courtyard and the sound of a motorcycle winding out its gears.

I wiped at my eyes. I tried again to speak. And if I can't have her, I said, then I don't want anyone. Not in that way.

She laughed, a dry hard laugh. A man among men, she said. I wanted very much to hit her.

And you plan to live like this? she said. To wait for her?

I do.

And to pay for it? For the other?

Yes.

She laughed again, less bitterly this time, and I felt her laughter as if it were mine. For how long, she asked?

I saw how my life had led only to this moment but after led to nothing at all. A puff of wind blew at the covers and the girl was chilled. But she only sat on her hands in the bed and didn't move, waiting for an answer. I saw the dry pity in her eyes then, and it angered me and I grabbed at her hands and brought them up from her pretty ass. She shook her head and turned her face away from me, and I let her. For that one time, I let her.

YOU LOOK DIFFERENT

People, maybe your friends, notice. You've been wondering about this. Each day it seems that you look different from the day before. There's a consistency thing that's missing here, in the looks department.

Your wife leaves for work, her first day back since the accident. She is concerned about you. She has reason. There are things she would like to ask.

Into the cold February morning with your wife goes your remaining child, a daughter, fifteen, past the age of riding a bus to school. In two months she will drive herself to the nearby high school. Coatless and petite, she moves gracefully past you, pausing to peck your waiting cheek. Her eyes are moist but hopeful. The carpet holds the traces of her footsteps. Stephanie. Sister of Steven, daughter of Peter and Irene, grand-daughter of Patrick and Elaine, Thomas and Marybeth, cousin of Seth, Karen, and Jeffrey. So many ways to name her, so many relations we bear to one another. Family relations, you think, are like logical or mathematical functions in the naming, but not in the living. To name is not to live, life not imitating logic. So much spills out and over, bursts its containers and tumbles free, staining the world.

From behind the wheel of the car a kiss is blown. The kiss flutters across the length of the garage, past the carefully hung garden utensils, ladder, lawn mower, shelves holding screws, nails, nuts, bolts, all labeled and contained in shiny plastic cases, past the workbench with its clean, uncluttered surface, till it reaches you, exhausted, drooping, heavy with knowledge.

You stare at your wife through the windshield. Her face looks wavy, distorted, a circus funhouse face.

The house is quiet. You won't go in to teach today, you decide. Take some more time. Let your assistant teach the logic class.

Make a mental note of the rising number of people that know you. Vow to trim the list.

Go into the kitchen to wash the dishes. There are three of them: three juice glasses, three forks, one coffee mug. Wash them carefully, watching the jetted water splash against the aluminum sink, feel it ricochet up and onto the sleeve of your shirt, warming you. Turn the glasses upside down and place them, dripping, in the cupboard. Return the plates and forks to their places, their gleaming surfaces free of the clinging grit of food.

Walk the house, close each door. All but your son's, which, you see, is already closed. The phone rings. It's your assistant. Twist the cord in a tight knot as he talks, then lift and swing the phone in the opposite direction so that it's twirling madly.

Try to locate what's been lost, try to get a fix on yourself. There's this day after day sameness across time and space that gives us our identity. Our substance. We depend on sameness; without it difference makes no sense. This sameness, you wager, is what's been lost. It's not like you're deliberately trying to change anything, this much you understand. It's just that you wake up, you shower, you brush your hair in front of the mirror, and there's a different guy each day looking back, as perplexed about the whole thing as you.

This is the way you live now.

What is happening to you? You wish you knew. You're unrecognizable to yourself. There's probably a word for this, some Latin medical term no doubt that would sum it all up.

Your wife's minister had drawn you aside into his office after the funeral service. He told you that it is during the disquiet of our lives, during the turmoil of the difficult, that new ideas come. Transformation. He quoted a German philosopher: *Better a mended sock than a torn one; not so with consciousness.* In hushed ministerial tones, the kind you imagine is used in confessional booths at Catholic churches, he spoke, using an economy of words.

You glance at the pile of student papers lying in a stack on the floor by the kitchen table. You pick one up, surprised at its length. As you read you see words that are misspelled (missed by a spell-check program? Or just more human error?) and you move quickly to correct them, your pen a sense-making instrument, a machine for correction. You understand this process; the processing of words. What you don't understand is how to correct you. What the steps are, what this all leads to. That's where you're still a bit shaky, you'd say. Sure.

You get up from the table, lay the student's paper aside. You walk into the darkened hallway of your house. You are alone in the house for the first time in days. People related to you—sisters, mother, father, brother, uncles, cousins—and people from your wife's church carrying armloads of food, their voices clattering in the old house, all have left. They have gone back to where they came from, leaving behind in the house only their familial smells, and flattened dreams. Three people will sleep in this house tonight. It was difficult for you, for a while, to sort out those two sets, relatives and strangers. For a time all was confusion, meals were taken in the presence of strangers, women would knock at the door of your bathroom and call to see who was inside.

You pull open the door to the attic and climb the ladder to the gloomy elevated space of memory. What you seek: the remembered light of childhood. In the dusty box of old photographs you find the one you want. It is a sunny day in New York. A boy of eight or nine, at the height of childhood, stands outside the walls of the Central Methodist church, near the black wrought iron fence. He is dressed smartly in a gray wool suit with matching cap, knobby knees showing below the gray shorts. There is an inscrutable look on his face, not, it seems to you, the look of a child; as if he knows more but is not telling. There is no childish smile on his face to soften his features, nor even a silly schoolboy grin, just a serious little boy, his dark eyes averted from the sun (or is it from the picture-taker). In the corner of the picture a bride can be seen, her back to the camera, and a small crowd of people dressed in 1950s finery. The boy looks unrelated to it, and to everything else.

Steven was a neat and orderly child. He gave you no trouble. He thought before answering. When he spoke, the room often grew silent. He had few friends. He liked his bus driver, a plump, jolly woman. He was the first to be seated for dinner in the evenings. He was a timely child.

You remember a scene from your childhood, when you were seven. In that church, in the last pew, you paid no attention to the service until the end. When everyone had their head down in prayer, you saw the minister make the sign of the cross over the bowed congregation. How blessed you felt to have seen him make this ancient silent symbol on your behalf, unseen by all the others, unnoticed. You alone had seen, and that tall handsome man with the flowing yellow hair winked at you and smiled. All for you. How you loved him, loved his god at that moment. You learned later, from your unimaginative parents, that he was not a very good minister, and had as a young man wanted to be a forest ranger. Probably he should have, said your mother at the time, his preaching certainly leaves much to be desired, but this new information only endeared him to you all the more.

On the ground floor again, you head for your son's bedroom. You pull the door open slowly, and glance around the room. The bed is unmade. From where you stand, hand still on the doorknob, you can see the small imprint of his body on the sheets, curved toward the wall. At the foot of the bed is a book. You move slowly toward it, stalking it, as if it might disappear. You study the title. It is a library book. Its plastic protective cover feels cool to the touch. You pull the book up to your face until you feel its surface graze against your skin. Its musty smell you take in manfully. There will be no tears. You will refuse them, even when you realize this is the book you checked out with Steven weeks before. You look inside the cover. The book is due today.

You hadn't wanted to leave the house today. That was not your plan. The work you need to do is not outside. These are your thoughts.

You flip on the TV, clicking past talk show guests with tales of woe until you find Mary Tyler Moore on Lifetime. Mary's at a party with Rhoda. Rhoda pretends to be the wife of an astronaut. A woman inquires, which one? Rhoda declines to answer. You know how it is, she tells the woman, You tell someone his name, people all start wanting moon rocks. The laugh track kicks in. You hit the off button on the remote.

You find the vacuum cleaner and vacuum for forty-five minutes, the entire house, making sure that the thick pile faces in the same direction. When you finish there are parallel grooves in the carpet the length of each room. You sink into the soft chair in your study and stare absently at the books on your shelf. When the phone goes off in the kitchen you count the number of pulses: fourteen. You make not even the slightest movement. You disturb no space.

Driving to the library you try for no sudden movements. You wish to go unnoticed. You realize that you are already fading, you're thinning out, with any luck soon you'll be invisible, your childhood wish. A shade. You drive down streets with no name, the signposts long since defaced, past boarded up factories and the block long brick building that once housed a prosperous magazine. You wonder if anyone can name these streets now, if that was the idea behind the defacing.

If you can keep from speaking, this task, too, can be accomplished.

You wait as a car backs out of a space at the crowded parking lot of the library. A woman in a sleek black Buick tilts her head, wants to back up, asks with her eyes if she has clearance. You fumble with the many buttons of the stereo till you find the one you're looking for, to disconnect. The automatic antenna slips back into its hidden hole with a muted thump. To a silent count you wait, eyes averted, till she moves the Buick. You glide into the space she has vacated, and kill the engine.

You stare at the dashboard. A smile plays at the corners of your mouth as you read the embossed silver lettering on the Panasonic stereo system: FULL LOGIC CONTROL. You think of your computer at work, the message you once found after a series of false prompts: UNRECOVERABLE ERROR.

All errors are not unrecoverable, you think. Full logic control. You recall from last week's logic lecture what can be done with words, Aristotle's categorical propositions in standard form. Some S are P, No S are P, Some S are not P, All S are P. No errors are unrecoverable. All errors are unrecoverable. Some errors are unrecoverable. Some errors are not unrecoverable. You try to remember which is a contradiction, which a mere contrary. It escapes you. Unmoved mover, you think. That was Aristotle too.

The book is titled, *Mastering Instrument Flying*. Steven was ten. He had found this book, as he did all others, by himself. He wanted to be a pilot. Flying was what he wanted, for himself, for you. To soar, you think, above all this, out of harm's way. This was before the accident. Before he took his last step, the one you'll remember most, viewed from the safety of your kitchen window while grading at the table, the one that set into motion sirens and ambulances, and the startled, sobbing faces of fourth grade children, the one the driver with the thick fingers never saw as he swerved on the ice to avoid the yellow school bus, in his panic not seeing the small dark form that was your son.

Later, in the emergency room, after the doctors pronounced their verdict, brooking no discussion, you listened stoically to the man's sobbing story, the police waiting dumbly nearby, then the bus driver's, until you heard someone say, What's that, Mr. Thick Fingers? (absurdly, you called him this to his face), Excuse me, Mr. Fuckin' Thick Fingers? What's the matter, you can't see lights, the color yellow doesn't register with you? You walk out your door and you don't think, Shit, there's ice, I should slow down? You have children, Mr. Thick Fingers? Yeah, well I did too, once, I had a son.

Stop, Peter, please, your wife pleaded.

You ignored her, started on the bus driver, followed her out to the hospital parking lot where her bus sat stupid and empty, idling merrily, its children packed off to meet with school psychologists.

She cried, this bus driver.

You let her.

Names of lawyers raced through your mind, unbidden.

It was then that you had glanced at the big shiny bus mirror. The mirror held an image, but it wasn't yours. You were unrecognizable. Unrecoverable? This is how it began.

Death, you realize, is what people tell you it is.

You remember now, sitting in the library's parking lot, that you had been looking at books, killing time, when Steven had called you to the circulation desk to check out *Mastering Instrument Flying*. Past the many aisles of fiction written by skilled liars living failed lives, spin-doctored histories written to support the lies of those in power, the stacks of false, outdated science, paperback romance novels, philosophical ideas with half-lives much shorter than rumored, stale as week-old bread, you had walked. Following his voice, with no great urgency, you had snaked your way to that desk, noting the dust upon each volume, light but unmistakable. Useless knowledge.

Now you hold the book in your hands, as he had held it. You caress its creamy white pages, running your fingers across entire sentences, tracing the outlines of commas and question marks, dreading the periods. You feel what he had felt; touching the pages of this book, a third skin unites you.

You enter the library, head down. You walk to the counter. You're prepared for this. The clerk takes the book from your hands, with it also the note. On it, you've written, This book is on time.

You sit in your car, waiting. You check the mirrors.

When you walk back to the circulation desk the clerk acts surprised to see you again. She asks if she can help. You spot Steven's book, not yet shelved, recoverable, and you point to it with a steady finger. The clerk smiles at you, then asks simply, Renewal? You nod, your head bobbing idiotically, and then onto your tongue you feel the word drop, as if from a great height, sudden and with remarkable lightness, and it pushes its way out past you, to her, leaving both of you laughing, that peculiar, hissing, affirmative, Yes, you say. Yes.

CHASE

Humphrey wants more from me, would like to be the brother I never had, but we both sense that we can't top our first conversation, when I wandered into town, lost, looking for someone to talk to about my wife, who was hunched over a corner table in Humphrey's bar talking to his wife, Jan, whom she'd just met. We closed the place down and spent the night with them. The next day Frankie drove back to L.A. and I started teaching at my new job. Now, six months later, when Humphrey and I talk it always comes down to women, but the story about Frankie isn't as edgy as it was. It sounds boring to me, and worse, predictable, something you'd want a friend to censor, out of mercy. And now there's Chase.

At the mall I'm thinking about Chase, who spoke in class today for the first time, when I see a retail art director with big hair undressing a mannequin in the window of Victoria's Secret. The guy has his hands on her breasts, which are razor-sharp, fitting a purple wired bra over her simulated nipples, and there's a crowd of kids booing. He dips her, lays her out flat, and when he kisses her there's an enormous clap of laughter.

I search the mall until I find a hair place, and ask for a shampoo. A woman with a name tag that says "Charbe" leads me to a back room and motions me to a chair. When she puts her hands to my hair I shudder, startling her. Charbe asks if the water is too hot. I shake my head, embarrassed, and tell her I've been cold for three months. She smiles and tilts my head back further, so that the warm water pours over me, then trickles lazily into the sink. I cross my arms around myself in a hug, trying to get warm, and smile back at Charbe. I want to tell her about Chase, but when I start up she puts a pretty finger to my lips and says, "Sorry, I don't do girl advice anymore." She bats her eyes a few times, then says, "Oops. I'm not reading from the script, am I?" I tell her it's okay, I'll figure it out, and she says, "Sure you will." Then she lifts my damp hair off the back of my neck and starts to blow it, waving the drier back and forth like a wand so that the warm air hits my neck, shoulders, and ears as well as my hair. As I turn to leave she gives me a top to bottom look, hands me her card and says, "For later. When you need this mess cut."

Later, I sit in bed and re-play the day's events. Before today, Chase hadn't said a word for seven weeks. There had been plenty of looks, and once, walking around the classroom as I lectured, I had glanced down and seen my full name in her notebook, with two dozen question marks arranged neatly around it in a square: North, east, south, west. Then today, she hands in her mid- term and says, "So. You got your coat and hat at Nick's, right? I shop there all the time. Nick's a friend." Her voice is whiskey and soda, sexy. I turn towards her but she's already gone. It's confusing, with students swarming all around the desk trying to hand in exams, and I have difficulty recalling more about this non-conversation. There's the voice, sure.

I live alone. "Freelancing," Humphrey calls it. When it's not crowded in the bar Humphrey sometimes pulls the Springsteen tape from its place next to the Frito stand, picks up his four month old kid, turns him upside down like a guitar and plays him while The Boss does "Born to Run." The kid wails but what's he going to do? About then Jan will come up and give Humphrey one in the gut, tell him to put the kid down. Which he does. She kicked him out once, and he spent a week camped out on some land his father owned. When I came in the next day he told me that Jan was busting his balls again. "She's pissed because we didn't do mega-thousands on the Femme promotion, so now I'm freelancing."

It's an eight block walk from my apartment to the Humanities building, but the blast of cold that blows off the lake adjoining campus is pitiless. On the way is Humphrey's bar. Mid-mornings, I stop there to get warm. I help him set up, he gives me a shot of Jameson. We talk. To be fair, he does most of the talking. Frankie calls the bar a lot, usually late, and if I'm not there she'll talk to Jan or Humphrey, then call the apartment. The next day the three of us hash out what it all means. Two of us have positions.

Humphrey thinks I need to go back out there, claim what's mine. "Show up during one of her rehearsals, rock her socks," he says. Jan's skeptical about this. "What's the hurry?" she says. "You do that, she'll know you're desperate. Frankie's cruising, she's trying out her new girl stuff. This guy Dominic's necessary to her now, he's Transition Man. Let 'em dance the dance, it'll make a man out of you. Besides, what can you do?" Dominic is Frankie's producer, a guy with a gold Mercedes and big teeth. Frankie says he's been hanging around rehearsals, looking hungry, but that she can handle him. "You want my advice?" Jan says. "Get a divorce, then give her a call. Marriage is a beast, it's ruined otherwise normal people. It's totally overrated, everyone knows that. See if she wants to date. After you get a job out there, of course."

All of this tends to depress me, so then I walk to campus. Jesuits dart in and out of offices in darkened hallways. They look at me like maybe they should know me. Sometimes they ask if they can help, thinking I'm somebody's student. It's a huge department, and this is my first job. I was lucky to get it. Tenure seems, at the moment, unthinkable.

Frankie didn't want to leave L.A. We argued about it some, said things we'd come to regret, and finally I just left. We didn't talk for a month, and I made no travel plans, not even for the holidays.

This is my first winter in the Midwest. On Christmas Eve

I bought myself a black coat at a thrift shop, along with a gray scarf and a gray Greek fisherman's cap. That night Frankie called. Scattered on the bed were letters from the big journals, with much white space, telling me that the projects I was working on weren't what was wanted. I had them arranged, these letters, according to style, from mildly interested to vaguely hostile. When Frankie called I was getting set to burn them. I had a Windex bottle in my hand, filled with water, in case things got out of hand. It was midnight in L.A. and she was calling from a pay phone at the theatre where one of her plays was being mounted. The play was called "All Those Crazy Sweaters," and had Evel Kneval's son in the lead role, with sisters fighting over him and swapping clothes a lot. I asked what she was wearing, and she said, "You mean right now? Mmmmm. Panties, white. Black bike pants over a black lace leotard. There's a skirt with that, maybe eight inches worth of skirt. Silver on the wrists. My orphan boots, you remember, the Oliver Twist ones? A black Doors T-shirt I made with gold glitter letters over Elmer's glue."

"What's it say, this T-shirt."

"Fuck Oliver Stone," she said.

"Cute. So, how's Dominic?" I asked.

"He's still got the teeth, if that's what you mean. He's being separated from his money. Theatre-wise, of course."

"Of course," I said.

I light up one of the letters. It breaks into fiery pieces, moving upward in a dozen directions. I blast them with the Windex bottle and in the process drop the phone.

"Jake? What was that?"

"It's okay, I'm back. Small fire crisis here, some flames, possibly some burn damage, nothing serious."

"He likes it. The theatre, I mean. He's in real estate full time, so this is a new venture, here, for him. The arts thing, he calls it. He tells me he's starting to feel a little human."

"Great. I mean, considering the alternatives"

"He reads all my shirts. He can read."

"Maybe I'll send him a card," I said.

*

I don't hear from Chase Whitney again until two weeks later when I find a note in my campus mailbox: *Professor DeFrancesco: Can we talk? Today? Especially today. 6 PM. Your office.*

It's signed simply Chase, but it needn't have been. I know it's from her. I'm expecting it. I say that because at the end of that mid-term, two weeks earlier, she had written on the last page of her original screenplay, in tiny handwriting:

> *You who never arrived in my arms, Beloved, who were lost from the start, I don't even know what songs would please you. I have given up trying to recognize you in the surging wave of the next moment. All the immense images in me—the far-off, deeply-felt landscape, cities, towers, and bridges, and un- suspected turns in the path, and those powerful lands that were once pulsing with the life of the gods— all rise within me to mean you, who forever elude me.*

I remember thinking at the time: This is a bit much, no? The professorial moment. Then: O God! O shit! O shit! This was pretty much the sum of my thinking at the time, as I recall. Luckily, I had assigned a grade to her essays before I found Rilke's poem written in that cramped, childish hand. I closed the booklet and placed it with the other W's. Strict alphabetical order.

At five minutes past six o'clock Chase knocks lightly on the door of my office. She's wearing a ripped up pair of Guess jeans and a heather ski sweater that brings out her eyes.

"Look," she starts out, "I don't know why I'm here, exactly.

Shit, that's not true. Shit. This isn't going to work. Did you read the poem?"

I check it out with the part of me that approves, then silently I rehearse Rilke's poem, looking past Chase to a point over her left shoulder, to a spot I imagine myself sucked into, without remainder. Then I give her the second stanza.

> *"You, Beloved, who are all the gardens I have ever gazed at, longing. An open window in a country house–, and you almost stepped out, pensive, to meet me. Streets that I chanced upon,– you had just walked down them and vanished. And sometimes, in a shop, the mirrors were still dizzy with your presence and, startled, gave back my too-sudden image. Who knows? perhaps the same bird echoed through both of us yesterday, separate, in the evening. . ."*

What happens next is what I'm still thinking about, what makes me think. It's like a test. I wait to see how she'll do. If she speaks too quickly. If she makes a sound. If she talks about how she really likes Rilke, how she can't get enough, how he speaks to her directly, how he *is* poetry, or anything like that, I'll be embarrassed for her, for us, I'll lose interest, there won't be room to audition even one more word.

She reaches across my desk and grabs my keys. Then she stands and takes my coat off the peg, grabs my hat and scarf, turns off the light.

Most of my life I've spent waiting. Not waiting for something– a taxi, or the waiter to come to your table–no, just waiting, like whatever the wait was for would soon be announced. Before long. A vocation of waiting. This is what I'm thinking as we walk out on the frozen lake, trying to keep our footing on the sleek black surface. The northerly wind at our backs blows us faster and faster. We're holding on to each other in a half-run when my feet go out from under me. I know right away that Chase is going with me, we're falling, falling, and there's this exquisite moment when we're both suspended over the surface of the lake, in movie time. I think we're never going to hit, we're going to stay up here for as long as we want, for as long as it takes. But of course we don't. We land heavily, and the unyielding ice feels malevolent and sinister as I turn my head to look, seeing it really for the first time, this element of life gone cold, undrinkable, suddenly strange. The ice is scarred from the blades of skaters. I place an ungloved finger in the wounded, glassy surface and feel a chill pass all the way through me. Chase laughs. I turn in the direction of laughter and see her small white teeth fully exposed, the pink gums gleaming, the tip of her tongue tilted upward against the roof of her mouth. I imagine her mouth pressed against my ear, firing hot moist pockets of air into the cold, warming me, those teeth closing on the skin of my neck, spitting out gray and black thread till they find human flesh. It is snowing. In the silvery winter air we sit there on the ice, mute and expectant. We haven't said a word since the office.

"Is there a word for this?" I finally say.

"Selection," she says. "I've selected you. It's really out of your hands." She studies my face to see how I'm taking this, then says, "Hey, you're a lucky guy."

Humphrey's Amstel neon lends a softness to the street below that I hadn't noticed before. We climb the three steps to the bar, stomping our feet clumsily as we enter. Chase's green mittens are clumped with snow from when she made a snowball and hurled it at a stop sign, hitting it from twenty feet between the S and T. She tells me she played shortstop in the Whitney infield with her father and two older brothers. This would be Nantucket. It's a close family. She's Dad's girl.

Too late I try to steer her to the left, into the restaurant section, but Humphrey's quick, in a Ralph Cramden way, and he's on us before we can sit down. He peppers me with questions about the Bulls-Lakers game and makes furtive glances at Chase. Finally he pulls himself into his full butler pose and goes, "Ahem."

"Oh, uh, Humph, this is Chase. Chase, this is Humphrey. He owns this dump."

"With the claw," Humphrey says. "Over there."

"With Jan, he means." I give Humphrey a look, but it must have been too professorily correct because I can see him tugging on his ear diamond, which is our code language for "Listen to this shit." Humphrey wears a large red button on his XXL rugby shirt that says, "Sounds Like Bullshit To Me." I try not to think what Humphrey would think about my Rilke quoting earlier.

"I've been in here once before," Chase says, smiling. "For the turtle soup. Can we get some? With some brandy, maybe?"

"Excellent choice. My mother's recipe, three generations. She cooks it herself in the back room," Humphrey says. He looks pleased. "Mom!" Humphrey bellows, "get your elderly ass in gear, these people want the soup!" and waddles off. As he turns the corner I catch Jan with hands on hips, making this impossible-to-imitate face at Humphrey. She's radiant. The bar is humming. People are in their whimsical blizzard mood. It reminds me of a scene from Little House on the Prairie. I expect Pa to come in next, maybe with Victor French, singing Old Man Tucker.

Jan delivers our order herself, waving off the waitress. She looks at me, maybe a little too tenderly, then puts the food down. We drink a pitcher of beer with the meal, follow that with Irish coffees, then shots of Frangelica with hazelnut Hagaan Daaz. It's snowing fiercely when we leave. We fall into the street, laughing like children, and walk a block to Chase's BMW. It won't start. We blow back into the bar. Humphrey is only too willing to help. He grabs his parka and steers us back out into the storm. Parked outside is his car, a hearse with a Ghostbusters insignia on the rear window, and an orange sticker on the side that says "Vacancy." I look at Humphrey, then at Chase. She says to Humphrey, "I'm going with him. To his place."

The hearse is roomy and dark inside, with the faint smell of honeysuckle. It is unbelievably cold. The three of us huddle together like soggy scouts in the front seat while Humphrey fumbles for the ignition. Snowflakes melt on Chase's lashes, and her whitened hair falls on her shoulders in disarray. Humphrey drives slowly through the narrow, darkened streets, aiming the hearse through deep troughs of snow on the straightaways like a slalom skier, then crossing through the wake on the corner turns.

"What are you thinking?" Chase says.

I'm thinking of Rilke. How he loved Clara, his artist wife, and Rodin, his mentor. How he slipped the knot of his marriage within a year, unable to work. And the letters they exchanged, letters about solitude and art and news about little Ruthie, whom they had abandoned to the care of grandparents. I'm thinking how dumb that was. I'm thinking how maybe I'm wrong, about this, about everything. I'm thinking of an alternate Ulysses, one loosened from the mast to chase the sirens, to chase the voices of a thousand distant fires.

"Do you know Rilke's definition of love?" I finally say, leaning into her so Humphrey won't hear.

Chase is direct. "I know about Frankie," she says. "Jan told me, when you were in the bathroom."

"I wasn't in the bathroom," I say. "I was on the phone to L.A., to Frankie. And I'm the one that asked Jan to tell you."

Humphrey is strangely silent. He stares straight ahead, trying to pick out my apartment in the swirling snow. Buildings that shelter strangers rise suddenly from the whitened sidewalks, which are empty of people. An abandoned car sits with its rear end jacked up, its grillwork grinning.

Humphrey steers the hearse to the curb. We get out. Wordless, we watch the hearse's taillights glow fainter, then disappear. The traffic light on the corner flashes yellow in what seems a miraculous way. Snow fills the mock Bernini fountain in the courtyard, giving it a false, fugitive beauty. Everything shines with a queer, antique light.

We climb the stairs to the apartment and shake ourselves off at the top of the landing. I find Chase a clean towel and an old flannel shirt and direct her to the bathroom. I hear her in there, showering. I turn on Letterman. He's got some woman on the phone, live, in her office. He asks about her boyfriend, wondering how serious they are. Is there a chance, does she think, for him, for Dave? She laughs, plays with her hair, tells him she can't believe he's calling her. He says, "Look outside your window." She does. He's got a high school marching band in the street playing Happy Birthday. "How did you know!" she squeals.

Chase comes out of the shower. The tails of my shirt hit her mid-thigh. Her smooth brown calves are beaded with water. She sits beside me on the couch, curling her long legs beneath her. I nuke Letterman.

"Rilke's definition of love is neighboring solitudes that border, protect, and greet one other," she says.

"You're young. You're supposed to say dumb, wrong stuff."

"Is that what you want me to do? And you're young, too."

"What I want doesn't matter. What I want you to do is sleep in my bed tonight," I say. "I'll sleep out here."

Chase yawns, lifting her arms high above her head, clasping her hands. There is a big dimple in the center of her chin. She smells good. It's my cocoa butter. She's used it as moisturizer.

"What'll happen to you and Frankie, do you think? I mean, what's the plan here? Jan says you guys are complicated."

"Jan only met Frankie once, the day before I moved into this place. We stayed with them one night."

"Will you get a divorce?"

She asks this with a perfectly even tone, mild inflection at the end. I choose to hear it as a child's question.

"My parents almost got a divorce, I think. Last year," she says.

"When in America."

"How did you meet Frankie? I want to know."

"Frankie was a theater major at UCLA. I went to see a play on campus one night. Frankie played Cher in Nicaragua. I went backstage looking for Cher and found this woman in a Belinda Carlisle T-shirt and black jeans with a buzz hair cut sitting splay-legged against the wall, lots of cheekbone. I was dressed in black. She asked me who I was. I told her. She told me she used to like philosophy but that now she thought of it as 'Socrates, Inc.' I told her I thought pretty much the same thing. Then I said I know a place where they play the Go Go's and Bangles all night, not a contra is sight. She did this squinty thing with her eyes and hands, like she was sighting me along the barrel of some dangerous but still secret military weapon, then said 'Sure.' We spent the night in my car out in the desert, listening to the Ramones."

I stop there. I don't know how to continue, or if I should. It feels like I've been talking for a long time. I hadn't expected to tell this story again. The family voice in my throat sounds strange. My words seem suspended in the air between us, as frozen as the fountain outside. Beneath them, the space of memory.

I look over at Chase. Her eyes are clear, her gaze steady. She listens like this is the most natural story in the world, like if there's more and I want to tell, then she's the one to hear. Everything passes softly through us.

"What do I call you? I mean, it's awkward, isn't it. Can I call you by your first name?" Chase says.

"Look, Chase, I'm sleepy. What time do you want me to get you up in the morning?"

"It doesn't matter, silly. It's Saturday."

"Right."

I go to the kitchen for a glass of water. I run water from the tap, searching all the cabinets until I find a blue glass that I like. I put the glass under the stream and try to understand why I feel so lost, why I have trouble locating the simplest things. Listening to the water run, overflowing the glass and spilling out over my hand, I think about the playful way Charbe had tousled my hair after telling me she didn't do girl advice any more. Her girlish giggle after she said that, and her smoky, bubblegum smell, but mostly her touch. Two weeks ago. I start to think about Frankie, try to imagine what she's doing or what she's wearing, but decide to kill that thought before it gets going. I turn off the water, draw the edge of the curtain aside and try to look outside. The window has frosted, and I have to scratch a spot clear with my fingernails to see the snow, still faintly falling. Covering everything, what wants covering and what doesn't. I let the curtain fall back and feel the draft circle my wrist. Shivering, I go back into the living room with my water. Chase hasn't moved.

"Jake?"

"Yes?"

"About Frankie. She loves you, you know? I promise."

I put the glass of water down. I lift her, sliding my hands under her back. Her legs stick out over my outstretched arms. She laughs, and tucks her knees into my chest to keep from knocking pictures off the hallway walls as we head to the bedroom. I smell my scent on my shirt, on her. I lay her down on the bed, pull the covers up to her neck, fan her long hair out over the pillow. She sighs contentedly, smiling up at me. I turn off the light.

In the night, what will happen is this: She will get up to use the bathroom and get disoriented in the strange space. She will grope for the hall light. I will look at her, startled, the harsh white light framing her shadow on the wall. I will get up and go to her, watch as she sits to pee, then guide her solemnly back to bed. Neither of us will say anything. Minutes later I will return to the bed, stand over her, and study the line of her legs beneath the thin cotton sheet. I will crawl into bed beside her, noiselessly. Breathless, I'll put my hands to her hair, raise it to my face, feel it tickling my skin. The perfect ends I'll put in my mouth. I'll curl up alongside her till we're shaped like spoons in the chilled night air, my stunned fingers resting in the small of her back.

MISSIONARY

> "So they drew near to the village to which they were going, he appeared to be going further, but they constrained him, saying, 'Stay with us, for it is toward evening and the day is now far spent.' "
>
> ~ *Luke 24:28-29*

Right after high school, I spent almost a year at an evangelical Christian college in upstate New York, where I seduced my English professor and got C's in all the courses not in my major, which was psychology. My papers in Paul's classes were all weeks late, which explains the C's, if you believe in explanations.

I wasn't dumb. I left before we were caught. They didn't have anything on us, but they would soon be on the scent. Paul was hopeless at deception, and they had ways of finding things out, a whole legal machinery of sin detection, complete with informants. Leaving was something I could do for him, at least. I never got to say goodbye, which was the way I thought I wanted it at the time. Just check out, like a rehab gone bad. Failed fundamentalist. Don't look back. Lead him not into temptation. Deliver him from evil.

I know what people think when they hear all this, and it's okay – maybe I think some of that myself. But it's been six years since I left, and I still don't know what any of it means, or even how to make this sentence keep going until it made sense to anyone who wasn't there. Or to anyone who was.

Like Garbo

Winter is my favorite season. I've always known this. It seems wrong to speak of other seasons. I liked it there in winter. The sky was low like a snowy roof and in the brilliant woods adjoining campus a furious wind was blowing, always. The lake was frozen three straight months. Sometimes Paul would walk me across it, laughing and moving in a half-skate. We danced, a kind of tortured mock tango there on the lake, remembering bits from old movies that Paul had seen in videos that he rented and played late at night in his cabin, where I'd go late to him, breaking curfew with the help of my roommate Kit, who'd let me in the locked dormitory door at six the next morning.

When we stumbled and fell we'd lie in a heap on the ice, kissing. After, I'd pull away and stare at him, my face lit by moonlight, immobile, like Garbo. Like that, yes. I knew what he saw when he looked at me, his conflicted desire.

It hurt to look at him, seeing the shape of his care reflected in his cloudy eyes. Poor boy. It was then that I knew he was as lost as me. At these times and no others I'd let myself think, "he loves me," but then I'd remember that to him, as a fundamentalist Christian, love and rescue meant the same thing. He's big on salvation, I would think. Then: It's not his fault; it's all he knows.

Paul

Paul did his best to impersonate a fundamentalist college professor, but it was an unconvincing performance. He'd tell me that he didn't belong there at Redeemer College, that he took the job only because he was desperate for work in his field, that he got the job because the dean knew his father (a pastor), that he'd leave when he finished his dissertation, that something better would come along. And I'd say "What?," sweeping my hand in a dramatic gesture that took in the eight-by-eight square of his office with the droopy tile overhead and the blinking fluorescent lights. "And leave all this?"

Paul believed that leaving would be the best thing, after what had happened between us, but I observed that belief was precisely his problem, that he was excessive in his need for belief. Besides, I'd tell him, you're needed here. You're a missionary.

Mr. Darcy

When I was little, the single missionaries would stay with us at the parsonage, and my sister and I always dreaded it. The women, with faint moustaches and impeccable grammar in their fund-raising newsletters, always seemed to have the most terrible physical problems; they limped, they gave off a vague medicinal smell, they used no makeup, they wore K-Mart shoes and hose with seams. I changed the sheets when they left, holding them at arm's length as I threw them into the washer.

It's possible that the single men, however, were worse. Once, in sixth grade, a man named John Darcy stayed a week with us, and I never saw him come out of his room – that is to say, my room; I had to stay with my sister – until the last night, just before dinner, when he appeared before me and Cassie and our girlfriends and started doing calisthenics with an unholy enthusiasm. Amazed, we watched as he stood on his head in the living room, his glasses awry, his spastic mouth twitching with exertion. I was twelve, and horrified. I wondered what he had done all that time alone in my room. I grew up deathly afraid that I would become a single missionary and do calisthenics in the houses of strangers.

Class Notes

What I remember comes in pieces, like the soft doughy squares of bread my father served at communion in the Baptist church, the crust carefully cut away by deaconesses. I reach inside and seem to pick up a piece of Wonder Bread memory. *This do. In remembrance of me. This is my body. Broken for you.*

I remember Paul lecturing on the history of romance. It was a morning in early January, Missions Week at Redeemer. Slouched in my seat against the pale green wall, notebook in my lap, I sleepily took notes. Tall titled columns of them. But when I look at my notebook now, it looks like the haphazard ramblings of a bright but disorganized deity:

happy love has no history
Tristan lands in Ireland
Iseult the Fair love has always been nourished by obstacles
romance only comes into existence
when love is fatal, frowned upon doomed by life
what draws us is the story?

It surprised me that an evangelical college would offer courses on Shakespeare and the age of Romanticism, lots of Keats, Byron, Shelley, but I've learned that evangelicals are very big on love and romance. They're suckers for tales of conquest and heroism, evil dragons slain, fair damsels rescued from distress. They don't really believe in happy endings, at least not in this life. They want to believe that all are sinners, all are lost (they're right, there!), that everyone and everything can be saved through a personal relationship with Jesus.

I'd say: Jesus saves. Moses invests. Lead us not into Penn Station. Deliver us from Evel Knieval.

This was not what Paul wanted to hear.

Mother, Milky

I had sex for the first time at fourteen, and by the time I was eighteen I had had four lovers, a drinking problem, and an abortion. My parents were oblivious to what was going on in the house. They were never home, always at church, organizing, or practicing the cure of souls, and Cassie and I quietly became famous in the Grand Rapids underground, a loosely knit criminal network of mostly pastor's kids. It was fun, until Cassie fell off the back of a speeding motorcycle on the Gerald R. Ford Freeway, and my parents remembered me, and started to use my name in sentences in a way that seemed to me excessive, and began asking to spend time with me, their cadaverous eyes haunted, their skin stretched tightly over remaining flesh.

Late one night I got up for some milk. My mother, drawn like a moth to the light of the refrigerator, sat down in the middle of the kitchen floor, naked. I dropped the milk. She called me Cassie, then sobbed uncontrollably. I laid down next to her, my head in her lap, and kicked the carton away, then drew my milky legs up until they were under my chin.

There was no money for college, but Redeemer offered free tuition the first year for the children of pastors, so there I was. I figured I'd do one year, then transfer some place. It wasn't much of a plan, but it was what I could manage at the time. My parents said they'd find a way to help pay for a secular school later if I gave them that one year at Redeemer. They'd say it just that way, like a prayer: "Give us this year."

Like it was a gift.

To them, I guess it was.

To me it was a life. Or half a life. A half-life.

I was eighteen years old.

Chapel

The first week of winter quarter was missionary week at Redeemer. We were required to attend chapel twice a day during missionary week, in the morning and again at night. The missionaries that came to the conference were the real item, all the way from Chad and Brazil, Zaire, Mexico, the Philippines, Japan, England, France, you name it. And "Home Missions" people too, from Grand Rapids and Atlanta.

I found it odd that they would have missionaries in a lot of these places, especially England, Spain, France, and Grand Rapids, where there's a church on every corner. Kit said the evening sessions were a great time to catch up on your homework. We'd sit in the back of the chapel in the part we called "The Zoo." We'd pass notes, giggle, set off the occasional alarm clock, and make fun of the nerd boys they had there, who carried gargantuan designer Bibles with their names printed in gold block letters on the cover. (They prayed over ice cream cones when they'd venture out on dates, which were rare.)

One night I asked to look at one of these Bibles. A nerd boy had come in late and had to sit in The Zoo, so I reached over and opened it to the inside cover, looking for the inscription Kit said was always there, in the five line space Zondervan made for this purpose. Sure enough, there it was: "To Travis, in the hope that this book will keep you from sin. Remember, son, 'This book will keep you from sin, or sin will keep you from this book.' For prayerful study at Redeemer, where we trust you will get a safe education, by the grace of God. Your loving parents." I gave the Bible back to Travis and squeezed his sweaty hand, dragging it into my lap. I pecked him on the cheek. I put my tongue in his left ear and smiled sweetly. I did not ask him how safe his education felt then.

Sex

I didn't tell anyone about us, except for Kit, but I knew that we were being watched. At Redeemer points could be scored for bringing someone down; a sexual fall was a biggie. Sex was preached against on a daily basis in chapel, but all that did was call attention to it, heightening anxiety and, of course, curiosity. Lust was everywhere. The place was a hothouse of love, love, love; everyone was a possible victim, anyone could fall. It was the most sexually democratic place on earth.

Paul

Somewhere in here I concluded that Paul belonged there. I say this because I watched him pray (while safely disguised as a good-attitude coed in a navy blazer and plaid skirt). Paul sat up front on the right side of the College Chapel with the other faculty. His head cradled in his beautiful hands, the long slim fingers threaded through his wavy hair, when he prayed he seemed to be lifting off the pew, as if elevated by an invisible wire. Afterwards, students and colleagues would gather around him to ask what he thought of the sermon. Even if it was a disaster – say the preacher had gotten off one-liners on abortion, the ACLU, how God made Adam and Eve not Adam and Steve, liberal apostate theologians doomed to hell, all in a commentary on the first chapter of the Epistle to the Romans – Paul would look each of these petitioners in the eye and speak carefully, without condescension, giving his careful critique. Evenhanded. He must have known that it was killing him to be there, that he should leave, but I began to feel that this was because of me, not because he had outgrown the place. How could I take him away from all this when I didn't even know what it was, the life he had there?

I'd think: If anyone finds out about me and Paul, we're

fucked. He wanted to turn himself in. He was unprepared to live in the world, that was pretty clear.

One day we went to the post office in Albany. He wanted to mail a package to his grandparents. We were in the downtown office, it was crowded, and he drifted from counter to counter, unable to settle anywhere, until finally he found the right one. But then he realized he didn't have the right zip code. He stood there, turned to stone. He was ashen. I asked what was wrong and he said it was impossible, we'd have to return home and look up the address. I told him that was ridiculous, it was a thirty minute drive back, and besides, one of the clerks at the window could look up the zip code. He stared at me as though I were a Martian, as though this were news from another planet. Finally, he got in line, the clerk addressed the package complete with zip code, and Paul paid him. But when he counted the change, he saw that he had one dollar too many, so he gave it back to the clerk. Then he walked away slowly, counting again, and in the middle of the staircase he realized that the missing dollar belonged to him after all.

I stood next to him, at a loss, while he shifted his weight from one foot to the other, wondering what to do. Going back would be difficult; a crowd upstairs was pushing and shoving in line.

"Just let it go," I said. He looked at me, baffled.

"How can I let it go?" he said.

Not that he's sorry about the dollar, money in itself is of no consequence to him. But it is the fact that there is one dollar missing. How can he just forget about something like that? He spoke about it for a long time, and was very unhappy with me. And this repeated itself with different variations, in every shop and restaurant. Once he gave a homeless person a five dollar bill. The man had stopped him and asked for a dollar so he could eat. Five was all he had, so Paul asked the man to change the five, but the man claimed he had no change. We stood there for a full two minutes trying to decide what to do. Then it occurred to him that he could let the beggar have the five. But we hadn't gone ten steps when he began getting angry. This is the same man who would have been eager and extremely happy to give the poor man five hundred dollars with no questions asked. But if he had asked for five hundred and one we would have spent the day trying to find a place to make change, he would have worried himself over one dollar.

His anxiety in the face of money was almost the same as his anxiety over women. Or his fear of things official. Once I called his office in the morning, begging him to take me away from there that day. I was beside myself, I needed to get away, just for half a day, somewhere, anywhere. I cursed him when he said he couldn't. Afterward, he didn't sleep for nights, he tormented himself, wrote me letters full of self-destruction and despair. Why didn't he come? He couldn't ask for leave. He was unable to bring himself to ask the Department chair for release from his one remaining class that day, the same Department Chair he admired in the depths of his soul – I'm not kidding – because of the Chair's skill with computers. How could he lie? he'd say. To the Chair? Impossible.

Lying is possible for most of us because it gives us a safe place, at least momentarily, a refuge from some situation which would otherwise be intolerable. At one time or another all of us have taken refuge in a lie, in blindness, in confusion, in enthusiasm or despair, or something.

But Paul had no refuge, nothing at all. He was absolutely incapable of lying, just as he was incapable of getting drunk or high. He lacked even the smallest refuge; he had no shelter in the world. He was exposed to everything that most people are protected from. He was like a naked man in a world where everyone is clothed.

This is why he could not continue seeing me, and also why he could not continue teaching there. He knew this, but was unable to leave either me or Redeemer. Like at the Post Office,

I thought: He will move from counter to counter, trying to find a space to work it out, a place from where he can see through to tomorrow. He couldn't leave because of me, but he couldn't stay either. What would be his reasons for leaving? He loved what he did there; he felt he was needed by his students. And of course he was. If he were to leave, where would they go? Had he left last year, he would have never met me, and then my suffering would have been greater. I know that he thought about this, but for him it was more than a practical problem, it was also a theological issue: How could God do this to him?

I told him: lying is inescapable. If he stayed there he lied, because he couldn't remain and be the type of person that he was. But if he left that was a lie too, because there was part of him that very much belonged there, that would be misplaced anywhere else.

I told myself: Maybe we are all searching for places where we can stay the longest without lying.

Later, I thought, who knows? Maybe he reached his place of optimum truth there.

Cabin Stories

When we met Fall Quarter, Paul was a virgin. He told me there was a girl once when he was in high school, but they broke up before it ever got to that. One had to know how to listen with Paul. He tended to leave things out.

One night I followed him home to his house on the north end of Main Street. The street was lined with run-down shacks, with broken down cars on the dirt driveways and little kids playing tackle football in the street. No faculty lived on this side of town. As we walked our shoes clacked on the concrete pavement, then afterwards crunched on the long cinder path that led up to his little cabin at the edge of a dark wood. Dry leaves rustled. It was Thanksgiving break. I'm sure, to him, I was a waif, lost and errant. It's true that I had nowhere to go. Everyone else had gone home, most to their parents' houses. For many reasons, my parents' house was out of the question. I called and told them I was staying with a friend. They sounded relieved.

Over wine at dinner I got the rest of the story out of Paul. It turns out that he had never even kissed this girl, whom he had met at a dance when he was sixteen. She was the great love of his life, there had never been another, and he hadn't so much as kissed her.

There was a black coal stove in the center of the main room, but the bin next to it was empty. The tiny bedroom was in the northwest corner of the cabin. The bed was covered with animal skins. It was funny to see Paul's white hands shooting out of those dark skins at dawn, like some prehistoric creature with good reflexes. We'd laugh and squirm around to get warm, grinding ourselves into the cotton sheets while Paul re-positioned the skins above us. I'd ask him to tell me a story, and he'd tell me how he used to tug his little brothers on a sled up a snowy hill in Poughkeepsie, above the Hudson, or about the time when he was four and his older brother's dog bit him, and his parents made Matt destroy the dog in the back yard, in front of him.

Right here was when I told him about Cassie. I mentioned her wavy dark hair and did her laugh for him and made him get up to get my jacket, which had been hers, for her scent, and we both put our noses into the collar and rutted around, and when he cried I knew I wanted a different story. After that he began telling stories about God and I got less and less interested, and finally I told him to stop and then there were no more stories.

We stayed in that cabin almost a week. Paul found some coal for the stove, and it was a good thing, because on the second day it snowed. The windows frosted over, and snow blew in through small gaps between the logs. When we talked we could see our breath. Paul said it looked like something out of *Dr. Zhivago*. I took his word for it.

We got into a routine: wake up, cook breakfast, back into bed, up for lunch and long walks in the woods, drive into Albany for dinner at a different restaurant each night, feed the fire with black coal, bed again. There was no talk of Redeemer College.

The day before classes resumed we were lying in bed. We talked past noon. I took a deep breath.

"Paul, how did you get into this whole fundamentalism thing? Why are you here? I mean, you can't really believe all this stuff?"

" 'Jesus made as though he would go further.' "

"What?"

"That's it. That's why I believe."

"What are you talking about?"

"Luke 24. After his resurrection, Jesus is on the road to Emmaus and he meets up with two of his disciples, but they don't recognize him. They think he's just another guy and they're amazed that he hasn't heard about this Jesus person, so they say, 'Haven't you heard? You must be the only one in town who hasn't! He's risen from the dead!' Then Jesus finally reveals himself to them, going back through the Old Testament and showing them how all this was speaking of him, how he really is the messiah. The first time I read this story, Zoe, I thought to myself, this is sad, this is really so sad. I mean, to have to explain yourself like that. After all the great things he did, all the miracles and the healings and to top it off Jesus rises from the dead, and here these guys that claim to be his followers don't even recognize him. He was traveling through the world incognito. Even the ones who claimed to know him best didn't recognize him, or denied him, they all somehow missed him, or betrayed him with a kiss. After three years they still didn't know who he was, they still didn't get it."

"But what is this, Jesus made-as-if-he-would-go-further stuff?"

"After Jesus goes through this whole routine with them, and now they recognize him, and believe again, it's dinner time, and the disciples were going to spend the night somewhere. But the text says that Jesus made as though he was going further, and they had to persuade him to stay with them. I think that's why I love him. I think that's why I'm here. He was just so incredibly polite, he didn't force himself on anybody, he had the most incredible manners. He didn't want to offend. He wanted to help them to see. Jesus – "

"Wait a minute. That's why you're here? Because Jesus made as though he was going further, because he had good manners? That's a reason? You're saying that you came to teach at an evangelical college with weirdo rules and a pervert for a President, and you choose to stay here, the whole thing, because Jesus was polite to these bozos?"

"Because Jesus goes unrecognized in the world, Zoe. Because we've been in the presence of grace and we didn't even know it. Because the greatest mysteries in the universe have been revealed to us and we've forgotten or overlooked them or somehow screwed things up but he's too considerate of our freedom to embarrass us again. Because he travels through the world, travels through us, incognito. For me, it all comes down to hospitality. Some have entertained angels, unawares. We keep pushing him away, out of the world, out of our lives, and he lets us! Because he's been right there with us, hell, he's carried us and we didn't even notice."

He sighed, and looked into his hands.

Outside, the wind was picking up. Voices of children could be heard at play in the street, and farther off, the low rumbling of a train. I watched the grimy curtains move toward us, disturbed by the wind, then lie limp against the window pane, suddenly still.

Paul got up and threw some more coals on the fire, then

came up behind me and waited. I didn't say anything.

Then he said, "I know I'm not saying this very well, Zoe. I just think I can help here, that's all."

Kit

One day during missions week a Vice President of one of the big missions boards used maps and charts to share with us missionary possibilities all over the world, particularly in the former Communist bloc, and could it be that God would like to use us in Russia for His glory? Five hundred students raised their hands and come forward down the aisle to go to Russia. That's one third of the student population. I thought: What are all these people going to do in Russia? I felt sorry for the place. I pictured all those Bible thumping classmates tearing up the countryside, knocking on doors and handing out tracts in poorly translated Russian. I thought, if I were in the Kremlin I would pass laws immediately to stem the tide of evangelistically minded American students with large Bibles. The way I looked at it, the country had enough problems.

But then, Kit and I figured that 498 of them would change their minds. They'd get married, get a mortgage, have kids. Most of the students I knew would rather die than think of themselves in a country without shopping malls. And what would these students wear? Kit and I tried to imagine the Redeemer girls with their blazers and pearls, trying to talk to vodka-smirched Russian women waiting in line for brown bread. We cracked up.

Besides me and Kit, there were our trainees, Alix and Jennifer and Sara. After the missionary conference ended at 9:30, we'd sit around complaining about how we were expected to get any homework done when they had us going to meetings all night. We'd trade favorite missionary stories. Sara thought she had the best one, about this missionary from

Brazil who used to tell repeatedly, every time he spoke, about how this giant beetle was burrowed in his skull for three weeks, how they eventually prayed that bug right into oblivion, and Alix recalled a missionary who somehow failed to tie up the livestock on a plane and wound up with goats chewing things up and raising hell in the cockpit, but we all sat there in amazement when Kit told us about her mother.

"I grew up in West Virginia, right, and down there we take our religion seriously. No room to fuck up, I mean you've got to toe the line, sister, or whump, they'll toss your sorry ass out the church. So my mom tries, right, really tries, to please my dad – who incidentally is the pastor of the church – you know, to be the total woman. She even wears only Saran wrap when he gets home from work, kinky sex to the Song of Solomon, the whole fundy thing. But she knows that she's going nowhere in that small town and she's itching to get out and back to school so she can get herself a life before she's too old."

Jennifer stopped looking at Kit, and stared at the wall, a vacant look in her eyes. I put my arm around her.

"So one Sunday night at church my mother shows up with three roses, each in a Dixie cup of dirt. One rose is completely closed, the other is partially open, and the third is in full bloom."

"What was she doing with three roses?" Alix asked.

"They were her props, see. She was about to give us an object lesson, just like she might have done in junior church or something, but that congregation was about to hear something it never heard before, I promise you. We kids are sitting quietly in the pew, we've got our coloring books, our Barbies, the whole thing, like a normal Sunday night. But nothing was normal that night.

"So now my dad, who remember, is the pastor, says it's testimony time, and the minute he says that my mother stands to her feet and in her hands she's holding her three roses, and she starts in on her testimony.

" 'My dear sisters and brothers in Christ, I want to share my heart with you. You see these three roses? They represent my life. As you can see, the first rose is unopened. It signifies my life as it has been for the first 33 years. All this potential, all of my possibilities, going to waste. Do you know what it is like to have a good mind, a sound mind that the Lord God has given you, but you are unable to use it? Well, that has been my life. This is the old me, a beautiful rosebud, unopened, yearning to burst out into bloom.

" 'And this second rose you can see is in bloom. Its petals have opened, all the world can see its beauty, but it is still a veiled beauty, isn't it?' My mom held the second rose aloft in her hands. I could see old Mrs. Bartle sitting on the edge of her seat, following that rose with her eyes. 'But something is still wrong,' mom said. 'This rose is not all it can be. It has yet to become all the rose that God intended it to be.' Now she had her head bowed. She was weeping. 'This is my life now, this rose. I've opened up to the Lord, I'm willing for the world to see me now, but not all of me, just a part. I'm still only half a person.

" 'But this rose.' She waved the third rose in the air now, triumphantly. 'This rose is in all its glory! It is the rose in full bloom. Nothing can be more beautiful than a rose that has completely opened to its possibilities. And this rose is what I want to be. What I shall become, by the grace of God.' "

"God, Kit, that is so beautiful," Jennifer said.

"Yeah, they all thought so. Mrs. Bartle was bawling so loud you could hear her across town. But what no one knew is that I had heard my parents earlier. They had a huge fight. They thought I was outside playing with my sister. My father was pleading with mom to stop having the affair, to stay with us, and she kept screaming, over and over, 'Leave me alone, you're smothering me!' That woman was heading for the door long before the trinity of roses speech, I'm telling you. It was a great performance, and it bought her some time and a lot of sympathy afterwards, when she left town. *Masterpiece Theatre."*

"God, Kit," Jennifer says. How did you stand it? Did you tell her that you knew?"

"I've never told anyone," Kit said, "till now."

On The Ward

Kit was the rebel. I didn't have the energy for rebellion. For that, you had to care. I was just there for observation. I told myself constantly, "You're on the ward, pay attention." But it was weird, since they all thought the same thing, they were observing you. After all the services at home, all those Redeemer chapel messages, all the Bible classes, I had internalized a fundamentalist voice. It talked back to the other voice, my voice. I heard these conversations all the time.

—It's wrong to have sex. The Bible says so. Whoremongers and adulterers God shall judge.

—That's ridiculous. Sex is the most natural thing in the world. You see a gorgeous guy, you think you're going to live forever. God gave us sex. It's his fault. He made us this way.

—You must learn to overcome these lustful thoughts. God will judge.

—Then God's judging himself, since he gave us these bodies in the first place.

—That's blasphemy.

—Your God's perverted. Do you really think he's hanging around the Ramada Inn, checking out what's going on in Room 208? Shouldn't he be more interested in Northern Ireland, or Lebanon, Bosnia, Haiti, something more worthy of his time?

—He's working on that. Besides, God knows everything about everybody. He is not only omniscient, He is omnipresent.

—So he's got the Holiday Inn covered too.
—You have a bad attitude.
—So what?
—You're headed for hell.

It's like fundamentalism is a double-voiced sickness, but the ones who observe it are themselves observed, so no one knows how to chart it. It's a standoff.

Chapel, II

I did some math: if you stayed at Redeemer for four years, and went to chapel and the special bible and missionary conferences at the beginning of the semesters, and to church twice on Sunday and Wednesday night prayer meetings you would have heard 255 sermons per year, for a total of 1,020 in four years.

Redeemer was in session for thirty weeks a year, fifteen weeks per semester. This means that a student could hear 255 sermons in 210 days in one year; graduating seniors will have heard 1,020 sermons in only 840 days. If you want the prayer figure, take the sermon number and double it: 2,040 public prayers, minimum, not counting required dorm bible studies and prayer meetings.

Many of these were about sex. Not having it was the idea. There was no mention of child abuse, homelessness, racism, or sexual harassment. Math was not my strong point, but I checked my figures three times. I thought these figures were not widely known. When I told Paul he suggested I write a letter to the school newspaper. When I told Jennifer, she said that's not counting the summers, when you attend church and prayer meeting at home with your parents. She went off to calculate the number of times that worked out to in terms of hosiery bought and put on. When I told Kit, she said, "What'd you expect, that they'd leave anything to chance?"

The President

The president of the college frightened me. His name was Jack Sampson. Since Redeemer was so small, we all got to see him way more than we'd want. Every time he looked at me it sent shivers down my spine. One day, waiting for Paul after Chapel, he looked at me; well, not at me, he looked at my body. At my legs and butt. It was a "degree day" today, meaning it was below zero and the girls got to wear pants. Pants on girls were so unusual that when we got to wear them, we'd flaunt it, whatever we had. So I had on Jennifer's too-tight striped pants and he looked at me in this really ugly way, and I knew he wanted to undress me. I wanted to take Paul's hand and run out of the building.

That night's topic of dorm conversation was President Sampson: Was he a pervert? Kit thought so. "Think about it. This guy comes right out and says he is a friend of Jimmy Swaggart, I mean this guy knows that weirdo! He has Swaggart's home phone number, can you believe it?"

"Did you see the news when Swaggart asked forgiveness from his congregation? Wasn't that nauseating? His poor wife."

"I saw the interview they did with the prostitute Swaggart was with. She has a kid. She said the stuff he asked her to do, it was sick."

"I don't know, Zoe. I don't think Sampson's a pervert. The president asked for prayer for him, is all. And besides, we're different from Swaggart in doctrine, right? So Swaggart doesn't really represent the Christian community. I mean, Swaggart is a charismatic, right? We don't believe that stuff about tongues and all."

This was Jennifer. She was somewhat in awe of us.

"Right, Jennifer." Kit said, "Sampson doesn't speak in tongues so he can't possibly be a pervert."

Paul

I worried about Paul constantly. It was unbearable. He was wracked with guilt. I didn't believe in guilt. I thought it was a false emotion that we manufactured to torment ourselves. I watched my parents manipulate each other and my sister with guilt. Evangelical Christians are expert at guilt, but this is a cliché. What's not widely known is how much they suffer.

I looked at it this way: I'd been around evangelicalism enough to have received an inoculation. I think I'm immune to it now, that enough distance has been created, but it's still in my blood, traveling in me, silent and potent.

Saved Sex

Paul sometimes wondered if he was still saved, what with all that we had done together. I'd tell him we need saving from something every day, what makes this day any different? And take his hand and place it on my breast.

Kit and Me

One of the weirder rules at Redeemer was that if two girls were on a bed, they both had to have both feet on the floor.

I ask you.

So one night Kit and I were lying in bed in our underwear with the door locked. Kit was admiring my panties, which were red, with white hearts. My mom sent them to me for Valentine's Day, but they were too big. I knew Kit didn't have much money. After her mom ran off her dad lost his church. He got another one but it was a small congregation and couldn't afford to pay him much. I said what the hell. I gave her my Valentine panties. The matching red bra too.

Kit gave her professors fits. That day in New Testament she had embarrassed her prof by asking him if he had sex before marrying his wife.

He deserved it, he kept going on and on about the biblical view of sexuality and Kit just couldn't take it anymore. I had to put my head on my desk to keep from laughing out loud. The prof asked if he could see her after class. He questioned her attitude. She had an appointment with the dean the next morning at eight.

Anyway, we're lying in bed, me naked now, regretting my decision to stop seeing John outside of class, when Kit jumps me. We wrestle till we're panting with exhaustion, our sides splitting with laughter, but she has a good twenty pounds on me, and it's clear I'm going to get pinned, so I decide to just lay back and enjoy it. Kit pins me, then counts slowly to three in a referee's voice, and calls me a wimp. She lip synched to the illegal tape I had playing: "Got it bad, got it bad, got it bad, I'm hot for teacher." Then she kissed me on the lips, and asked me out to dinner.

The next day when I returned to my room after classes there was a note on my bed from Kit. They'd kicked her out. I ran down the hall crying. I found the Residence Hall Advisor and asked her what happened to Kit? She looked at me like I'd dropped in for the day from Jupiter. Then she said out of the side of her mouth, "Kit had an attitude problem. As you know. She's gone."

*

It's been six years. I made my escape the day Jennifer was kicked out for attitude in The Zoo. I piled all my Redeemer clothes in the middle of the floor with a note saying "Help Yourself!" and caught the next bus out of town. I didn't say goodbye to anyone. I called my parents from the bus station and they freaked. But they didn't ask me to come home, I'll give them that.

I stayed with Kit in Ithaca until I got a job cutting hair and an apartment. I took some night classes and tried to get into a degree program at Cornell, but I couldn't get my Redeemer credits to transfer. Whenever I said that word, Redeemer, I'd get this look, like I was bad meat. There were fights with the Registrar, and scenes in the Admissions office. Finally I just gave up.

That was years ago.

I am twenty-four.

Last year I got married to this guitarist. We're on the road a lot. It's okay at night, when there's so much set-up work to do and then the band is playing and everything is moving by so fast, the lights winking at the dancers on the crowded floor and the crashing wall of sound that seems to flatten the room, picks us up and throws us down again. But the days are slow. Sometimes, after dinner with the guitarist and his friends, I stand up and walk outdoors, and keep on walking till I'm in sight of a church.

I just found out that I'm pregnant. I haven't told the guitarist. I haven't told anyone, yet. I've given a lot of thought to what I'm going to call the baby if it's a girl. Katherine Anne, after Kit and my grandmother. And if it's a boy? That's easy.

There's this song playing at work. I hear it all day long. The one about God on the bus, trying to make his way home.

I think: What if God *was* one of us?

I don't know what happened to Paul. For a while Kit received Redeemer newsletters mailed to her house but she called and told them to fuck off.

I never got any. I guess to them I never existed.

I still think about him sometimes, and yeah, about our conversation that last day in his cabin. And I see Paul's point in the Luke story. But I think Jesus made as though he would go further because he just wanted to get away from those two guys. Maybe that's the difference between believers and non-believers when you get right down to it: the believers think it all comes down to this one person, and they know how to hang on to what they have.

And then I remember: We were in bed when he told me that funny story about Jesus walking on the road. Paul's hands were there on my belly, like mine are now, soft and warm, and he was sobbing, shaking so hard I thought he would break apart, and he kept saying my name, over and over, Zoe, Zoe, Zoe, Zoe.

I tell myself I may be remembering this all wrong, that things change and your life plays tricks on you, but I mean, there we were, in that little cabin at the end of the road, and I was in his presence and I never knew what it was, what he meant, what was mine.

GAIL

In seventh grade Gail Romano was the girl we all wanted. She was what our mothers called "well developed," which to us meant that she had big tits. She also had long brown hair and huge brown eyes which even too much blue eye shadow couldn't ruin. Her skin was creamy white, as though she never saw the sun, and her skinny legs were often encased in black fish-net stockings, the rage in 1967. But I liked her voice, which was uncertain, like she was afraid to let the words get too far away from her, and tiny for such a big girl. Talking to Gail was like an invitation to get closer to those tits.

She liked me, I thought. She liked to flirt, especially in Mr. Cyr's history class, where I always got into trouble. I made her laugh. One day Cyr caught us passing notes. "Mr. Thomas, come forward," he said in his theatrical baritone. Everything with him was such an event. I reminded myself as I walked up to the front of the class that this man was the eighth grade bowling coach, for Christ's sake, that I couldn't let him break my dignity. He grabbed my shoulders, squared me up, then turned me around and kicked me. It hurt, but I didn't make a sound. After, when I turned around to look at Gail she gave me this look that I wanted to save forever.

One day at Bobby's house we practiced what we would do when we finally got Gail alone, how we aimed to kiss her and feel her up. We made up a clumsy code of words and moves that we thought might work, stuff I'd heard guys talk about in metal shop class. We had signals for when to French kiss, when to grope her tits, when to take the beaver shot. I watched Bobby squirm around on the couch, grinding his hips and kissing the pillow, and I called out the code words at what I thought were the right moments. Later, he did the same for me. We were men.

The next week she got kidnapped and raped by a man in his thirties. When they caught him they put his picture in the paper so we could all look. There was a story under the picture, I remember, though I noticed they left out the rape part. I studied the words, the peculiar black and white pattern they formed on that awful page, the way they referred somehow to Gail: minor, undisclosed location, allegedly, protect. When Gail came back to class all she got from us was silence. She limped, and every time our eyes met I would look away, or at the hospital gauze on her white thigh that kept slipping down her leg as Mr. Cyr talked. The stockings were gone.

It's funny: I don't remember seeing her again after that, not in high school, not anywhere, though I'm sure I must have. We lived in a small town. How could I have missed her?

I'm older now. I have two sons of my own. I've never told them about Gail. What would I say? *When I was your age I knew this kid, a classmate. I was really hot for her, you know? We never did anything about it, though. We were kids. Then one day, she was gone. Just like that. I don't know what happened to her. I can't find any of my high school notebooks, or my notes from college, even. Yearbooks, graduation tassel, gone, all of it. At the time you thought it was important. You thought it would all be there for you, somehow. Life is like that. Things change. You don't know how or why but they do. You just look up one day and everything is gone. Cells of your skin die every minute, second by second, from the time you are born, brain cells decay, you lose what you most wanted to save, and the ghosts carry the rest away. Trust me on this.*

Now, I sit at home late at night and try to imagine what she looked like. I sit at this keyboard and try to remember her into existence. I tap her back into my life lovingly, one keystroke at a time. Gail is at our twentieth year high school reunion, drinking by herself at a corner table, and her voice hasn't changed. I still have to lean into her to hear her.

CHRISTMAS: 1972

My first girlfriend had blue Christmas lights strung on trees in front of her stone house. My family had all gone to bed. When midnight came, it was snowing. The streets were silent as I drove. Snow filled the lumberyards of Peekskill along the Hudson River. I'd gotten a wool sweater, gloves, a navy blazer with gold buttons, gray pants. A wet kiss from my father, his holiday tears. She was in her wooden bed, high on the second floor, beneath the dormer. I parked in her driveway, cut the engine, listened to it tick. Her house was filled with brilliant surprises, narrow white feet and her girlish sleep. It'd be years before I returned. She'd be a teacher, I'd be married, my grandfather dead, my grandmother still in the kitchen in her worn housedress. The lumberyards along the river would be empty. She'd hold me all through the night. We'd try to sort the past, but everything had fled, her innocence, small chin, the thinness of her wrists. She'd lay beside me on the couch in her terrible insignificance, the life we never lived dissolved to tears. But that Christmas in her driveway snowflakes like diamonds stuck to the curved windshield of my father's Ford. I waited for the sun to rise, like a story.

THAT'S GRACE, TOO

My son lies on the sofa bed in the living room with a red and yellow sleeping bag pulled up to his chin. The same bag, it's true, that I used to cover Colleen the night we slept in the tent in Vermont. Rain falls faintly on the tin roof above our heads.

I like it that this blanket that once covered Colleen now covers him.

Rain fell that night in Vermont. We drove around the campground looking for the slot we'd rented, joking that two college graduates should be able to count. We had rented lot 45 but couldn't find it in the dark. Laughter was a relief. I started in on the tent while Colleen pumped up the air mattresses. She looked over at me. I was having a harder time. The tent was new, it was dark by now, the instructions were useless, and it was coming slowly. I didn't want to ask our new neighbors for help. Or worse, her. When I finally got the tent up she looked pleased. We kissed in the light rain, then went inside to our new home.

We made love that night, safe and dry and happy. The rain all night. We had travelled a long way to arrive completely in that moment. I swear to you, I was happy.

The sleeping bag covered us both like a blanket, but as we slept she got most of it, and I shivered beside her, glad to give it to her, happy that this was something I could do for her. It pleased me that I could keep her warm, even if it was only for this one night.

One of the tent poles collapsed. It waved like a dog leg in the wind and the rain in the chilled night air showed no sign of stopping. Colleen got up to pee. She tapped the broken pole with a manicured fingernail. I wondered if the tent would collapse. We shrugged and went back inside.

My son talks to me about a book set in Montreal, but I am thinking of the first meal I bought Colleen, the little cafe where we kissed for the first time, admitted we were scared, and tried to see the future.

My son remarks how comfortable it is, this sleeping bag, and this pleases me. It pleases me that the bag that warms him once warmed Colleen, even if it didn't warm me. The night that Colleen and I used it (she more than me) I stayed up most of the night watching her. I combed my fingers through her hair, placing the long ends in my mouth. I smelled the smoky woods, heard the fire hiss as I stroked her arms, kissed her fingers, admired the swell of her breasts through her cotton shirt. We were lovers. And something else, we were friends.

Later, we exchanged the tent for a motel room by the interstate. I'd lie in bed and listen to her shower, then ask if I could watch her do her makeup and hair. She'd brush it one hundred strokes, humming softly, standing absently in front of the mirror, planning her day. It was summer. I'd made this time for us, and we were happy. An interlude, she called it—she was giving me this *interlude*, giving it to us, and it was clear from the way she said it that it was full of grace, this moment. I tried to take it in, the way you look at the mountains when you're from the flats, not knowing when you'd get out west again, if maybe this was your last sight—how could you know? This is the way I looked at her at first light. I tried to memorize the way that she moved in that early morning motel light.

But things change, don't they? Some things you give up. If you're lucky you get more. And the *more* never replaces what you once had, it just stands tenderly beside it, guarding it maybe—or maybe it just makes it easier, I don't know. A new sight comes along, new memories, new ways of seeing. New people enter your life to move you on. No, the things you give up you don't ever get back, but if you're lucky you get new things, not replacements, exactly, but just new things to keep you moving. To keep you whole. And that's grace, too.

ITCH

On the day he learns of his wife's affair Tom Friendly watches the girl drummer of White Stripes wail away at it somewhere in Canada. The girl is good, her long dark hair matted against her pale skin as she bounces up and down on her seat and keeps the beat, joining her brother in the vocals at the chorus. He hadn't known the two were related, and while he thinks it kind of creepy, the way they look at each other on stage, he had just been admiring her pale white legs and strappy shoes walking the tarmac in the Yukon.

Tom nods on the phone, even though Elise, who is 1,000 miles away in Chicago, cannot see his nods. She explains how sorry she is and Tom elects generosity, accepting her apology but not requesting details even when proffered. They have been separated for three months and Tom has himself proposed an affair with a young woman he has recently met in Boston on a book tour.

Tom replaces the phone in its cradle, grabs his car keys, and goes to the Rite Aide. For two days he has been itching without relief. It is late August and his skin is dried out from too many days lazing at the pool, exhausted from his book tour. He asks a clerk where to find the health and beauty products and is directed to two long aisles cluttered with products whose names he does not recognize.

He hadn't expected to meet anyone so soon, or maybe ever. But Anastasia had looked up at him from the first row of the auditorium where he been giving a reading and it was not what she said—she hadn't said a word, too shy to ask a question in the exchange afterwards—but just the way she had allowed others to crowd forward in front of her, knock-kneed in her clumsy Doc Martens, the way she looked up at him and then stepped aside. She'd buzzed off her hair, a beautiful girl tired of false attention, and placed herself in the background, but Tom saw and understood her as a woman willing to do what was necessary to start again.

Tom knew that Elise had been having the affair but kept his mouth shut, knowing she would tell him when she was ready. And now he has nothing to say. He can't tell her about Anastasia because nothing had happened. Just that graceful stepping aside, the taking of an auditorium seat while she waited for him, a cup of coffee afterwards, and a few hundred emails between distant cities.

Tom Friendly walks slowly down the aisle lifting products from the shelves, struggling to read the small print on bath oils, beads, salts, scented body wash with aloe, topical creams, cocoa butter. He doesn't know what he needs and feels too foolish to ask for help. His skin appears normal but feels harsh and irritated. The itch travels, reconstituting in a different place on his body each time he scratches. He gathers one item from every shelf and leaves with $82.89 of merchandise. The pretty redhead who takes his money—he has only a hundred dollar bill—makes change and attempts a joke about self-medicating, but Tom is itching so badly he smiles grimly at the girl, and speeds home.

He strips off his clothes and draws a bath, dumping in a $20 package of salts from the Dead Sea and lavender bath oil. While the water runs, Tom adjusts the small TV mounted on the bathroom wall until he finds the station with the boy and girl band. The documentary is still playing. Sister and brother are visiting with the Inuit people of a small village in Canada. Then they are giving a concert, and now the girl is singing, earnest and off key, and her skin so white and plain, and he thinks of Anastasia feeding her child eggs at the breakfast table, her husband rushing out the door to work and it cracks open his heart.

Tom dabs his eyes and reaches behind in a futile effort to scratch his sore back, then grinds his shoulder blades up against the doorpost for relief. He steps into the bath. Leaning back in the tub, he stretches out until his head rests on the shelf behind him, and his toes reach up into the cascading hot water. Brother and sister sing "Jolene, Jolene, please don't take him," and later, the girl is speaking in a subdued tone, embarrassed by the two cameras capturing her every word and gesture in a botched impromptu interview, and her cloying brother—is he really her brother or is this too an act?—teasing her for her shyness and speaking over her.

Tom opens a jar of coffee-colored cream. The cocoa butter smells sweet and inviting. He slides his fingers deep into the cool cream and lavishes it up and down his arms, his chest, his inner thighs and calves. The jar holds the trace of his fingers in four parallel tracks matching the scratches he has placed on his body with nervous nails. He pulls out the plug and feels his cracked skin relax, tired pores open. Gravity sucks away the gray used water. He watches the girl, perhaps a wife, twirl her sticks and pound her drums.

THE WONDER SEAT

We met at a writer's conference in Yellow Springs, Ohio. She stood on the sidewalk licking an ice cream cone as I drove past in my blue convertible. She was tall but walked slowly in silver ballet flats with ribbons attached in bowties, as if she had nowhere to go. Her light summer sun dress flattered her form. Her hair was a shade of light brown streaked with blonde; the day before she had twisted a cut daisy into its long tresses. She stood still beneath the movie marquee, licking her cone and watching the traffic (there wasn't much) move up the street.

I parked the car and walked back. I hadn't said a mumbling word to her at the conference. Nervous now, I said hello, then asked, "Where did you get your ice cream cone?" An idiotic question. It was a small town with one ice cream stand. She pointed down the street, and her voice—I remember this so clearly—her voice was that of a child. A musical child. It was a voice from childhood that I had missed.

Returning with my ice cream, we exchanged pleasantries, made inquiries about what kind of writing we did, or wanted to do, and then I asked her bluntly, "Do you want to go for a ride? It's a beautiful night and I have a convertible." She shrugged her high shoulders and said sure.

It takes only a few decisions to make an affair. Someone sees, someone is seen. Call and response, two voices call, deep to deep. The ancient machinery of desire is activated from well-worn cultural codes, the codes of the western world—the way hair hangs or holds the light beneath a movie marquee, say. The way a woman moves when she walks down the street beside you, the sight of her mouth, moving, eating an ice cream cone, that way that women have of lifting their legs, knees rising and the smooth tan legs of summer swinging into the passenger seat, swinging parallel from hips sheathed by the thin white cotton of her dress, legs together out of the night and into your car. A woman feels the intensity of a man's gaze and knows that she has occasioned it and that it is all for her; knows too how to keep this gaze directed on her. She has a power over him now, has reduced him to this elemental moment of wanting, waiting.

She positions the toe of one ballet shoe to the heel of the other, and the shoe falls to the floorboard and now her one foot is bare, and the fuchsia painted toes shuck the other shoe aside and now a barefoot woman is beside you in your car on a warm summer night and you are moving down the street with the top down, the smells of summer cookfires blending with the faint scent of her perfume, her hair swinging as you accelerate into a turn on a country road where children jump rope in a driveway, and she is talking while you listen in the wonder seat, reading her face and long body for clues and you are underway, both married to different people, and in trouble. You know you are in trouble, and that if either of you had any sense you would stop, but you can't. Because you are going to have an affair and if you hadn't wanted that you wouldn't have approached her on the street and she would not have gotten into your car and she certainly would not have removed her silver shoes.

What will happen is what usually happens, the talk of family and children and jobs and bruised dreams and busted hopes, what he said, what she said, and soon enough a husband who doesn't get her and a wife who is restless but unable to say what is wrong, exactly. Words of negation (I couldn't, shouldn't, wouldn't) give way now to words of affirmation. He thinks to himself: she gets me. She thinks: he doesn't talk like any man I know. The idea occurs to you that the two of you are in a car moving fast, you are already coupled aren't you? And a thought about time, how malleable it is, how moments from a marriage can be borrowed if promised to replace.

Soon you are lost in a forest of desire. A search party is formed. You are discovered by swinging lanterns lighting inquisitive faces from the village, walked before the magistrate, met by her husband, your wife, your children, your earlier, wiser self. Everyone has questions you do not know the answers to. You stand there dumbly and when asked, even by a friendly voice, *why did you do it, what in the world happened,* all you can manage to say is, I do not know, it just happened. I was out eating an ice cream cone, I was driving my car home from the conference one night, and because you are both writers you will find a way to finish this awkward sentence, yet no one will believe you.

THE GROCERY GIRL

My wife Frankie may be joking about doing the bag boy but I'm afraid to ask. There is a loopy grocery logic to these things. Late in the Reagan administration we lived for a time in St. Louis, where I fell into some things with a checker at the grocery store. She had the 80s big hair, the good bones, the big brown eyes. Frankie had moved out, leaving Jade with her mother, citing a need to get some fresh air, maybe in L.A., and an unspecified need for something she thought she'd be able to put her finger on once she got there. In time she confessed that the thing she had fingered was Dominic, her agent, who was also fronting a play she had mounted at the Beverly Hills Playhouse. I chose to ride it out, checking in by phone from St. Louis.

The thing with Frankie and Dominic made me feel like I'd been knifed in a back alley. It was the first real affair for either of us. Although we couldn't know it at the time, the marriage would survive. But it was as if the tip of the blade had broken off, was lodged deep and working slowly deeper. The days were unbearably long. I vacuumed the carpet with a loud machine, banging into furniture and cursing. Nights I had trouble sleeping. That wore off, in time, but everything seemed diminished. My world shrank small enough to drown in the bathtub. Eventually we got back together, and not long after that I got even.

The checker girl stood beside her cash register in her tiny

orange vest. She held her arms above her head as she yawned and twisted her hair into a French braid. Her vest pulled up, baring her flat, tan belly. She held my gaze steadily, with a smile that said, "That's right, pal, I'm right here and it's hopeless now, isn't it?"

There were no customers in her line. I was standing in the picnic aisle. Throwing some charcoal, lighter fluid and matches into my shopping cart, I went through her line, then went through again twenty minutes later with a small Weber grill. The girl who was bagging for her whispered into her ear, loud enough for me to hear, "Girl, this one look like he want to eat you up."

Her name was Cindi with an "i." Cindi Jean. Her mom dealt blackjack downriver on a riverboat that never left shore. Her dad she didn't know from. She lived in a 16 x 80 Southern Elite three bedroom, two bath trailer that she shared with her mother when mom was around, which wasn't often. The trailer was ancient. It sat fifty feet from the railroad tracks, just above the Mississippi River. Someone had retrofitted it with a screened in sleeping porch, which Cindi kept filled with cactus and coleus plants.

A crooked bridge just to the east crossed the river at a forty-five degree angle. The bridge was closed to traffic. An earthen mound, covered in weeds, blocked it off from anyone dumb enough to drive up to it. But kids would park in front of the mound and hang out there, partying, and climbing the bridge when they got drunk. Every year one of them would drop into the Mississippi and be brought up, dead as a mackerel. Towering two hundred feet above the river, it looked terrifying at night, this unlit cantilever bridge to nowhere. Aircraft warning lights mounted at the top of the bridge had long ago been shot out and never replaced. A new four lane bridge stood downriver. Just outside the trailer, freight trains rumbled past, rattling every pan and dish in the place. It was like living inside an aluminum can. It was best to be outside when the train passed through. When the engineer pulled his whistle we would go watch, seated on some cinder blocks that Cindi's mom had stacked in the miniature dirt yard.

One night we sat smoking cigarettes in the trailer. Cindi was unusually quiet. I had just come from a university function that had required me to dress up, and I hadn't stopped off at my apartment to change clothes. She looked at me as if we were meeting again for the first time. She played with my hair, and then my necktie. I shot my cuffs, and she fingered my gold watch, which had been my grandfather's. She pulled at my cuff links, clasping and unclasping them. I asked her if she had ever made love to a man in a suit. She shook her head no. "How do you tie a knot like this?" she asked. I undid the tie and put it around her slender neck, which was brown as a nut. As I demonstrated the four in hand knot I chose that moment to tease her about the spelling of her name, the bad professor hitting the easy target, and she locked eyes with me, then shrugged, and said that was her mother's doing. "My mom wanted me to have something in my life that wasn't plain," she said. "That's what she came up with, I guess."

I remember her saying this to me. The silence afterward. The way we held each other, then, her head nestled against my shoulder. Revenge sex had felt cheap and dirty and exhilarating. I knew it could only end badly. But they say every love affair has one moment that comes to represent all the others, one that will stay with you if you let it.

HE WASN'T YOU

This is you, this is me.

Her voice gravelly with sleep, the woman traces the outline of her body and her husband's as if at a crime scene, her hands the yellow chalk of police. She wets one long finger and massages his eyelids. He registers the peach scent of her hair, newly washed, sighs, digs deeper into the sheets.

There had been affairs. First him. Then, he suspects, her. They separated. It went on like this for eight months, then last night he called. And wound up here. Her house. Their old house.

He wakes to find ten sharp nails swinging lightly in his face, each perfectly shaped and painted Ferrari red.

"Kathleen," he says. "What time is it?"

"Blow them dry."

Martin blows lightly on each of her nails, careful not to touch them with his lips. When he finishes, she taps them lightly on his forehead, then reaches over, flips on the lampstand light.

He shoots her in this new light, his eye an unblinking camera, taking his time, as if he has never before seen this woman. He sees her chipped front tooth, the small scar on her temple, the gentle rise of her neck, the slope of her shoulder, the curve from hip to waist, and the way her legs, half folded on the bed, seem painted on the white sheets in a sexy angle.

"Stay there," she says. "I'm not finished here."

She twists to reach his thighs, the muscled calves, his feet, where the sheets lie bunched. He lies perfectly still until she completes her tracing, his strong surgeon's hands clasped and resting on his chest. From where he sits he cannot see the clock; his pants block the lighted dial. Dusty morning sun slants through the raised corner window. He props his head with a pillow and waits.

She grabs at the reading light suspended over their heads and adjusts it skillfully, like the doctor she is, so that it shines brightly into his eyes, blinding him momentarily. She lies back in the bed, adjusts her pillow. They are naked under the covers.

"What time is it," he asks again.

"True confession time. Time to pony up some answers. Like, for instance, why you called me?"

Martin had been out driving. He drove across the north shore, onto the Lake Pontchartrain Causeway, twenty-four miles into New Orleans. Then turned around and got back onto the Causeway. Fifteen miles out he had pulled over, set the flashers and cut the engine. Cars roared by, honking and flashing their brights. He had gotten out of the car, moving carefully to the railing, buffeted by the wind of the flying cars. He was out of the sight of land. Under the light of the half moon, the black water beneath him rippled in circles of light. He spat into the darkness, considering. Then removed his blazer and let the wind kite it down, down, the sleeves swirling out then folding in and out of sight. He twisted the gold ring off his right hand, another gift from the New Orleans woman, and threw it over as well. Past midnight he found himself in a parking lot, looking in the window of an all night convenience store. The light was strange, that funny amber color that seems to paint things more than light them, that makes you believe for a time that maybe it's a different world and that this is no ordinary convenience store, no ordinary night.

"So, Martin" Kathleen asks again. "Give me a sentence.

The truest sentence that you know. Then another. And another one after that. Lay them down"

Martin clears his throat. He starts. "So I was at this convenience store on the north end. I was parked there somehow, I don't why I was there and not somewhere else. And I saw this woman carrying stuff to the counter, piles of stuff in a basket. She wore a yellow bikini, this woman, one of those thong jobs that makes your crotch hurt just looking at it, and she had lots of muscles, but she threw that stuff up on the counter like it was some great effort, with way more arm movement than you'd think was necessary for a small basket like that. And the thing is, I was parked head in, right up in front, so I had a good view. She had a bottle of peroxide and some rubbing alcohol up there on the counter, two cans of Band Aids and a big economy box of Tylenol, an Ace bandage, a tube of Coppertone and a six pack of Miller."

"Big night. So, what'd she look like, your woman?"

He frowns and gives the big stare. Then says, "I don't know. Like your average woman in a thong at midnight getting ready to self-medicate."

"That's the B answer," she says.

"Okay. She wasn't hard to look at. Sculptured. Good bones. Chiseled from the Cosmo prototype. Huge heaving breasts, wasp-like waist, that one perfect mole just above her pouty lips, which are lipsticked the color of—"

"Of these," she says, holding up her fingernails, which have dried but still have that nice wet look, and waving her toenails in the air, which she has done in the same color.

"Exactly."

"And after she made her purchase there at the counter she drifted out of the store and toward you in some big, final way, like an Obsession ad, like she's built for speed, like all your days hereafter will be filled with a modicum of happiness and just the right amount of danger, like the grail is in reach and all the brothers notified, like—"

"Like you."

"That's sweet, Martin." she says. "Pathetic, but sweet."

Martin managed a smile.

Kathleen's eyes narrow. "Now, are you going to tell me the fucking truth about the New Orleans woman?"

Martin considers, checks her face, to confirm, but she's pokered up. "What's to tell?" he says, stalling. "It's over. The New Orleans woman got deep- sixed, over and out, tossed over the Pontchartrain, buried deeper than Jimmy Hoffa."

"And that's why you're here."

"Sure. Yes. Well, no. Actually, I had a dream."

"A dream."

"Yeah."

"You and Martin Luther King. Lincoln Memorial stuff."

"Not that kind of dream. I'm being serious, here, Kathleen. I really did. I mean, maybe it doesn't mention you directly, this dream–"

"Dreams don't mention, they enact. Your unlived life. Your shadow self. The whole coulda, woulda, shoulda thing. Basic Carl Jung."

"Didn't Oprah do a show on that?"

Kathleen ignores this.

"So anyway," Martin continues, "it's a Pope dream."

"A pope dream!" Kathleen doubles over, in apparent stitches, but stops her laugh dramatically, looks at him hard, with mock seriousness. She's clearly enjoying this, but Martin cannot figure her angle.

"Was the popemobile there?" Kathleen asks. "I always wanted to ride in the popemobile."

"No popemobile," he says.

"Isn't the Pope in every dream, technically? I can't remember."

"Wants to be, maybe. Anyway, you're the Catholic," he says.

"Was the Catholic," she says. "Tenses, Martin. Watch the

tenses. My girlish patent leather youth. Okay. So there's the Pope. What's the Pope doing?"

"I was in a classroom–"

"Tell it in the present tense, like it's happening now."

"I'm in this classroom, alright? It must be that I am back in high school because I recognize the colors of the walls and where my locker is. The Pope has come to our school to answer all our questions and to talk to us about, dunno, what Popes talk about, I guess. This is a dream, remember, so some of this is sketchy but it's still all true, I swear. True to the dream."

Kathleen blows on her nails and looks bored. She picks up a bottle of moisturizer from the night table. She starts with her legs and moves up. Martin watches her pale hands for clues.

"Okay. I get it. Continue with this dream, Martin."

"And I'm scheduled to say something to him, you know, the Pope. To make some kind of scripted remark, like it's a photo op or something. Like they had out in Denver or wherever it was."

"Stick to the dream. Don't editorialize."

"So then, for some reason, I'm on the ground, crawling around. I mean, I didn't start out crawling around in the dream, I did one of those deep knee bend things that Catholics do–"

"Genuflect."

"Right, I *genuflect* to the Pope, and then I seem to like it, because I stay down there a long time. I'm crawling around on the ground not being noticed by the Pope, who is busy blessing everyone and doesn't see me."

"What are you doing down there?"

Martin takes the moisturizer bottle. He caps it, and continues his story. "Well, this is the funny part. I'm crawling around on the floor near the Pope. And I remember I'm trying to feel something. With the Pope there and everything, I figure

I should be feeling things more intensely. Maybe even religious things, or spiritual, you know, but not just that. I have this idea that everything will be intensified."

"But it wasn't happening."

"Right, it wasn't happening. It's just not there, I mean, I don't feel anything. Nothing about anything. So then I see this other kid, like me, on the floor, crawling. Except he's cut his thumb, and I can see this raised bead of blood on it, and he's looking at this blood and at the Pope, and it's like I start to feel through him, you know?"

"Uh huh. Weird."

"Yeah. It's like I feel for him, bleeding like that, and then I began feeling like him, and then I *was* him."

Kathleen drops her gaze. They both look at her hands, which she has placed them on her pale belly, fingers laced. She locks eyes with Martin, and frowns. "And now you're thinking–what?"

"That– you know." Martin looks down into the bedsheets. "I'm–I'm thinking that it might be a sign or something," he says softly. "For us."

"For us?" she repeats.

"Yeah. Like we're going to be okay. now. Like, I was this one person, you see, and now I'm another. I'm different. I can feel again, can feel another person, the whole range of things. The emotions."

"Just like that."

"Just like that. Why not?"

She sighs, and turns away from him and toward the wall.

"You know, Martin?" she says. "You didn't have to work up a dream for this, you could've just bought the Pope's book at the mall."

He bites his lower lip. "Knock it off, Kathleen."

"You are such a shithead."

There is a long silence. Then she turns back to him, reaches for his hand. He lets her take it.

"Look, Martin," she says. "I am trying here. I would like to believe that you are trying too. I am working to believe you, what you're trying to say here. That it's over with what's her face. Miss November. But there's something you should know."

He bites his lip again. And waits. But there is only silence. He looks again at her new red nails. She has man hands, freckled on top, and large.

"You've met someone. Is that it?"

"Well, what'd you expect, that I'd crash the convent? It's been eight months! You didn't call. I didn't call. Then I called and you didn't want to deal with it. Then you called and your timing, once again, was off."

"Who is he?"

"Who is she?"

"*Was* she. Miss November, remember?"

"Well, he's Dr. November, okay? A guy at work."

She spits the words clean, till she registers his wince. "No one you know. Why don't we just leave it at that?"

Martin raises his voice, rotating in bed so that his shoulders and head face her, while his lower body remains still, in a golfer's coil. He finds her eyes, which have narrowed again, and speaks to them. "So what was the big attraction for you with this guy? He's the master swordsman? He touches you in all your deepest places? He's the one we've all been waiting for?"

"You shit."

"Well?"

"He wasn't you."

Martin gets up, puts on his pants. He reaches under the bed and finds his shoes. He starts to lace one on, then slings it at the wall. The shoe ricochets off the wall and knocks a vase of flowers off the end table. Kathleen suppresses a scream. She tries a smile, then retracts it. Remembering a day at the beach when they first met, she recalls that she wore a T-shirt and black bikini bottom and she stared at him and he stared at her, and she waded out into the waves and waited for him to do something.

"Are you finished?" she says.

The water from the vase has soaked Martin's socks. He peels them off slowly, and lays them methodically on the bedspread.

He leaves the room. She tosses her hair and clicks on the morning news. He comes back in. She clicks off. He holds new socks from the dryer in the basement.

"Look, Kathleen," he says. "I'm sorry. I'm sorry as shit. Look, I guess you had the right. And who am I to blah blah blah. It's not pretty, any of this, and the worst part is I feel like we're reading off a bad script."

"Ditto."

"And the weird thing," Martin says, "is that nothing really happens in this story. I mean *something* happened, something big took place here, but in a way everything is still in place. You're you, I'm me, the house is still the house and these are my clothes and our friends are still our friends–it's just that all the meanings have gotten jumbled around, out of order or something. Stuff that normally goes with other stuff has just been knocked out of place, you know? Emotions. We don't know where to put this other stuff that we feel, right? The bad stuff, I mean."

He considers this. None of it sounds right. He knows what he wants to say, but the words feel like dust motes in the morning light, visible and small, floating. He tries again.

"And divorce is the ultimate cliché, isn't it? I mean, then we'd join the national rap about personal growth, the word space would come up, repeatedly, when we're out with our respective support groups, in this priestly tone our therapists use, there'd be the usual talk about us, the allowances made as to how at least there were no children, our parents and friends would do just the right amount of tactful commiserating, or they wouldn't, but the whole thing would be so boring and predictable we'd want to fucking kill ourselves."

"Death before divorce, is that what you're saying, Martin? Take the long view. Play the hand you're dealt. Be adults. Stop whining, take what you can get, pray the St. Francis of Asissi prayer or whatever it is, 'change what you can and don't sweat the rest,' get a dog."

He laughs. "Something like that. Maybe without the dog part."

"The dog, I think, is critical here." Kathleen's mouth is open in a wide smile now, showing teeth that have been capped and bleached.

"Could we start with a hamster or a gerbil or something? You know, work our way up to the big stuff?"

"Sorry, pal. Nothing in cages," Kathleen says. "You get my drift?"

"Right. Check."

Martin punches the TV remote, surfs to CNN. There's an update on the latest disaster haunting the world, some wildfire footage out West. The firefighters look grimy and weary. Like they'd rather be somewhere else. A place without heroics.

"So, this was good, right?"

"This, meaning what," she says.

He waves his arms vaguely, spinning now, around the room, like a child's top whose string has been pulled.

"This. Our talk. Our understanding. I fucked up, you did what you had to do. Now we go on. Right?"

"Sure," she says. "We go on. Thoroughly modern. But here's the deal."

"What," he says, taking a seat on the bed next to her.

"I'm going to continue to see him. Tuesday and Thursday nights, same as before."

Martin claps his head. "What! You're fucking kidding me."

"I kid you not."

"What the fuck, Kathleen!" he bellows. "Why are you doing this?"

"Relax, I'll bring him by. Introduce him. You'll like him, I promise. Think of it this way, I'm back to seventeen. It will be like you two have joint custody."

He stands up, turns around, and looks at her. Her color is up, and he can see her lightly freckled shoulders, the delicate collarbone, twist away from him, then back. The first two fingers of each hand are crossed. She sits up tall, and cups her hands under her small breasts in a mock Playboy pose, but he registers her hands, which she's moved behind her back, with her fingers still crossed. He laughs, relieved. She is a redhead, all the way down.

"Gotcha." She sticks her tongue out at him, uses the wide smile again. She looks so small to him, then, sitting there like that on the wide bed, so present, so completely within reach.

"Deal," he says.

"You like my hair, yes?" She fluffs out her hair, which has dried to the color of a copper penny. She lies back on the pillow so that it fans all around her face, framing her.

"I do," he says softly.

"Hair I am!"

He laughs, and they grow silent. Martin starts to speak, checks himself. Then starts again.

"We'll have our moments, though, am I right? It's not this easy, is it? There'll be things I'll want to know that I shouldn't, words will be said and I'll piss you off and we'll get off kilter, do stupid shit. That the arrangement?"

"Pretty much. And one more thing."

"What's that."

Kathleen sticks a piece of gum in her mouth. She chews it slowly and deliberately. It is Autumn, a violent season in the emergency rooms of New Orleans. The hospital employs extra workers to clean bloody laundry. An unmarked hamper collects demolished sheets. Sharpened scalpels drop to the floor during the panic of this season. Dark drops of blood falls like tears to the sterile floor beside his blue papered feet, meaningless blood. He was not schooled in regret or remorse. Regret costs the next life. To heal, surgeons inflict pain. Most surgeons finish med school near the bottom of their class; their genius is in scheduling, and appearing, godlike, to give news to waiting families. They require more sleep but cannot get it. Not everyone can be saved. These are thoughts he falls into, until he is called back by Kathleen's voice. She is saying something.

She is saying: "I see her around, or you see her, and I do her. Then you. The full Hoffa. You tracking on this?"

He stumbles into the kitchen. Opening the back door he watches neighbors up and down the street getting the paper, taking out the trash, setting the flag on the mailbox, ordinary stuff he's seen a thousand times. He watches them get into their expensive cars to pull them out of their cluttered garages to go to their important jobs.

Martin studies the careful way that they move. He stands on tiptoe, lifting his eyes and craning his neck. He strains to see past where his street turns out of the development and connects to the main road into town. He can barely make it out.

SCRIPTS

Beat Sheet

Mother is late again. She pulls up and Zach throws himself on the floor. She's promised a treat if he behaves at the beach. He has Bobby's soft Augusta drawl. "Ass cream, Gramma, ass cream."

We stop to give Jenna a lift to the airport. She knows how mother feels about her work. So, on the drive over to her apartment she texts me, "Contract girl 4 Vivid=No anal and guys wear condoms." Jenna is five ten and sculpted. Guys in high school creamed when they saw her.

Mother drives while Jenna sits beside me and continues to text. "New name Savannah Haze. My brand re-launch." Zach reaches his dimpled arms for Jenna/Savannah, and she gives him a big kiss on his neck. He giggles and that does it, she's giving him busters now, loving all over his little neck.

Jenna tried to get me to go with her to the audition, but Bobby got shipped to Afghanistan in the surge. We could use the money. Mother wants to help but Bobby has his pride. I have no earthly skills. Jenna does girl girl but she never made a pass at me. I kid her about it and act offended. One of the Vivid contract girls fell in love and refused boy girl for a long time. Word got out and she lost lots of money. She's back to anal and feet now, Jenna says.

We drop Jenna curbside. She has just enough time for her flight to LAX. I get out and walk her inside. Zach keeps screaming for ass cream. Mother says don't be long, dear. She has a long frown for Jenna.

Jenna pulls me into a hug and tells me Bobby will be okay, she swears. She'll say a novena. It must be all over my face. She asks me to water her plants while she's gone. She's away a month at a time. She bought a new condo in Studio City when her agent got her the Vivid gig. She's relieved. She says she has sex less than me now, her contract is that good. I tell her I'm happy for her but no one has sex less than me. I miss Bobby awful. Jenna tells me I can jill off to her movies, she'll send me some. I tell her no thanks. She has new peep toe shoes. Her toes look like ruby candy. She's my friend since second grade.

At the beach an old man watches from his balcony. He's got binoculars. I tug at my top, then flip him off and run after Zach, who is barking. He thinks he's a dog.

A+Treatment

The Director watches from the balcony of his high room, tracking the women and their little boy as they make their way to the island beach near Savannah. The mother is fair, pixie cut, the daughter tan, free of affect, connected and purposeful.

Ten a.m., the sun scorches. The Director says that we are too afraid of death to love wisely or to discover beauty; forfeiting beauty in exchange for love we begin to die before we have learned to live. To cast and crew he says what torture it is to play opposite an actor who looks at you and sees someone else. He grabs the actress, the actor: *if everything around me were true how would I behave?*

The Director lifts his binoculars. A man walks past the two women, who struggle with the toddler's seat buckle. The girl is quick.

The Director sits in a raised chair at the pool. Below, on the beach, the women pull the boy in his red wagon. The mother shakes her head, rolls her shoulders, cracks her long neck. The girl looks twenty-two, too old for the part. Elise, his producer, texted him that his lead is back in rehab. Her boyfriend too.

Every action has a purpose. The beach girl bends at the waist to help her son with his pail and shovel. She is within reach of her little boy, available to him, a terrible beauty promising connection but remaining essentially unavailable. Nothing we do is neutral. The Director believes that only what happens before the age of eighteen is essential, he wants to be that buried child. Girl as Mom. As actress. Every actor's life is broken in half trying to escape self-awareness. At the moment you lose it you diminish your receptivity to experience. The best actors learn to hide as creative life becomes a shield, a way of keeping life at a distance. It saddens him. The girl is ruined, he thinks, even while embracing her beautiful distortions.

Better to watch her bury her boy in sand. Buried child. His delighted squeals, the easy grace of the grandmother's smile. A day at the beach, and nothing more.

Certain tribes of aboriginal descent believe that a photograph can steal a soul, imprisoning it within its amalgam of polyester, celluloid, salts and gelatin. The Director smiles to think himself a thief of souls. He leaves the Pentax camera around his neck. The girl will go untouched, unnoticed, unremarked, the perfect line of her body undisturbed. A role must have continuous being and unbroken line. He watches her, preserving all necessary distance, until at last he raises his weary arm and makes the sign of the cross over her, over the mother and the boy, and the beach, as if in a papal blessing, as if his heart is not rent.

Shooting Scripts

She has two dimples just above her perfect ass, dimples you

have seen before, in a woman you once knew in a life long ago. You order a chair and umbrella to be placed alongside her encampment: a large pile (monogrammed Louis Vuitton waterproof canvas bags, cooler, red wagon heavily laden), and you wait.

The young woman, when she approaches, looks like Kate Moss at twenty. Tousled blonde hair below her shoulder blades. Four-inch silver teardrop earring, left side, closest to you. Her mother lovely as well, her hair in a blunt cut, a two-piece swim suit. The little boy is delightful, curly blond hair, uncut, a boy of two. For him they pull the big red wagon on the beach. They arrange their lives around him. They follow his every move, the male of the species. He carries pail and shovel. Women without men, at the beach.

But the girl is twenty-two – can still be called a girl, before the sadness of twenty-four, or worse, twenty-nine, before the requisite changes of twenty-five, when the world calls women like her to account, to questions she does not now entertain, the girl at twenty-two, she stops your heart.

You have known her, you know her now. You smile at the mother and go on watching behind your summer hat of straw, your large striped beach glass. Under the ocean-blue umbrella in the summer sun.

The girl wears a black string bikini and as she watches her boy, places both hands on her hips.

The little boy has a sturdy body. He digs his shovel into the wet sand, then abandons his toys to chase a dog into the soupy surf. Both women run after him. You lift your fork to your mouth, then stop, exhausted. Eating seems like work, is there no end to eating, must we go on doing this simple act forever? The girl bends at the waist to help her boy. Her breasts do not separate nor do they hang. Her line is perfect.

Her chest is small, her thighs and legs, everything well proportioned, but her ass and hips are kept from being too small, she has escaped looking anorexic and depleted only by giving birth to that boy.

Her boy has run off again. He kicks a ball under your chair. Now she moves toward you, smiles.

"I'm sorry," she says.

She is sorry. A lifetime of apologies. They simply can't, and never do, apologize enough. Beauty and her shade, sorrow. Her mother looks and smiles too. We go on smiling. You lift your weary arm.

When they go you'll keep coming back for her. You will wait. A week, a month, she may be nowhere in sight, yet present, still. Each day you will see her more clearly. She has made every last person on earth seem unnecessary.

WHAT YOU DO BEST

You're auditioning women to replace Alison. Her part apparently has come to an end. Veronica's ended months ago. This is sad, these cast changes. As Director you can say that it touches you, you're moved. You do appreciate their years of devoted service, the selfless way they performed their roles, read their scripts, threw themselves into their assigned parts, assumed their characters. At times it was difficult to keep up with them, an almost daily writing on your part, scripting their lives to suit your desire.

Now that they're gone you try to imagine your life without them. It is the performative element that you'll miss. Talking to Alison you went before the interiorized camera, assumed an identity and constructed a self just for her. With her as spectator and participant, audience and actress, your life seemed a work of art.

You're going to miss her, sure. You miss them all. You missed them before they left. You missed them before you met them. You'll miss them even if you somehow get hold of them again. Missing, you've come to believe, may be what you do best.

You call Chloe. She has, you're prepared to believe, the look that is needed, what's more, the name. First things are so strange. The first phone call is a rush. The phone rings. You wait. Once, twice. Then, connection: that familiar clicking sound that tells you someone's picking up. You anticipate the voice. Hers sounds low, cautious. When she realizes who it is, you can feel the smile break through. Next: the laugh. You wait for this, thank God for it when you hear it, tender and unrehearsed, try to make it last.

"Not impossibly," Chloe says, when you ask if she could possibly inhabit the space of the word lonechill.

"What are you wearing," you say.

"Beautiful, Estee Lauder. Victoria's Secret, bottoms only."

"All the good names," you say.

"Some blood, the result of a collision with a kitchen appliance. While phonebound to you."

"Blood is good," you say. "We can do blood."

"We must be in love before we can care that all women are not virtuous," she says. Proust. Excellent choice.

"Take them off," you say. "The bottoms."

Into the receiver she hums what you recognize as a Natalie Merchant song, "Gun Shy." It works nicely with the scripted lines. You remark on the improvisation. Then the line goes still.

You consider: Her voice, the sly metallic glint of it that still rings in the receiver, is perhaps too carefully modulated.

"The beloved is successively the malady and the remedy," Chloe says. "Both the poison and the cure."

"No news there," you say, your voice courting resignation, tottering on the edge of something else entirely.

"They're off. My bottoms, I mean. They're in my hands now. I've gotten blood on them, I'm afraid."

You line up the shot, taking care to see that she is backlit. Her hair, a lemony blonde, is pulled back severely and lies close to her scalp in a single French braid. Her skin is tanned and smooth, her body slender. Her bare brown toes grip the kitchen counter as she leans back precariously on the tall stool like some giant bird of prey. From this angle you can see the light hairs around her navel. You study the line of her left leg, the leg closest to you. She holds the phone with her chin, the blood-flecked panty draped over her near shoulder. Both arms are wrapped around herself in the chill morning air, crushing her breasts together.

The trickiest part now: to feign indifference. Your humanity, that part you feel tugging at self-betterment, you experience as both task and episode. "I did God's work in approaching you," Veronica had said, and Alison: "I was ready to follow you anywhere."

Which you hear as: impossible, un-writeable.

Chloe hums, deep and off key. You adjust the lens, check the sound levels. Somewhere in here you'll lose your way, abandon the script. Maybe you never much believed in the script, anyway. You're looking, always already looking for the ending. You wish to keep this scene short, very short, make it almost a non- event, and yet one that cannot be forgotten. By her.

All ways out: You select one, mumble goodbye, citing difficulties with the lighting, when what you're thinking of is the blemishes. It's best to exit before the physical blemishes are noticed, best to stay ahead of all partings. Spiritual blemishes come later, of course, when it's too late, when your two lives have shipwrecked somewhere off the coast of hope.

You make a mental note for Chloe to do the Kafka reading, the conversation with Max Brod.

We are nihilistic thoughts, suicidal thoughts that come into God's head, a bad day of his.

Then is there no hope? Brod asks.

Oh yes, Kafka says. Plenty of hope, an infinite amount of hope. But not for us.

You're off the phone in a flash, traveling faster than she can move, faster than she'd want to, you're gone: Where you want to be. Where she'll find you.

THE PRINCE OF ARTHUR AVENUE

They're in Arlington National Cemetery, father and son, not far from Kennedy's grave. The older one. Then the younger brother, where there is only a simple white cross, low to the ground.

It's a warm day in April and they've shed their jackets. The son wants to know what it was like in those days. He's a tall boy, taller than his father. Around his neck are purple beads and a guitar pick with a hole in it, the bead string snaked through so that it looks homemade.

Tell me a story, he asks. Anything you want. Just so it's about me. You can do that, can't you?

The father drags his sleeve across his brow, checks his watch. We have time, the son says. Later, we'll go find something to eat, see the town. But first, tell me this story like I want.

I'll tell you a story, the father says. I'm not sure if it's what you want, but it's one I know. It concerns you, in a way.

Shoot. Whenever you're ready. We've got all day.

I worked for Tuck Tape in those days, on the loading dock, down in the Bronx. There was a bakery not far from there on Arthur Avenue, where they made Italian bread. I liked to smell the bread baking as I pulled into the lot. It was the smell of home, made by hard working men in the dead of night. It was an honest product, that bread. Sometimes after work I'd stop and pick up an armful of bread just to smell it on the drive home. Your mother would slice it up and serve it that night with salad and pasta and maybe a bottle of red wine. We had the life.

I worked graveyard five nights a week and caddied on the weekends at North Redoubt Links because we needed the extra money. North Redoubt is still one of the better clubs, though I haven't been there in years. Caddying was good pay if you got the right member or some happy-assed relative from out of town, but it was lousy hours, ate up the whole damn day, and I didn't get to see your mother much. She was pregnant at the time. We hadn't planned on it. We had barely enough for our own selves. In those days it seemed like every time I turned around someone needed money. Her two older brothers had managed to run a perfectly good tire business into the ground and got sent to Riker's when the feds got into their books. So there was that, their families to look after, and we were supporting my sister, who had MS and needed pretty much around the clock care. Things were tight. But hell, we welcomed it, the news about this baby. We thought maybe this would turn things around for us. I told her I'd just caddy on Sundays, or if I needed to I'd get a third job. I knew a guy who fished the Hudson for crabs. It could be managed, I told her. We'll be fine. Let's have this baby.

We rented a small house in Yonkers back then. We had a back room that I used for storing my tools and fishing gear. I cleaned it out and she set to work, cleaning, spackling, painting, wallpapering, you name it. She put a blue border running along the top of the wall. She was sure it was going to be a boy. In those days you had to wait to find out what you had.

She asked me one day, Joseph, do you think we can afford a crib? This baby is going to need a crib. I said sure, let's go get us a crib. We poked around antique stores on Broadway until we found a crib that suited her. It was mahogany, stout as you'd please, with fine woodworking, all hand tooled. That crib could have held the young Paul Bunyan. And a set of drawers, she said. This baby will need a place for his things. So we bought a set of drawers to match the crib. We put it all in the baby's room, the room that was my old tool and fishing room. She said to me one night, Do you like the baby's room? I said it was the finest baby room I had ever seen. There wasn't a finer baby's room in town. And I meant it. It was a fine room. We had everything just so. At night sometimes, before I went in to Tuck Tape, we'd sit on the floor in that room with what was left of the bread and wine and we'd talk about baby names, about who it'd look like, what side of the family it would favor. She wanted to know what his voice would sound like, and how it would feel to hold him that first time.

This one night in particular we were sitting there in what was to be the baby's room, past ten o'clock, talking, like we would do, and she looked so pretty sitting up against the wall like that, like a child herself almost, except for her belly, where she had begun to show. She had her hands propped up on her belly, just holding them there steady, when she started sobbing. Not loud, you understand, but so I could hear her. I asked her what was wrong.

Nothing, she said. I'm just so happy, I guess. I'm happy that you want this baby.

Sure I'm happy. You're going to be the best mother any baby ever had, I said. It was true.

She was quiet a long time. Then she said, this baby is going to be loved, Joseph. Not like me.

What do you mean, not like you?

I never told you this. I didn't think it mattered. But now I see that it does.

What do you mean, I asked her.

You never met my father.

I know that. He's dead. Drowned in the Hudson, you told me. Fishing accident.

He's not dead, Joseph. I told you that because I was ashamed. Or because he's dead to me. He's drowning all right, in booze. He left when my mother died, cut out just like that. That's why I was raised by my grandfather, not like I told you, because my father never died. He's still here in this shitbum town, a drunk, Joseph.

Well, of course I knew that her mother died of cancer when she was seven. But this news about her father made me wonder about her, about what else she hadn't told me.

The boy looks at his father, then looks away.

You want to hear more? the father asks. The breeze presses against his face. Tourists shuffle around the graves, with somber faces. They shake their heads and walk off, a steady stream.

Sure, the boy said.

I saw him one day, her old man. I asked around at the union hall. Some men who had worked with him, all good men, they told me where I should look. He wasn't hard to find. I went to one of his watering holes. I staked a position at the far end of the bar, and waited. Along about midnight this one Friday night he shows up, still in his work clothes. I remember how he leaned into the bar, standing the whole time, one foot on the dented brass rail to steady him. His bartender lined up three shots and he downed them one after the other, then chased it with beer and ordered up another set. I ordered another one myself, careful not to catch his eye. He was a mean drunk, loud and loose-limbed, and he had a wicked laugh that ended with this high little trill. It sounded funny coming from such a big man, but no one laughed with him. No one tried to talk with him, just his bartender, who kept feeding him the drinks, washing his glasses in the sink and drying them with a towel he kept slung on his shoulder.

The crowd is still six deep at the dead President's grave. The boy plays with the guitar pick around his neck. He puts his jacket back on. The sun has ducked behind a cloud, lower now in the western sky. The wind shifts, and the eternal flame at the dead president's grave turns toward them. The breeze holds the smell of the underground fuel.

His father studies the boy a long time. Then starts again.

I knew it was him. He looked like your mother. His jaw had the same set to it, and besides that there was that laugh, the way he broke it off with that high lonesome sound, which to me that night sounded like a small animal in pain. It was a laugh designed to mock people. Women, in particular. I had heard it from his brothers, the Riker's crooks, and I hated him for it, hated all of them, and looking at him that night in the bar I knew, I could feel, how much she hated him, hated the very sight of him. Hated him so much she had snuffed him out in her memory, even though he was all she had in the world after her mother had gone and things went to the bad for her family. But to hate your father and bury your mother as a little girl—where does that leave you? I felt awful, watching him that night, and there was something else, besides, something I hadn't counted on. I began to understand, finally, what I meant to your mother. It was a burden to have to mean so much to someone who had so little. I began to feel like it was a weight I couldn't handle.

The boy stops fingering his pick. He looks at his father, then looks away.

So anyway, I followed him home that night. After last call he staggered out the door, and I went out after him. I had it in my mind to hurt him, to hurt him like he'd hurt her, and everyone else he'd ever known. And no one would've blamed me if I did. Hell, they'd thank me. I walked ten paces behind him and he didn't even notice me. I don't know how he knew his way, he was blind drunk, and reeking of booze. His smell stuck to the air.

Did you tell my mother you found him? the boy asks.

No. Not right away, at least. I followed him for a few nights, debating whether I should tell him what a certified asshole he was, that he had a beautiful daughter no thanks to him, and a grandchild about to enter the world. But then I thought no, that would make him a grandfather, put us in connection in a way I didn't want to be connected. Right then was when I understood how your mother had felt, understood the way she had refused to let him exist even though he clearly did. For a minute or two I might have thought that news about his girl and her new baby might change something in him, knowing that he had someone to care for—but I shook that off when I remembered how he'd left his own blood years ago, and how would any news change him, anyway? It would all be the same to him. I saw I was just being a fool. But I trailed him for days, looking for signs or clues or something, what I should do, or shouldn't do. It bothered me that your mother was from such trash, I'm not ashamed to tell you. I wish I could tell you different. And it changed something in me. I can see that now. Though we managed for another few years.

The boy looks at his hands, puts them in his hair, then cradles his head in his clasped hands as he leans back and tries to find the sun. He straightens up then and looks at the rows of white crosses, marking the lives of the famous, the unknown, and the dead.

Is he gone? the boy asks his father.

Yes. But I didn't do it, I'm pleased to say. Much as I would have liked to. He fell down drunk on the job one day is the way I heard it. Never got up.

What was his name? the boy asks.

Not yours, says his father. Not yours.

They walk around the twisting road, past the tall gates, aiming for the car. The cemetery is quiet, it's secret knowledge safe beneath their hurried feet.

When they are in the car, before his father can get his keys in the ignition, the boy tries again.

What was his name?

What's it matter? his father says. And reaches to start the car.

The boy grabs his father's right arm and holds it. Tell me,

he says.

William. His name was William, same as yours. Your mother wanted to change things. She believed in the redemptive powers. Absolution, you might say. I think she just wanted to be able to say that name with love again, to love a person with that name, William. There was never a woman with a bigger heart than your mother, I can tell you. What's happened between us is all on me, I've told you that. There's things you can change in this world and things you can't. We have to figure out which is which. Though I never was much good at it, I guess.

They sit in the Virginia night, father and son, exchanging thoughts without speaking. The parking lot has emptied.

I never liked my name, the boy says. I'll change it.

No. Don't change it. And don't tell your mother I told you, either. This isn't a contest, see? She never told you about him, right? That's the way she wanted it.

The father cranks the car, eases out into the traffic headed back into the nation's capital.

And I bet she never told you we called you William, Prince of Arthur Avenue?

The boy shakes his head no.

Then don't tell her, don't talk about it. Just leave it be, son. You wanted a story and now you have one. It doesn't mean anything's changed, or that you have to fuck anything up because you know something new. It's just a story.

Yeah, says the boy, rolling with it now. William, Prince of Arthur Avenue.

Just a story, his father says.

BEAUTIFUL GIRLS

I was trying to figure what it was about women's feet when a cop stopped me. This cop had the full Cleveland look, and he wasn't playing. I fingered my Native shades while he approached my car, lumbering. He said remove your eyewear. I said okay. He said you from around here? I said, well, I guess.

He studied me and went back to his car with my license. Wait right there, he said. Here? I said.

I voicemailed over to my outgoing message, to see what I sounded like when I was sober.

The cop came back and said did I know I was doing 85? I couldn't feature that, so I said so. It was a time for honesty.

I was thinking about women's feet, I said. What is it about them?

The cop had a badge that said Danny. It looked like Dandy.

In *Vogue* the women's feet are strapped and loaded. The colors make me weep. Do they put makeup on feet? I see a heel on a cool blonde I wanna cry. I told this to Danny.

My wife has corns, he said. She makes me rub them. I have this special rub I do only for her. He shakes his head. God damn. When we first married I would give her foot massages. You see what I'm saying? He shakes again, hands me the ticket. His hat is off and his head is pattern bald. He replaces the hat and shakes my hand. Thank you, I say.

She can't wear heels, now, Danny says. Sensibles only. She goes around everywhere in flats or flip flops. She has the veins. Three kids. Christ, it's probably my fault.

I nod, but am afraid to use the voice. He's on to something.

Michelle Pfeiffer, Danny says. You remember? That mob movie? She gets a foot rub?

I try my voice. Uma Thurman, I say. The great debate with John Travolta and Samuel L. Jackson. about did she or didn't she get a foot massage from thus and so. That didn't sound right. I waited.

Now Uma, Danny says, she has the flat feet. Funny toes. I dunno about her.

Beautiful Girls, I say. You ever see that movie?

Nope. Danny checks his watch.

I pocket my ticket. I smile and replace the Natives. Then I salute. That doesn't seem right, so I slurve my hand over to part my hair.

But Uma, Danny says. She was amazing in Kill Bill. Real scary. I like that.

Beautiful Girls, I say. She is the perfect girl from Chicago. In this movie, see? She says to the guys, I'm looking for a man who can say to me at the end of the day just four words. Good night sweet girl. Just that.

Just like that.

Like that.

Women's feet, I say.

It's the arch, Danny says. She hangs her foot by your mouth. Beyond the reach of tragedy. Speed dial the pope. Sweet Jesus.

We nod in agreement.

QUIVER

"Our love still matters," he whispered on the night she left him. They were at the Russian Tea Room. He kissed her wide forehead and her doll's eyes, wet with tears. She walked off into the December cold. Her high heels clattered on the sidewalk. He watched as she hailed a cab. Traffic was heavy on West 57th but she leaned into the wind, her arm outthrust. She ducked entering the cab. He smiled; they were the same height and he had taught her. She slid her bottom in first, then swung her hips and longs legs, resting her heels on the floorboard. Satisfied, Vincent returned to his table. He nodded at the dancing bear above him, tipped his hat, and ordered Irish coffee in honor of Aisling.

He had found her in Connemara, lace curtain Irish girl with dark hair, blue eyes and alabaster skin. She worked as a waitress at a tiny inn by the sea. She walked fast, moving about the room with a purposeful intensity, but Vincent's eye was drawn to the narrow waist, where an oxford shirt tucked neatly into black pants. A busboy carelessly spilled coffee onto his lap and in one long movement Aisling came from behind, moved the table forward, placed a light hand on his arm, dropped a cloth into his lap, arched a perfect eyebrow at the unfortunate busboy, and refilled Vincent's cup.

They conversed at the table, he her last customer. At nearly ten o'clock, the June sky through an open window retained the pale light of Ireland. Vincent imagined her in New York. His one gift, complementing his visual intuition, the capacity for sudden and intimate conversation with a stranger. She was the youngest of aged parents. She commuted by boat to work, was an accomplished amateur golfer but had done some acting in her coeducational secondary school. The school crest dated to the twelfth century. She blushed when asked about a boyfriend, but allowed as how there was someone she'd been seeing, nothing special. When the bill had been settled, a sigh escaped Vincent. Aisling laughed to hear that, a light laugh that stayed in her throat, as if unwilling to travel farther. She asked, did he find her company that boring? Vincent issued a denial. On the contrary, he said. There was talk of Galway and Dublin, and where his work would take him next.

When the room had emptied of customers, she locked the double doors with a skeleton key, then turned to him and said, "Will we have a drink, then?" They moved to the inn's small bar, which stood beside a winding staircase with a banister made of cherry wood. Two stuffed chairs and a sofa were lit by a soft lamp. A small fire was laid in the fireplace. Aisling threw peat into the fire and laughed when he showed her his business card, saying, "Sure, I'd be lost in New York, wouldn't I, a girl like me?"

For Vincent, the scent of the peat turf fire conjured memories of Elysian Fields, the hooves of heroic horses striking fire, and stone castles long abandoned. She sat prettily by the hearth. He reached into his briefcase and brought out a copy of the magazine where he worked, last year's issue of "Women We Love." She thumbed the pages looking at the girls, reading their bios and asking questions.

When she gave her consent (she was of age) he sent for a crew and they arrived within the week. Vincent had shot the scene in his mind long before they set up for it and knew what the final print would look like. They shot her in the grey light of Connemara on Derryclare Mountain, one of the Twelve Pins in the west of Ireland. It was wild and windy country, protected by mountains and surrounded on all sides by lakes and rivers and the ancient Irish sea. Her long hair blew free.

She posed on a rocky outcropping with an seven iron in her hands, her long body coiled in a perfect follow through. She was clad in a black bikini. It was so cold, and the mist they blew with giant fans so effective, that her sleek skin goose bumped and her nipples stiffened. Her eyes were pools. She was a sensation. "All these eyes on me," Aisling said, without complaint. Vincent left his editing job to manage her career. She soon had all the big magazine covers.

Vincent finished his drink and moved to the door. He hailed a cab and headed south to Greenwich Village. At Bleecker he walked into the narrow cobbled street. Stepping up from the curb he entered a small boutique. Dressing Aisling had given him pleasure. In the early days he bought off the rack, later commissioning pieces from emerging designers. Vincent, who all his life had dreamed of being more beautiful than he was, dressed her and watched her go.

The next day and the day after that he returned to the boutiques of Bleecker Street where he had made his first purchases for her, years before. He stood before a plate glass window, behind which stood two mannequins, children fair and blonde, she in a sporty dress of colored blocks with darling bows at the shoulders, he in a sailor suit.

Vincent took particular delight in teaching Aisling. Once, he allowed her to pay for their meal: Never leave silver on the table with the tip. Always lead with your best side (her left) walking slant into a room, camera ready. Sit against the back wall with everything in front of you. Know where the exits are, all ways out. Cabernet, never Merlot. An inexpensive Italian red may be quite good, but this is never true of a French. Patiently, he explained the placement of silverware, and taught her the vagaries of light in New York: *"Winter street shoots use tons of foundation and fill light to fight shadows. The kindest light is October in the park or the West Village but never sit in window sun at a restaurant–you look bleached from the street."* He selected her hair stylist and advised on makeup. He took care when feeding her, using only the freshest ingredients and cooking her meals when they stayed in. They took a large apartment on Central Park West and lunched in the Bronx, using service elevators and slipping out side doors of little Italian places where Vincent knew they would be left alone.

Aisling spoke often of children. The youngest of eight children, seven of them brothers, she wanted two, a boy first, then a girl, and was quite certain about their names: Gabriella for the girl, Gareth for the boy, celebrating their Irish-Italian union. But she landed a contract with Estée Lauder and after that came her first movie. Her pale skin and heart shaped face seemed to invite audiences directly in, or so the critics said; but Vincent understood that her look was of the land, Connemara's sparse and solitary places. Viewers filled in what they desired. No one in Hollywood, it was said, held a close up better.

When she fell in love with her leading man, a Scandinavian with frosty skin that twinkled like diamonds on screen, Vincent had no difficulty understanding the attraction. The man was beautiful to look at, like sun passing through ice of a winter's morning. They were north and south, he and Vincent, Nordic and Mediterranean, a study in contrasts. Aisling offered no explanation; none was needed. Only that once had he made his simple declaration: *Our love still matters.*

For two weeks he returned to Bleecker Street, turning off each time onto streets that carried scented memories of girls in their summer dresses: Perry, Christopher, Cornelia. He looked for women he would like to dress, then undress, but soon got bored and returned to the shops of Bleecker Street, to the mannequins with their vacant gaze.

One day he returned to the Central Park West apartment, his arms laden with packages. His doorman greeted him with a smile and a wink. "Been out shopping again." He helped Vincent carry everything to his door.

Vincent threw the bags one by one onto his big bed. The shopping bags hit the pile of other bags just like them, dozens of bags, and fell to the floor. The bed was strewn with gift boxes, gloves, jewelry, evening dresses, skirts, tops, scarves, belts, carton after carton of women's shoes, and four dozen children's outfits of all colors and designs, from onesies to 4T.

He lay down on top of all of it and listened. On TV, the History Channel narrator spoke of the Eternal City. Having outlasted mongrel hordes and hapless fascists, the ancient aqueducts carried sweet tasting water to the trattorias and ristorantes near the Pantheon, arched vault of the heavens. Close ups of Rome's fountains: the Trevi where tourists threw coins, hoping to return, and at the Piazza de Spagna, Bernini's boat shaped Fontana della Barcaccia. Men tossed their caps onto the statue and placed their noble Roman faces under the clear streaming water, understanding, as Vincent did, that art is not intended for sterile museums, that love is written on the body, that all roads lead to Rome, that women must be treated as carefully as shotguns, that children are arrows in a man's quiver.

ECHO PARK

for Emily Mortimer

The film industry began here southeast of Hollywood. The streets retain traces of the footsteps of Laurel and Hardy, Charlie Chaplin, the Three Stooges, and before that, a horse drawn streetcar trundled down the dirt road. Nicholson and Polanski shot Chinatown here. Later, Tom Waits would come, Michael Jackson shooting Thriller. From your garden you can see a hummingbird and a coyote. At night the police helicopter circles overhead shining its powerful beam on real life criminals, though what's real in Los Angeles? A perpetual mystery. For six years you lived out of the same suitcase, filling it in London, pulling out an outfit a day for the acting jobs you started getting, finally. Such a strange place, so close to downtown where no one can be seen walking the empty streets. A cartographer might have mapped you dancing on the upturned edge of the world, lit by the famous light, or cavorting in a Ridley Scott scene from Blade Runner, the glittering rain and shattered sound of a future world well lost. You escaped to the fog and damp of London when you felt you could not take another day. A city where one could take a walk, a city of parks. But no longer yours. You felt a stranger there, and then another audition, another job, Echo Park, suitcase. But in LA the seasons never change, the filmmakers' adoration of light never stops, the years go by and you were scared you would not be able to leave. People in LA live in denial of death, pretending the light, the wheatgrass, the pill, the new enema, the hairstylist's guru, the botoxed face—until the earth moves and you think, bloody hell, give me New York, a city on bedrock. But you stay in LA because it is possible to do nothing, and it is easy to avoid a hangover because no one wants to get drunk and besides you need to drive, even if it's just down the street. So you're in bed early. You wake in the morning and can actually do things, can read and think, without feeling oppressed as in New York, by the Next Big Thing which must be done. But today someone recognized you at Il Cielo, a perfect stranger, and interviewers hang on your every word, or ask the same idiotic questions, and look at you, almost forty now, but still the raspy voice, now sexy, now squeaky, and there is nowhere to hide. As before the camera, then projected onscreen, nowhere to hide, nowhere to go, the room you've entered a dream of this room you now inhabit, for now every boy, every lost man teetering on the edge of a train that runs into the night through Echo Park and lays in your underwear drawer, the palms and the endless fiery plants and the layered levels of the nameless shining mountains, the important people and the filler people, and the parties that make you quiver like a bright paper streamer blown in the breeze, every last one of them will ask, "Must I follow her too?" Whatever it says you must do you must do. Now is the time for you to go out into the light to congratulate whoever is left in our city, and look, I am totally taken with you, light a candle and place it here in my death wreath and let me blow you a crazy kiss. Oh, wow, I love you so much in so short a time, I'm yours, now what are you going to do with me? Why do I tell you these things, you are not even here.

STYOPPA

I was looking for Styoppa because I didn't know who I was. I had lost my identity during the war. A barmaid at The Dancer's Nightclub gave me a card: R.M. Snead: *Private Enquiries*. She blew me a kiss and called a taxi. The lights of the city were an endless sheet of glitter. High above the faint clouds a searchlight prowled. We passed the oil well that stands in the middle of La Cienega Boulevard, then turned off onto a quiet street fringed with palm trees. "Wait here," the driver said. The driver went into a drug store and returned with a pack of smokes. He offered me a cigarette. "No thanks," I said. The driver shrugged. "Suit yourself," he said.

The taxi dropped me off at the corner of Hollywood and Cahuenga. I walked the six flights up to Snead's office. Dark wooden shelves covered the walls. The shelves were filled with city directories and yearbooks. A calendar on Snead's desk was lit by an opaline lamp: December 21, 1947. Snead sat behind the massive desk, wearing a black raincoat, giving the whole room an air of departure.

He offered me a job at once.

"Just the kind of man I need," Snead said.

"A man who doesn't know his own identity?"

"In this business you learn to recognize an asset when it walks in the door," Snead said. "Los Angeles is a great wrong place. Not being known can be an advantage. Let's get dinner. You can tell me about Styoppa."

Snead drove a 1940 Cadillac Fleetwood. His hands were shaky on the steering wheel. The Caddy finned like an eel through the streets of downtown Los Angeles. We passed into

Echo Park.

"I wish I could," I said. "But I don't know who Styoppa is. I found an old photograph from the war with a picture of a man standing next to someone who looks like me. The name Styoppa is handwritten next to this man's picture."

Snead stopped at a traffic light. He rested his hand on my knee. "And this guy standing next to Styoppa, you say he looks like you?" "Could be," I said. "But he's looking down in the picture and he has his helmet on, so I can't be sure."

We arrived at a restaurant. Two middle aged women supported a very old man by the arms. The man wore a white suit. He had skin like white plaster. Behind him walked a tall man wearing a loden cape. Was this Styoppa? I pulled the picture from my jacket and handed it to Snead. Snead glanced at the picture. Then he stared at the caped man, who was just my height. The man stooped as he entered the low covered porch of the restaurant.

Snead's friend Jean greeted us at the bar and led us through a courtyard to a private cottage in the back of the property. We walked silently behind Styoppa and his group. The French windows of the restaurant were brilliantly lit and I could see couples moving behind them. The tables were dressed in white tablecloths with white cloth napkins and gleaming silver. A single chandelier hung from the ceiling.

The caned chairs were upright in the French café style. Jean pulled out my chair, nodded to Snead, and ordered an expensive pre-war Bordeaux.

"It's not a large crowd tonight," said Jean. "But there's a wedding party that may end in an orgy." Styoppa was helping the plaster man with his cane, talking to the two women. They were across the room from us, part of the wedding party. The music was loud, and the dance floor was full.

A woman was seated alone at one of the tables. She wore a pale blue dress and her chin was cupped in the palm of her hands. What was she dreaming of? I wondered. "The bride," said Jean. I called to a waiter. "What is she doing there," I asked. "I don't know, he replied.

"So, you're going to work with Snead," Jean said. I nodded. "Tell me how you came to know Styoppa." He winked at Snead and curled his lip. We sat and drank our wine. Jean ordered another bottle of the Bordeaux for dinner and attempted to draw me into conversation. We'd both served in the Second Army. I kept my eye on Styoppa but he never returned my gaze and the cape never left his broad shoulders.

After dinner we followed his group out to the parking lot. They moved slowly. Styoppa half carried the plaster man, whose white suit was blotched with red wine. I got to the car ahead of Snead and opened the door. Someone was huddled up on the front seat, leaning against the window. I bent down and recognized the bride. She was asleep, her pale blue dress drawn up to the middle of her thighs. One shoe had fallen to the floor, the other dangled from her small foot. Styoppa walked up. "We have to get her out of here," he said. His voice seemed familiar.

I shook the woman gently but she remained asleep. Styoppa and I pulled her from the car. "We can't just leave her on the ground like this," Jean said. Styoppa took charge, just as he had during the war. He ordered me to carry her back to the restaurant. Her head lay against my shoulder. I stumbled to the restaurant in the dim light of the parking lot. Her dark hair was loose and hung over my arms as we walked. She was wearing a scent I remembered but what? I wanted to ask Styoppa but he and Jean had vanished with Snead into the night.

WITH MARY

Downstairs was crowded and too many voices were speaking at once. I lost sight of Mary. Some people huddled in a corner by the stage. The microphone was still on the stage but I did not know where Mary had gone. A couple looked at me as though I should know them.

A woman threw her arms around me. She thanked me. Her voice was hoarse and she coughed into her starfish hand. She apologized for coughing but her perfume was lovely. It hung there between us. I wondered where Mary had gone. The couple by the stage continued to look.

I left the room with my bag under my arm. Mary was at the bar in the next room. She came up to me and took my arm. A photographer wanted to take our picture. Mary sent him away after one flash. My eyes stung. I wondered where our picture would appear.

A waiter went for a taxi. Outside it was hot and bright from the camera lights. They were filming the outside of the bar. Equipment and cars filled the street. The street was shaped like a little square. A fountain had appeared in the square and water tumbled. There were trees and grass and on the grass taxis were parked. One drove toward us and the waiter opened the door. Mary got in. I tipped the waiter and got into the taxi beside Mary.

I told the driver where to drive and he shot out of there. Ruts formed in the wet grass as he accelerated. We entered a long tunnel. I told Mary what she had said to me the last time

I saw her. That I made her laugh. She frowned at me and said, did I say that? She smiled then and I saw her white teeth.

The tunnel was dark. Mary moved close to me. We sat close to one another and were quiet. I put my arm around her and tried to see where we were headed. At the end of the tunnel was a long hill and we climbed the hill in second gear. Outside the houses were white stucco lit by floodlight.

We crossed a bridge. The water was black beneath us. I told the driver to stop. I got out of the car. I took Mary's hand and she got out. I told the driver to wait. With Mary, I stood on the bridge and watched the black water move. A bat flew into the open window of the taxi and the driver yelled and the bat flew out. We watched the bat fly off into the night. I asked Mary if she felt alright and she said she felt fine. It was hot and dark. A light went on in a house across the river and then it went out.

FUNERAL

Patrick Quinn fingers his collar and watches the funeral director instruct the pallbearers. The grave site is steep. Two days ago the widow had joked with him, Father, you'd better wear your golf shoes with cleats.

Quinn follows six beefy pallbearers to the rear of the hearse where the funeral director, a woman, gives directions. She is dressed in a smart black pants suit, contoured at the waist and hips, three quarter sleeves, high-waisted pants with flared leg openings, and sensible black pumps. The pallbearers look like high school linebackers. They can't take their eyes off her, either.

Quinn has worked with the director before, but where? His parish draws folk from three rural counties, cradle to grave Episcopalians who line up for death and are plucked monthly from the back rows of the country church where he has served for twelve years.

A small plane drones overhead, and a late summer breeze blows through oak and maple trees. Below, a creek flows steadily to the Little Miami, from there to the Ohio River, and eventually into the Mississippi. Reared in New Orleans, Quinn has never gotten used to the staid funerals of these stoic Midwesterners.

Veronica left him for a podiatrist in town. In bed watching a new vampire series, she'd turned to him and said, "Jesus, Quinn, I thought you knew? We weren't exactly discreet." But Quinn hadn't known. In the parish, he is always the last to know. People hide bad news. Quinn has booked a flight to Connemara, County Galway. But first, this funeral. This woman director. What is her name?

He opens the Book of Common Prayer and recites the opening sentences. The psalms and the prayers he intones solemnly, in plain song, as the widow had requested. Quinn is conscious of his brittle tenor, and of the young woman who stands beside him, watching.

Freddie. Her name is Freddie. They had ridden out to St. Paris in the black hearse for the Bleeker funeral, not long after Veronica moved out, a week before their twentieth anniversary. Which he will spend in Ireland, alone.

Quinn listens to Freddie's voice rise beside him, a low alto. She uses the old language, forgive us our trespasses, as we forgive those who trespass against us. Placing his right hand on the casket, above the silent head, he stands on the narrow spit of land between the casket and Freddie's small feet, on green Astroturf that covers freshly dug earth.

Quinn pronounces the benediction. He plucks a white rose from the spray on the casket and gives it to the widow, who breaks into tears. Quinn comforts her with the ancient wisdom of the church, aware that Freddie has not left his side. His parish is comprised of mostly post-menopausal women, and Quinn feels the heat from Freddie's body, not two feet away. He recalls that her boyfriend is a body builder, a hypochondriac unable to sire a child. She is the lapsed daughter of a deceased fundamentalist minister in town, a man Quinn despised for his narrow-mindedness.

Birds sing their late summer song. The creek moves fast, the current deep. An orange kayak floats downstream. Quinn has parked his BMW in the shade of a live oak. He gifted himself with the convertible after the divorce.

The family scatters. Happy to be done with the funeral, Quinn thinks of his upcoming trip to Connemara. Freddie trades war stories with two cemetery caretakers, men Quinn has worked with often. Quinn laughs at their recycled stories. He would like to take the BMW's top down and follow the creek around the cemetery.

Freddie recalls a picture-taking ceremony. Family members took turns leaning into the casket with their faces next to the corpse, she says. They had big cheesy grins. They handed me a camera and made me snap away, till everyone had a keepsake. I'm sure it all wound up on Facebook.

She has braces, the kind that blend in with the teeth, so all you see is a thin white wire. On the drive to the cemetery she'd confessed to Quinn that she was often accused of being too perky for funerals. She bares her right arm and shows them her new tattoo, a grocery list: bread, milk, cheese, eggs, pizza, beer. Quinn laughs. He tells her it would look even better if she'd crossed off a few items.

They admire the day, the gentle breeze, the dexterity of the kayaker. Quinn says it's a great day to take a ride in a convertible, and hears a trio of voices. "What convertible?"

Mine, Quinn says.

Oh, you didn't, Freddie says.

You got a minute? I can show you how it works. Freddie shrugs and says sure. The men walk back to their truck.

Quinn waves the key like a wand at the keyless ignition and fires the 300-horsepower twin-turbo engine. The BMW is fire engine red with a cream interior. The dual exhaust pipes play a throaty duet. Freddie taps her feet to the music coming out of the car's eight speakers. She has a small cluster of freckles around her nose, and that one clear line across her teeth.

Quinn presses a button and the red top begins to lift. The top slides back into the trunk. Four windows disappear.

Sweet, Freddie says. She opens the passenger side door.

Quinn punches up the volume and navigates the creek bend. He slows to a stop to allow a family of ducks to cross. Freddie's alto harmonizes with Springsteen, "the door is open but the ride ain't free." The goslings follow their mother in a straight line.

Quinn sets his clerical collar on the console. In one week summer will be over, and it will be Labor Day. Freddie is no more than thirty. All men are mortal, he remembers from logic class. Socrates is a man, therefore Socrates is mortal.

Freddie twirls Quinn's clerical collar like a Frisbee. The ducks make their duck noises, and the creek flows. Quinn lifts the collar from Freddie's pretty finger and places it around her slender neck. He prays every prayer he knows.

IN VENICE

They talked as evening fell. She'd appeared in the doorway at Harry's Bar in Venice, barelegged but in heels. It was her voice he remembered from their days in New York, scornful and warm above the shrieking subway.

The lights were blinking on in the buildings surrounding the piazza. She stared at a table of people, merry across the room and loud as Russians. Light gleamed from the polished wood of the bar. On narrow shelves lines of glasses stood like icy soldiers.

Something was missing in him. Women had always done anything to find out what it was. Across the room someone was saying, "When you've been married you want to be married again."

American college girls came into the bar drunk. A half hour later six girls in unison kicked their bare legs in the brilliant light, to scattered applause. They went on talking. She drank looking directly at him. Across the room the conversation continued. Americans. "Women fall in love when they get to know you," one of them said. "Men are just the opposite. When they finally know you they're ready to leave."

The bartender passed a dense icy glass to the man seated next to them. Summer was ending. Outside, the first winds of autumn ruffled the green water of the grand canal, wide as a river. A giant cruise ship was in port. Bilge water poured from its stern. He wished again that he was in love.

"In Barcelona," she was saying, "is a cathedral that was

never completed. Built by Antonio Gaudi, an architect more like a saint." She filled her lungs with smoke from her cigarette. "He was hit by a streetcar walking to church. He lay in the street, bleeding. No one recognized him." He reached for her. She let herself be held, but she was like a huge dog, leaping from his arms. "The cathedral that was never built," she said. "It has doors that lead both ways into empty air."

They walked out of the bar. A wave of pigeons rose into the air before a trotting dog. The lights in some palazzos shone. He imagined, in the curtained upper floors, the long legs of countesses uncoiled, shaved and smooth, slithering on silk sheets. The sky became violet. Two men sat at a small table trimming artichokes. The blue cars of the *carabiniere*. Bags of rice and dry beans beside the table where the men continued their work. A girl with a tailored coat walked past them with a scarf wrapped around her head. He felt that his life was clarifying.

A taxi pulled up and she stepped inside, pulling him in behind her. The car rattled the narrow street. They took the A4 highway west. In Verona, the points of the tall steeples. Schoolgirls in dark skirts and blouses blindingly white. One stood off by herself. Her pale legs shook like small sticks. The woman made the taxi stop for the girl. That was me, she said to him. She whispered words to her in Italian. The girl sat beside them in the taxi. The window of the Mercedes glided up. It started to rain. His room was on the corner. A long dark corridor, heavy drapes of forest green and matching cushions on the white window sills. The towels a pale green with the name of the hotel in white.

The girl did not look at any of this. He knelt to remove her shoes. She peeled a strip of pink paper from a menu on the nightstand. Her fingernails were short and clear. In the morning there will be breakfast rolls and cappuccino. A sliced pear. Gleaming spoons on a starched white tablecloth. His life was simple. In the morning the air will be pure and cool.

GIRL, INTERRUPTED

When his wife asked him for a divorce M drove down the New York State Thruway from New Paltz into Manhattan and checked into the Pierre Hotel.

Catherine hadn't been specific; it had been understood for some time that things were not working. M pouted, pleaded, tried to be charming, threw a fit, attempted to argue her out of it, and finally resorted to negotiating, but nothing worked. Catherine was firm. "Look, let's just forget it," she'd said.

M chose New York for its anonymity. He wanted to become invisible, his childhood wish. The argument with Catherine had discharged so many violent emotions that M had trouble remembering who he was. If he was no longer married then who was he?

He removed his wedding band and laid it on the dresser. Then he thought better of that and placed it in his billfold. He looked down at his bare hands, and wrists. The ring had left an indentation on his finger. He placed the thumb and forefinger of his right hand in the ring groove and traced the circle of bruised flesh.

Exiting the hotel, M turned north and walked alongside Central Park in the shade of the large overhanging trees. It was midsummer and everything was in bloom.

At 70th Street he looked across the Avenue at a tall black gate which guarded—what? He couldn't remember. He hadn't been to the city in years. Crossing the street, he joined a small group of people waiting to enter the building.

It was an art museum. The handsome building had been a

private residence that now housed a remarkable collection of Old Masters. There was an intimacy to the collection that seemed to invite M directly in. To look, undisturbed.

He wandered through the library and the family room and paused to admire an elegant staircase leading to the family's living quarters on the second floor of the residence, which was roped off. Standing at the base of the staircase next to the bust of a woman mounted on a pedestal, M looked at the forbidden second floor. A painting was hung on the landing, and two candelabras framed magnificent gold inlaid ornamentation that resembled the cabinets of a cathedral pipe organ.

M walked down the long dim hallway and stopped to look at a small painting. It was a Vermeer. A young girl sits at a dark table. Sheet music lies on the table, and a man holds with his thumb another sheet of music, which the girl also holds with both hands. But she is not looking at the man, whom M supposes is her teacher. Her face is turned toward the viewer, as if she had been interrupted at her music by M himself. She wears a look of mild astonishment. Her fine head, sheathed in a white head scarf, is turned away from her music. She looked directly at him.

Unnerved, M peered at the title of the painting: "Girl, Interrupted at Her Music."

Two weeks after the fall of the twin towers M had traveled with Catherine to New York, where they bought a grand piano at Steinway Hall on West 57th Street. In college, Catherine had majored in music and taught private lessons for many years. Over time she had stopped giving recitals, and eventually she ceased to play. Her Baldwin spinet piano held dozens of family photos, of their children and their dogs and horses, but no music. Making a present of the Steinway, it was thought, would spur her to play again. And she did, for a time. But then the grand piano stood idle as well. No pictures were mounted on it.

Now as he returns the gaze of the girl in the painting, M

thinks of his wife, whom he had left standing in the hallway of their house, she holding the mail, he reaching for his car keys. Her face was careworn, and puffy from crying. A strange, lonesome pity enters his heart to think of her. He had never known Catherine in her girlhood, had not in more than a dozen years asked her a question about how it was with her in those days when she was a child, raised by a widower, who managed to see to it that she continued her piano lessons after her mother died. By the time they had met, in college, Catherine was an orphan. He stares now, at the girl interrupted at her music, and he feels his soul run away, the solid world dissolve to tears. He tries to release his gaze but the girl goes on looking at him, startled.

OF COURSE WE'RE GOOD

Sybil and Zooey were friends and something more. The connection between them was solid but the *more* part added a nice tension and kept them guessing.

They met in high school English, where they dumbed down for cover but quoted lines of stories to each other in the cafeteria or lying out on the football field at midnight, stoned. J. D. Salinger was their favorite writer, "A Perfect Day for Bananafish" their favorite story. I like to chew candles. Who doesn't, Zooey would answer. I see you're looking at my feet, Sybil would say. Let me out here, please, Zooey joked.

Zooey drifted out west after college, working as a ski instructor at Jackson Hole and later Steamboat, and eventually found work as a session player in Los Angeles. He played guitar and harmonica. Sybil remained in New York and had a small gallery with a girlfriend, but sold it when she started a family.

Zooey was in town for a recording session in Greenwich Village. Sybil's husband was out of town for the weekend holding the hand of an indicted congressman, so she said, hey, why don't you come over? And bring that movie you're always talking about.

Zooey said okay. But he looked for the movie and couldn't find it anywhere, even in New York. He was in a store on Sixth Avenue with Halloween stuff . He bought a pair of handcuffs instead.

Sybil told Zooey to watch out for the doorman. He gossips like an old woman and sucks up to Peter who is president of the building, but he goes to dinner at eight and comes back at eight thirty. It's stupid, but I have to live here, you know? Eight fifteen is your sweet spot.

But Zooey had trouble with the subway. He fell asleep uptown and then got off at the wrong stop and by then it was eight twenty-five. He ran down Canal to Laight Street with a bottle of champagne sloshing in his backpack.

He stood by the West Side Highway and texted Sybil. Traffic zoomed by and the Hudson rolled. New Jersey was lit and the sky was low. A light rain began to fall. Zooey pulled at his hooded jacket and dropped the backpack with the champagne. He slowed it with his foot on the way down and that saved it. Sybil texted back and said *now*.

He punched in the number. She buzzed him in. The doorman was there. Zooey didn't break stride heading for the elevator. He half hid his face with the backpack swinging off his shoulder and blocking the doorman's view. He tried to think what to say. He wanted to give the apartment number but he couldn't remember it. Then he did. Five-o-seven, he said, reaching the elevator. Ah, the doorman said, Mr. Peter. He sounded like Boris Karloff. Yeah, Zooey said, from inside the elevator, Mr. Peter. The door slid shut, and Zooey slammed his fist into it as the elevator climbed.

Zooey swung around the corner. He saw her head, her dark hair pulled back, her body hidden by the big door. She waved him into the apartment and sat down with a cigarette at the kitchen table. He bummed a cigarette. She poured him a glass of red wine.

Shit, I'm sorry about that. Zooey laughed into his hands. I'm such a fuckwit. You are, Sybil said, and they laughed. But forget it, it's okay. That guy's not the doorman, that's actually the building superintendent, and he's cool. He called me and said you were coming up.

So, we're good, Zooey asked.

Of course we're good, she said.

They talked about his music and about her painting, where it seemed to be going, and the strange dreams she had been having, dreams of Danish officers in costume and teenage girls in masks and anonymous couplings in closets, and here is where Zooey gleefully produced the handcuffs from his backpack. Sybil took them in her small hands and unlocked them with the toy key. Too flimsy for me, she said.

The phone rang but Sybil was the kind of girl for whom a ringing phone did nothing at all. They poured more wine and smoked more cigarettes and talked long into the night and in time they came to the part about them.

Later, Zooey said, You're not wearing your boots. God, you have feet! He grabbed one bare foot below her skinny jeans and it felt to him like a small steel cable or an eel finning through a cove. What color, the nails? Zooey asked. Tomboy No More, she said. And they laughed at that, because it was true.

They moved to the sofa. She pulled at his backpack and he produced a season set of Mad Men DVD's. One of these and then I'm kicking your ass out, Sybil said. Zooey held out his glass for more of the red. She gave it to him, and poured one for herself. Zooey got up to use the bathroom while she slipped the DVD into the player. Her children slept two doors down from where he stood and washed his hands and studied the mirror. Zooey thought of the Dylan lyric he'd sung earlier that afternoon in the studio, "Yer gonna make me give myself a good talkin' to." He splashed his face and went back to the sofa.

She handed him his glass and patted the cushion beside her. Zooey settled in next to her and as they watched Betty Draper grow sadder and blonder, her face framed over the bananas in the A & P. Zooey reached again for her foot and she let him take it in his hands and he sighed and they went on watching. But Zooey couldn't follow the plot points, and despite Sybil's promptings he could not manage more than a grunt or a sigh. He buried his face in her neck and laced his fingers through her hands and she returned his squeeze and then stopped. She reached down to scratch her ankle. He wanted to lift her foot to his mouth and kiss the arch.

One more episode and this time pay attention, Sybil said. And Salvadore was getting laid at last and Draper was Draper and Joanie's mouth was strawberries in a bowl of cream and Zooey nipped at Sybil's neck and let his tongue go near her ear but then leaned back and sighed and then the show was over and she was packing up his DVD set.

Let me see the dress, he said. They were standing by the kitchen table packing up his handcuffs and the Mad Men set and he remembered the champagne and gave it to her. She placed it in the refrigerator.

Which dress, she asked.

The one you told me was the color of my car, Zooey said. The burgundy one you found in the thrift shop for the wedding last month.

Oh, Sybil said, that dress.

They entered the big walk in closet off her bedroom. She showed him three dresses and asked which one he wanted. There was her high school prom dress, a black beauty, but she said she didn't have the boobs to hold it up anymore, though it still fit everywhere else. What nursing does, she explained. There was another dress, off white and sequined, and there was the burgundy dress. He held it to his face. It was cool and smooth and felt like a mattress float on the spring sea.

I want to see all three. I can't decide, said Zooey, though he could.

Stand right there, Sybil said, and no peeking. Zooey stood outside the closet, but kept the door cracked open. She stood in the center of the room stripping off her skinny jeans. She had the same white stick legs and he nudged the door open wider with the toe of his boot. Then he said what the hell and walked into the room.

She had the prom dress on. Her small body was an A line, down to those cabled feet with the candy toes. She looked like a nymphet. Jesus, Sybil, he said. You make me feel like Humbert Humbert over here. Yeah, I hear you humming, she said. Go on, get out of here. Let me try the other one on for you, and then you really need to go.

From behind the closet door Zooey heard her say, Updike says that *Lolita* is the only convincing love story of the twentieth century. What a load of horse shit. He opened the door. She was bent over, naked from the waist up. She was lank through the chest and her nipples were long and fine. She looked at him and stood erect and said, Oh, what the fuck, come on in here and help me with this thing.

He zipped her into the burgundy dress and then she kicked him out and told him to wait in the kitchen. He realized that what he really wanted to do was shampoo Sybil's hair.

She wobbled out to him in gold high heels that tapped the hardwood floor and he laughed to see her and she frowned and then he smiled and opened his arms in a circle and she moved into them and stayed a few beats and then pulled away.

Okay, scram, she said.

Okay.

Okay.

Okay.

Sybil, he said at the door.

Yes, Zooey.

This is a *perfect* day for bananafish.

I don't see any, Sybil said.

That's understandable. Their habits are *very* peculiar.

Sybil stood tottering on her high heels and blew him a kiss from twenty feet. Zooey reached up and pocketed it. He had his hand on the door.

He really doesn't get it, does he, Zooey said. Mr. Fixit. Mr. Perfect.

Mr. Peter, Sybil said.

Mr. Fucking Peter.

Good night, Zooey. Sybil gave a short wave, and turned to the dishes. She stepped out of her heels.

He pulled the door shut tight, checked to see it was locked, and moved down the hall.

Zooey woke at three. He was at his cousin Raleigh's apartment in Brooklyn. Raleigh's cat jumped on the bed. Zooey got up to pee.

At three thirty he reached inside his underwear. He kicked the cat off the bed and felt his bare feet touch under the cotton sheet. He pulled the sheet off and then pulled off his underwear. He was sleepy but his mind was a pleasant blur from the wine and he had the sensation of being on a float out at sea and then he was in the air soaring looking down over a stretch of coastline from where he saw himself lying naked in bed and in his ears a reggae beat and nameless women passed through his consciousness in parts and in whole, the line of their bodies, and then his mind was a perfect blank of sudden concentration and the image of her in the dress and out of the dress and he reached over and caught it sticky in his left hand and held it there, and then cleaned himself and fell back into bed, where he sobbed softly for a moment and then fell into a dreamless sleep.

At 10 am she called to check that he had made it home safely.

Zooey said that he had.

Did you dream? Sybil asked. You always had the most amazing dreams.

No, Zooey said. I don't dream anymore. I don't get enough sleep to dream.

Well you should, Sybil said. Sleep, I mean.

Easy for you to say.

Well, what did you do if you didn't sleep, she asked.

You know.

Ha! she said.

Did you, Zooey asked.

Forget it, bub.

How long did you stay in the dress? What did you do when you took the dress off?

Cut it out.

I don't understand anything about women, Zooey said. I don't know what you guys do when you do it, what you think about. I can't imagine it's the same for you as it is for us.

You'd be surprised, she said.

So you did it last night?

I'm not saying.

Was I in it?

Of course, she said.

There was a long silence, during which Zooey pet the cat, who was back on the bed. The sheets were bunched at his feet. He looked out the window. A woman was arching her back, stretching out in a workout routine to the flat screen TV in her apartment. Her hair was pulled back in a pony wrap. Another women came up to her and handed her a baby. Zooey had never seen the second woman, and guessed her to be a sister, maybe from out of state. Though maybe it was her wife or lover. The baby appeared to be crying, or was in some kind of distress. The two women worked together to get the baby into a high chair. Then they sat down at the table. Zooey watched this and wondered how often Sybil thought of him. He didn't want to ask, but he thought he knew, well enough. He thought: normally in life it doesn't hurt to ask but sometimes it does.

So, Sybil, he said into the phone.

Yes?

I didn't mean to say that about Peter last night. I go in and out, you know? I mean, Jesus. This is sorta hard. Fucking Christ.

Sybil bit her lip and frowned. In eleventh grade, lying stoned on the football field beneath the battered moon, they'd always selected the fifty yard line. She couldn't remember why. Had there been a time when she'd chosen this? Or had she just followed him there? Their football team had been awful. They rarely advanced the ball beyond the fifty. Sybil brought the blanket, a green army blanket that had been her father's. Zooey brought the weed. Equidistant, Sybil thought, home and away. Dead center.

It's a perfect day for bananafish, Sybil said, but Zooey said nothing on the other end of the line. She hadn't read Salinger in years. She waited for Zooey, but there was nothing. She tried again.

Here comes a wave, Sybil said nervously.

GIACOMETTI

Giacometti reclines on the couch. He smokes my last cigarette and points to an object behind me, a spare structure of thin uprights and horizontal beams in which there is something like a flying bird, the backbone of an animal, a female figure, and a hollowed out spatulate shape with a ball in front of it. He tells me that only a few things had happened in his life but some of them he had felt deeply.

"I don't know by what terms my father came to terms with his grief," he says. "His sadness was of the kind that is patient but without hope."

My girlfriend enters the room. She crosses herself and kisses me shyly on the cheek. Then sits at Giacometti's feet. His shoes are caked with mud. She plays absently with the mud, scraping it from his shoes with her long unpainted fingernail. Giacometti ignores her, and keeps speaking.

"The artist conserves a splinter of ice in the heart," he says. "After I left my village of Borgonova in Switzerland, I was always a tourist, wherever I was."

Giacometti reaches down to play with Maura's hair. In a corner of the dark room stands a statue of Maura. Her body is elongated, thin as a nail and as big as a cigarette pack. When Maura has asked why he had done this he had said nothing, but shrugged his slender shoulders. To me, later, he had said, "When I look at a woman the longer I look the thinner they become. I work by paring away what is not essential, work until one touch more and things vanish. But do you love her, this Catholic girl?" I nodded my head, yes. "Very much, I said." Giacometti sighed. "I have no thoughts on this," he said. "All my thoughts are in the clay."

It was spring break in Cambridge. We had traveled two days and two nights to be with him in his studio. We carried letters of introduction, which he ripped up and burned in his kiln. Yet when he had answered the door he acted as though he knew us and had been expecting us for some time. Later he told us it was as if we had always been there.

"The artist must be taken in by his own tricks," Giacometti says. "He must begin by pleasing himself. This is essential. His mouth must be the first that drops open in surprise."

When he says this Maura reaches out her mud streaked fingers and caresses his cheek. She throws open the wide window. In the gloaming, a yawning face appears in the clouds. The sky is painted with a bruised lead and sepia tone that will afterwards haunt me, as too this room, with its objects alive and dead at the same time.

Maura is in his lap. She kisses him, repeatedly, but he makes no acknowledgement of her urgent Irish kisses. He only takes her hand and wipes away the mud.

Now, even the farthest windows have gone dark. We want to lie with Giacometti in his unmade bed on the floor in his studio.

The week before he died I confessed to Maura that I didn't think I could stand it without him. And she said to me, "I've lived with death my whole life. And I know that the people we love we carry with us, always. They are part of us."

WHY I WRITE SUCH GOOD SONGS, COYOTE

We got the job by lies and defended our honor by night on the Hill in Saint Louis. Jimmy was thirty and I was forty and we'd met in the state pen. The foundry was hot and shitty but the pay was good and the corner bar cashed your paycheck no questions asked.

The day we got the axe we handed our severance over to Annette and settled in. Annette was from the Illinois side. East Saint Louis but bled Cardinal red. She had two female cousins in town. Toward midnight they showed up and we knew we were in trouble. They heard us thinking and slid their stools closer. The blonde had a ragged way of breathing that sounded like there was a chain saw buzzing in her chest. Her friend had a hawk nose and the long waisted look that Jimmy fancied. There was one purse between them as they said they shared everything. They started out as threes but we drank them up to sevens and then eights.

We both had wives who'd gone on to other men while we were in the pen which of course held only men. Women made me jump and I mean any woman. That extra hole made a difference.

Since the blonde was mine I tried the Heimlich demonstration which I figured was both edgy and educational. Plus I wanted to hear that chest rattle. She sounded like a box of cough drops being shaken. After I saved her several times Jimmy tried out his pretty good coyote call which Hawk Nose captured on her cell phone camera. Then we started Tequila shots.

I inspected the women and gauged our chances. The blonde was called Roxy and the other was Michelle. Roxy rattled nearby. I knew if she was primed up she'd probably fuck a rock pile if she thought there was a snake in it. Then again, a hard dick has no conscience. If you live on the railroad tracks the train's going to hit you, Grandpa used to say. We hadn't been sober in a week. Hangover thoughts are real long thoughts.

We drank past closing time and then some. Jimmy got the idea to go to his ex's house. He formed a belief that she was out of town visiting her mother in Cape Girardeau. Annette informed us that we had to go somewhere and this elevated Jimmy's belief into one worth entertaining. What was astonishing was that the women thought so too. Which sort of endeared them to me.

Roxy drive her 78 Ford 150 pickup and I rode shotgun. She played a Bee Gees cassette tape and rasped along on the chorus of "How Deep is Your Love." Michelle and Jimmy were squeezed in beside us with Jimmy on the door and we crossed the Eads Bridge this way into East Saint Louis. The Mississippi was black wavy ink but the bridge held steady. Roxy drove with two stone cold hands. The pickup had one headlamp but it was a good one.

Jimmy had Michelle's shirt half off. Michelle had her hand on me but Roxy knocked it back off. We drove that way for a while. Hand tugging at zipper and hand smacked. Hand in waistband and hand smacked. Jimmy tried to help Michelle but got smacked too. I was hoping the house would show up soon but we were lost. We twisted around on some back roads and Jimmy called out the turns and worked Michelle's bra straps down. It was almost first light.

The house had burned down and all there was around the foundation were dry burdocks and chokecherries and one sugar plum the bears had broken down to get at the fruit.

Meanwhile the women were on their stomachs on a mattress that'd been left and both of their bare bottoms were showing plain as day. There was an old upright piano in the foundation square. The big sky was getting lighter and if their butts were cameras it seemed like they were taking my picture.

An Indian story came to mind from out west. Every time a man would screw he'd bleed to death because women had sharp teeth in their articles. It wasn't until a coyote came along and pulled the teeth out that men could screw without dying and get the human race started. This is why the coyote is thought to be sacred.

Well okay, but Jimmy's about as low down as a snake's dick. So he looks at these four women on the bed through his one good eye until he figures out that there's only two of them after all and only one for him. He asked the one if she'd mind getting up on the piano and could she lay out so he could sing to her. Michelle scrambled up with no problem and lay there leaning her head on a hand. He sang "Yes, we have no bananas" and she started laughing. It's what we sang to each other of a morning in the pen to keep our spirits up. I hoisted Michelle up on the piano beside her cousin. She looked right as rain. I stood partway up and she slid down. Her ass hit the keys in a nice way like the lost chord. We did it right there which wasn't easy.

CLOSE

I'm playing the Riviera in Los Angeles where my former wife still lives. She's married to the club's chef. I make the cut on Friday, sign my card and head for the bar. There she is. We haven't seen each other in five years.

Some years ago the paparazzi snapped long lens photos of two women dancing on a table in an adjoining hotel suite my caddy booked. The caddy had left the door ajar while refilling the ice bucket. Big noisy divorce, lots of drama. It came up in every interview. I joked to the press after my big year that I was the leading money winner on the tour and my ex-wife came in second.

It's seven o'clock. I'm moving slowly up the leader board. LA light streams through the blinds. I move toward her.

She looks up from the PGA tour guide she's reading, frowns, nods. She doesn't seem surprised to see me. But she doesn't offer her hand, and kissing is out. So I grab the stool next to her, drag it six inches farther away, and take a seat. She orders me a beer. Then she starts up.

She says I've caused her grief, a lifetime of heartache, made her feel humiliated and ashamed. Isn't that enough?

That's her opener.

Your picture sucks. She taps the tour guide with one manicured fingernail. It's hard to argue there. The picture was taken by my caddie, who was drunk. Tess never liked my caddies. That was an issue. A caddie is like a work wife. Still, I see her point. And then the dancing girls.

But then, you were into humiliation and betrayal early. She thinks a minute, or appears to think, then taps her head.

No, she says, not at the beginning. Not when we first met. You were different then. You remember, Fred?

We met in college. She was the blonde at the end of a long hallway. I saw her framed in the late Pacific light as I exited the Pepperdine Admissions office. They'd offered me a scholarship, sealed the deal at twilight, about this time of night, actually—and she was coming out of the cafeteria with friends when she saw me, looking. She stopped dead away in the hall and looked back. She was something.

You changed when you hit thirty-five, you know that? Like a switch went off in your brain. You really started up then. You turned on me. You did it up good, didn't you? Thought you were funny. You and your idiot caddie. You must be proud of yourself. The two of you.

She says, I'd love to sock you.

We had hard times and I stayed by you. When you were coming up. You remember? Mr. Fancy Pants. Ramen noodles, all we had, and who cooked for you?

She tosses her hair. She still has the hair. Her color is rising, and it's thrilling in a way.

But what's done is done. It is what it is. You're the one that keeps giving these idiotic interviews.

I said some things to the *Golf Digest* interviewer, it's true. Last issue. They sent a woman to do the interview, barely out of J-school, a real looker. It broke my heart just to look at her. I said more than I should. About Tess, about those early years. I babbled on and on. Even cried. The girl took notes and smiled. It was the smile that did it.

Some high school kids walk across the bar. Two girls in shimmering pink and green taffeta gowns, with a guy between them in a black tux. The one girl a blonde, the other a brunette, the guy between them happy as a clam. Above their high heels the girls' ankles flash brown to match their toned arms. In their swishing dresses they move by quickly, carrying it all.

You know something? I think you're sick. I think you're

nutty as a fruitcake. You and your idiot caddy. Oh, you've got 'em fooled, alright. The press, the sponsors. Nike would sponsor toad scum, if it did any winning. You think that means anything? Listen, I could tell them a thing or two about a thing or two. They can come talk to me, they want to hear a story. Don't get me started.

Tess somehow kept her head when the interviews came out. I always admired that. I don't know where that comes from, that reserve. But make no mistake, here at the bar, I know I'm back in town.

Think of me as dead. I'm dead to you now, you get it? I just want to live in peace. A woman in her forties, I'm entitled. Haven't I had enough of your bullshit?

Some more prom kids cross through the bar going to the party. Prom or something. I pull my hat down and try not to look. Tess watches me and laughs. I smile, and then I laugh too.

My ex is talking. She has the right. I listen, aware of the time. The LA light is fading, in that way I remember. I try to find an opening. But she's rolling.

I loved you so much. Once upon a time. Ha! Like a storybook. Like these poor prom girls you keep looking at, who think they're in a movie. My mother talked about love like that, my God, what we talked about! And sure, I believed it. Oh, I went for it, hook, line, and sinker. I was willing, I'll give you that. What else did I know? You swept in, with your boyish grin, your east coast ways, like you'd never lost anything in your life.

She sweeps the hair out of her eyes. She looks at me hard, there at the bar, until I know I've been looked at. The bartender brings us another set of shots and beers and turns away. There are no more kids passing.

We grew up together, for chrissake. I gave you everything I had, and now look. I'm an old woman. Forty, forty-five. Fifty-five. Sixty. Who knows. You threw me away. You son of a bitch.

She takes a long drink. Her fingers twitch. They'd like to be holding a cigarette. She's with me on that, at least.

I was young then, she says, and so were you. Maybe you were a better person back then, I don't know. You must have been or I would never have gone for you. I was so stuck on you. My God, I would have given anything. I stood on a thousand fairways for you, a thousand greens. I wanted you more than anything. Imagine that! We were so *close*. We shared everything in those little bitty motel rooms, you remember that? Driving all over the country in that old green Thunderbird, come on, I know you remember that. Making love by the side of the road. We were intimate once upon a time, Fred. God, I could puke! I could never do that again with anyone else. You got all of that, all those years you got off me, and what did you do with it? Threw it all away, that's what.

You were always lucky, though, I'll give you that. But you remember the wrong things, in your shameful interviews. Let me tell you something, buster, you don't fool me, or any other half sane woman in America. You hear me? I wonder if you feel any regret?

Regret is not something I feel, she's right about that. I don't use the word, it's been drilled out of me by swing coaches and sports psychologists. You can't win with regrets. Regret is for losers. I never liked losing. So regret? I don't think so.

Don't you have somewhere to go? Some big party, some main event somewhere? What are you doing here with me, with the filler people?

No, I say. Then I say it again. No, I have nowhere to go. I don't have any place I need to be. I don't have anyone to go back to. An empty hotel room and a drunk caddie.

I reach over and take one of her hands in mine. It feels light and insubstantial. A girl's hand. The hand is ringless and smooth. I hold it to my sunburned face and feel the heat. She doesn't draw away. She doesn't move toward me. She sits there.

I go to my knees. Right there at the bar, I drop down and hold her dress between my thumb and forefinger. I hold onto the hem of her dress like it's the body of Christ.

She sits still for a minute. I've shut out the noise of the bar, the people looking at us. As if studying a winning put, with that same degree of concentration.

After a minute she says, It's okay, get up stupid. What are you trying to prove? C'mon, get up, Fred. What are you doing down there? You are so dumb sometimes, I swear.

Look, I felt the need to vent, okay? I mean, Jesus. I don't see you for five years and you shooting off your mouth across America. What'd you expect? But you know, and I know, and the whole world, thanks to you, knows that it's over. It's history.

For a long while I was *inconsolable*. Put that word in your stupid yardage book! Inconsolable, you need me to spell it out? I was such a good girl, good, pretty and stupid. Raised to be that way, God knows. But anyway, I got over it. I learned, Fred, and I have a life now. It may not be the same as your life, understand, but I like it. He's good to me. He's home at night. He brings me organic bananas for chrissake. He doesn't send his idiot caddy to get me ridiculous presents, or to meet me at the restaurant when he's running late.

She takes her time. I'm still down on the floor, slumped over and holding on to her hem. I'm holding on like a terrier, like an ugly Jack Russell terrier, for all he's worth.

C'mon, get up. My husband will be coming in here soon to check on operations. How am I supposed to explain this? I know what you want. You want the magic words, don't you? Is that it? Okay. Look at me. *Look* at me! I forgive you, okay? I don't mind that you feel bad. Maybe a little bad. But sure, I forgive you. I *absolve* you. Like a good Catholic girl. You're free now.

But I'm still there on the floor.

Did you hear what I said? Hey, dummy. You have to go now. C'mon, honey. I said I forgive you. There's no need for more of this. You've got it made in the shade, you and your old lady. That's it. Hey, here's your hat. Don't forget your stupid hat, it's probably worth millions. That's it, get along now before my husband comes by.

Listen to me now, Frederick. I want to tell you something. She pulls me by the shirt, right into where she sits with her feet hooked around the bar stool. She gets my face close to hers, then closer. Till she's about three inches away. I take shallow breaths and wonder if she can hear me breathing. I lean in for what she has to say.

You just keep doing what you're doing. There's nothing more that can be done. We've seen everything. You just go on and tell it like you have to. I guess I never expected anything less. Just forget about all the rest. It's alright now. Really. I'm okay.

She walks me out. The white moon hangs sideways in the LA night. On the edge of the desert, night air envelops us. I don't think I have ever seen a moon like that. But I don't trust my lips. I don't know what might happen.

It was good of you to come. I know you don't usually play this event. I know you came for me. Maybe you'll come back some time, and maybe you won't. It doesn't matter. I'm happy here. But this thing that you're feeling tonight will wear off, you understand? Pretty soon you'll start feeling the old way again, and you have to learn how to deal with that, see? You don't have me to feel through anymore, to feel things *for* you. You have to get used to that, Fred.

That's her last word on the matter. She looks at her hands, then moves them into a defeated wave. She goes back into the bar and I stare up at the moon.

Kids get out of a car in the parking lot. The girl laughs and clutches at her white breast. Her date comes toward her with a long hatpin. His tux is awry. They look like they just got dressed. She finally gets his corsage pinned and they move into a long kiss. The moonlight frames them, just for an instant, and they move off into the clubhouse. I watch them go.

HAZARD

Playing alone on a sultry July afternoon at his club in Sag Harbor, Val Hollow had it at one under par on the thirteenth hole when it occurred to him that his wife might be having an affair. Dropping his bag to the ground, he fished a clean white handkerchief from one of the side pockets, and blotted his brow. Just yesterday, one of his firm's senior partners had remarked that he was mildly surprised at how reasonable Savannah had been. They had been in the library in the tort section, researching negligence in the Shinnecock tribe case. Val started to speak, he'd been filling the air with explanations and aimed to continue, but Vanderslice placed his hand gently on his shoulder and said, "Son, save it. You've made the common mistake of thinking your divorce is interesting."

He and Savannah had been best friends in college. They were part of a touring Princeton ensemble that performed at the tall steeple Congregational churches of Vermont and New Hampshire. Savannah was a soprano, he a baritone, part of a group of eight perfectly matched voices that sang French madrigals and holiday music. Val was taken in by Savannah's long, willowy frame, accentuated by a floor length cross-back jersey maxi which she had toughened up with a military parka and Doc Martens. With her pancake makeup and thick mascara, Savannah looked like Morticia Addams, had Morticia been a blonde. It was a joke between them, Val holding her pale arm aloft in the Princeton touring van as he kissed it in two inch intervals as the others cheered, and he proclaimed to her, only half joking, "Cara Mia!"

Val placed the handkerchief back in his bag. He pulled his

driver and stepped onto the manicured tee box. As he rehearsed his swing and tried to visualize the way he must shape his next shot, he saw instead Savannah in her skinny jeans, and then the way she applied night cream to her pretty face before climbing into bed next to him. One day soon that stops, Val thought. And someone else will watch her move in those jeans, watch her move through the Italian restaurant or pottery barn and into her car, into the seat beside him, knowing at the end of the day he can remove the jeans from her slim hips and watch her apply her night cream and count the seconds till she presents herself to him in bed.

He placed a white tee into the ground and wondered, how had they come to this? Just last month, lying in bed on a Sunday morning, he and Savannah had rehearsed a half dozen scenarios—married too early, two miscarriages, Val's meddlesome mother who had never approved of Savannah's couture, the numbing routine of a young associate at a historic Boston law firm, with longer and longer nights at the office and fewer opportunities to spend time together, their baby-less future. When they spoke of these things that Sunday their tone was one of sweet reasonableness, doctor conferring with lawyer, as if they had simply missed a question on their SATs. Married young, divorced young, no children, no worries. They would both go on. She in pediatric medicine, he at the firm. It was far from tragic. With all that was terribly wrong in this violent crazed irrational world, their problems didn't amount to much, even to them. They would use a mediator, one not from his firm. They would go on as best pals. No fault, win win, the ideal way to play it.

Val smashed his drive, starting it over the right side of the fairway, a high arcing draw. He shouldered his bag and tried to reason things out. If Savannah was really having an affair, everything changes. But why? Because deceit alters things. But why? What moral work does deception do? Why should it matter to him? The marriage is over. Yes, but it is also true that facts matter. However, if she denied an affair, he would have to establish the facts, which means an investigation. Does he want that? What if nothing happened? What are the grounds of his divorce, now? Is there a case that can be built?

He reached his ball. It had landed in the middle of the fairway, 270 yards from the tee box. He has 153 yards to the back of the green where the pin is tucked in the far left corner, guarded by a large bunker. A sucker pin placement. Val took his stance over the ball, made a few waggles with his eight iron. He concentrated on the shot before him.

But he had a corrupt swing thought, disturbed by the nagging suspicion that Savannah was seeing someone at work, and he comes over the top on the shot, slicing the ball into the trees. He walked angrily after his Titleist. It had come to rest two inches from a tall maple. Trees line the right edge of the fairway on this course, and he was in jail. With no other option, he took a five iron, punched out into the fairway, chipped onto the green, and two putted. Double bogey. Just like that he is one over par.

Val pulled his ball angrily from the cup and walked briskly to the ball washer at the fourteenth hole, a long par five. He pumped the ball up and down in the bright red washer, trying to remember the name of the guy Savannah had mentioned a few months back, a young intern at Boston General, the brother of one of her partners. Or was it a nephew? A guy who'd shown up with his stethoscope and blood pressure kit in a red and yellow Sesame Street lunchbox. What was his name? Halverson or Halverton? One of those. They had met, Val recalled. It was at an office party when he picked Savannah up at work one night when her car was in the shop. Deferential as hell, this kid doctor had been, he remembered that much.

He took the ball, dimpled and gleaming white from the washer, and promptly dropped it into a small patch of mud. Cursing, he washed the ball again and placed it, still wet, in his pants pocket. On the tee box, he took a few rehearsal swings, smooth and rhythmic, and addressed his ball. He hated the thought that something was hidden. That he has been so *not knowing.* He was not vigilant enough with Savannah, then hadn't bothered to put up a real fight for her. But why? Why had he allowed this Sesame Street kid to come between them? He had failed to *defend* her!

Soto voce, he hummed the Emperor's Waltz. Imagining himself gliding alone around a polished dance floor, he took the club back slowly, loaded his weight onto his back leg and haunches, and made a full turn. But his right elbow flew open and he sliced again, his ball peeling like a banana and landing in the next fairway. He hit a smothered hook from the rough, managing somehow to reach the green in regulation, but then three putts from thirty feet. Furious with himself, he takes his bogey and moved to the fifteenth hole.

Where he had a revelation. If Savannah *is* having an affair with Halverson or Halverton then she has surrendered to him the moral high ground.

All through their marriage Savannah had been the faithful one, the one whose steadiness guided their marriage, the one who had sacrificed her career while he advanced at the firm, the whimsical wife turned reluctant scold, who had tried to make babies while falling behind the pace in med school. And of course! It made sense that she was now the very soul of reason, now that she had proven unfaithful at last. But now he knew!

Sensing his advantage, and with the natural rhythm he had mastered as the captain of the Princeton golf team for two seasons, Val kept his left foot grounded on the turf, felt his spikes grab and hold, his lower body stable and quiet, while he rotated his upper body in a powerful coil and lashed at the ball, unleashing a beauty, a long powerful draw that splits the fairway 290 yards out.

He struck a perfect approach shot to the center of the green and drained the five footer for birdie. Back to one over par.

He birdied the next two holes and arrived at the eighteenth hole one under par. The eighteenth is a long par four, uphill, to a green that cants from top to bottom. It is important to keep the ball below the hole on the approach shot. Too deep and one finds oneself in a steep greenside bunker where it is impossible to get the ball up and down. Val Hollow cranked a soaring drive up the fairway. His ball came to rest 160 yards from the pin, where the fairway meets the first cut of rough on the left side.

There was grass between his club and the ball. Not a good lie. Val placed his gleaming seven iron behind the ball, hovering it over the grass, careful not to ground the club. He rehearsed what he planned to say to Savannah when he got home, all possible ways into his conversation about Halverson or Halverston. Halliburton! Ha! He waggled his club and tried to visualize the shot. He saw the lovely form of his wife, naked under the sheets, the sheets of Halliburton, the line of her long legs beneath the thin percales, the look of ecstasy on her face, and backed away from the shot. He shook his head and tried to empty it of every thought. Let the nothingness enter your shots, he recalled his Princeton coach say. The swing is the man. Relax, and feel it.

But as he built his stance and addressed the ball, his swing thoughts again are banished by the thought that he once had a wife and now he does not. The simple logic of subtraction: two minus one. Val recalled the look on Savannah's face when he presented to her on their first anniversary a diamond necklace with matching earrings. He had taken care with its purchase, scouring the stores at the mall trying to find something that would fit his law school budget. The young woman who had wrapped the gift in silver striped paper had beamed up at him and told him what a perfect selection he had made for his wife. His *wife*! How proud he had been of that word, how delighted he was with Savannah, the way she moved around their small apartment, carrying toward him two gold-rimmed teacups she had found at a church rummage sale, their tiny treasures. One morning, he'd carelessly dropped one into the sink, breaking the handle. Late for court, he'd thrown the cup in the trash. That night he came home to Savannah seated at the kitchen table, holding the cup and a tube of epoxy. Were you going to tell me? she'd said.

He flailed at the ball, his swing ugly as a collapsing lawn chair, and caught it thin. Too much club and he'd airmailed the green. From where he stood, looking unsteadily from his moistened eyes, he could not tell if the ball had found the bunker. If he managed to land it in the grass beside the trap he could still hit a lob wedge and save his par.

Val Hollow trudged up the fairway to the green, stabbing at his eyes. Captain of his golf team, student government president, rising young associate sure to make partner, he understood nevertheless that he had lost Savannah. When he confronts her tonight about Halverson—over what, a Sesame Street lunchbox? —she will look at him, in that way that she does, smile her Morticia smile, and say, "Val, you are so sweetly dumb."

He walked up the fairway toward the green, hoping for a break. Overhead, a lone red-tailed hawk soared, its broad wings beating, searching its quarry. As he reached the crest of the hill, Val saw his ball at last, sitting like a poached egg, buried in the hazard.

PERFECT EIGHT

Two weeks after Katherine and Niles went off topic and began to discuss the state of their union, agreeing that there wasn't any known marital doctrine that required them to live in the same house at the same time, Niles was hit by an SUV.

They were pleased with the friendly turn the aforementioned conversation had taken, and joked that marriage was an alternative way of being alone. Neither of them were given to making decrees, everything seemed negotiable. They felt no terrible rush for one of them to move out and take an apartment, though Niles allowed as how he was open to getting a place in the Central West End, if it came to that. Their house in Webster Groves was in good repair, and would bring a good price. The marriage was stale. Nodding their heads in agreement on this seemed fundamentally decent to them, thoroughly modern, and right. There was an underlying sadness to it, but tears, when they came, were not urgent, and were mixed with relief.

The SUV came up behind Niles like a thoroughbred on the rail, the driver neglecting to signal he was passing. Checking his triathlon bike mirror, Niles gave a hand signal, never seen, then started a left turn at the crossroad by the old Mansfield place.

Niles' body flipped up and over the bike like a ragdoll. He crashed through the windshield, shattering the safety glass, then orbiting clear of the car. The driver, a twenty-five year old male, jumped on the brake. Niles landed heavily on his right side, bounced off the pavement like a ball on a fairway, and skidded to a stop fifty feet away from where the SUV sat idling. The road was tracked with thick black rubber tire marks. The driver opened his door and ran back to Niles, got out his cell phone and called for help.

Katherine had been out weeding the garden when the first call came. She never heard it. She had shed her garden clothes and her bandana, soaked through with sweat, and was standing naked in the shower of the master bedroom, water streaming from her hair, when she heard the second call. It was James calling her cell phone, which she had placed on the white porcelain sink.

Without saying hello James asked, "What are you wearing?"

It was his favorite question. Sometimes he altered it to "Who are you wearing," if he knew that Katherine had a fundraising luncheon or dinner to attend. Katherine served on the board of the Saint Louis Symphony and chaired its fundraising committee.

"Nothing at all," Katherine said. She pulled a towel from the rack and draped it over her shoulder as she stared at the mirror. One of her girlfriends last week had observed that when a man goes by a mirror, he stops, smiles, and says damn! A woman looks into a mirror, frowns, takes out the equipment and gets to work.

"What is it you want, James?"

James was a lawyer in his father's firm downtown, a metropolitan male who followed women's fashion enough to be informed about hem length, seasonal colors and accessories. They had met at one of Katherine's fundraisers at the Chase Park Plaza Hotel. Looking at Katherine's body with a practiced eye, he judged her a perfect eight. His father having gone back to the firm after lunch, James stayed behind to chat her up on Debussy and Ravel, drawing on his music appreciation class as a Brown undergraduate. As the conversation turned to the symphony and it's mercurial conductor, Katherine sensed that she had been appraised and found acceptable. She guessed him to be ten years younger than she, and callow. By three o'clock that afternoon he had couriered over from Niemen Marcus a Kate Spade bow-waist dress for day, and a Betsey Johnson little black dress for evening. Unwrapping the box, Katherine calculated Niles' teaching schedule that semester. As best she could recall it was a MWF schedule. He had a three hour biology lab on Tuesday and Thursday afternoons. And then she remembered that he was training for his first triathlon. He kept his bike locked in his office at the university.

"What do you think, what I always want. Can I see you today?" James asked. "Doesn't Niles have lab today?"

Katherine liked the way James sounded on the phone. He had a musical baritone, a quick and ready laugh. Niles was a tenor in the Presbyterian church choir in Webster. "Don't you have anything better to do today, James, really."

James snorted in the phone. "Sure. I always have something better to do than what I'm doing. You're the better thing. Doing you, that's my thing."

"You're becoming tiresome, James, do you know that?"

James laughed and dropped the phone. He picked it back up and apologized. "Sorry. The secretary came in here and dad was close behind. I gotta go. Meet me at Balabans, the usual time. Wear the Kate Spade. Don't be late."

Katherine walked to the closet, trailing water drops on the carpet. She sorted through her dresses.

"Okay. Wait a minute, will you? There's the other phone."

"Sure, okay. I can wait."

And James did wait. Until he heard Katherine scream. Then he screamed "Kathie!" into his iPhone when she didn't respond, calling her name with an urgency that got the attention of his secretary in the outer office. James thought her voice sounded muffled, and worried that an intruder had gained access to her bedroom and was gagging her.

But Katherine had removed her towel from her bare

shoulder while she listened to the woman on the other end identity herself and then ask if she was Mrs. Katherine Mueller. Nervously, as the woman continued speaking, she placed the towel in her teeth and bit down hard. She screamed into her bath towel when the triage nurse at Barnes Hospital told her that they had been trying to reach her for a half hour regarding her husband, Niles.

When she reached the hospital Katherine was whisked to the trauma wing, where a team of seven doctors stood over Niles, their assistants attending. There was no room for her to stand. She was asked to step aside.

A nurse escorted her to the waiting room, which was nearly empty. A TV was tuned to CNN. A couple sat in the waiting room's drab brown chairs, ignoring each other, their gaze fixed on the television. Another crisis was brewing somewhere in the world. Katherine pulled her eyes away from the TV to listen to the nurse, who was repeating herself. Multiple trauma, did she understand? Yes. Her husband had a brain bleed. There were multiple breaks and fractures. His right elbow was shattered completely. His contact lenses had been shoved back into his retina. His skin, particularly on his right side, was scarred by road rash, and he was bleeding profusely. The doctors were doing all that they could. More than that, she couldn't say.

Katherine paced the waiting room. She paged through some magazines, then got up to pace again. Should she call Nile's Presbyterian church pastor, he could come to help. But she didn't know the number. Did she have her phone? Yes, she had slipped it into her jeans as she pulled them on in the bathroom. She could call one of her friends from the symphony. Her sister half way around the world in New

Zealand. James was unthinkable. She settled on her mother.

James sped over to Katherine's house from his downtown office, arriving in twelve minutes. He tried the door and it opened. He called for her, and then ran up the stairs. Nothing. He entered the master bedroom, then moved to the bathroom. He picked up her damp towel from the floor and sniffed it. Water from her shower pooled on the tile. He went back into the bedroom. Spread out on the king sized bed James saw the Kate Spade bow-waist dress.

Katherine feels the young couple in the room looking at her, looking with four eyes, the man's eyes a backup looking to the young woman's harsh gaze. The woman has stringy dirty blonde hair and a tiny black T shirt, sweat pants. Her paisley flip flops have a broken thong. The man wears the white shirt and checked pants of a cook. The woman addresses her, saying, "Who you here for?" Katherine explains how she is here for her husband but they will not let her go to him. Her cell phone rings. Katherine glances at the screen. It is James. She pockets the phone. The man is speaking, now. "Her dad, my boss. Cooked himself at work. Gonna have French fry marks on his skin for life."

Katherine bolts the room, heading for the ICU door, determined to get to Niles. They have moved his gurney into a room with drawn curtains and a huge overhead lamp. A doctor peers at her over his glasses. Nurses and technicians come in and out of the room. Machines whir and hiss. The light is very bright. When Katherine identifies herself as Niles' wife, the doctor nods her into the room. Niles is stretched out on the gurney. He is bleeding from everywhere at once. The phone in her pocket vibrates and stops. She goes on looking at her husband, unable to pull her eyes away.

The doctors have him stabilized. She asks about his condition, and the prognosis, she remembers the word prognosis. They tell her but she does not understand what they say. She wishes someone was here to interpret for her.

There is a new doctor in charge. He is able to get Niles into a sitting position. The blood continues to pour. Bandages are changed repeatedly. Niles is sitting up, and the doctor is saying that he has to get more light, he has to turn Niles toward the light, Niles can you hear me? The doctor trains the light on his bloody patient, and in that instant Niles' broken body goes rigid, then seems to elevate, electrified, as if pulled from an invisible string. His arms are spread-eagled like Christ on the cross and his mouth is open in a silent scream. The doctor looks shaken. The whites of Niles' eyes travel back in his head and the doctor is screaming something. Katherine looks in terror at the monitor in front of her, which has flatlined. She looks at her husband and thinks no, no, no, it cannot end like this, this cannot be the end of the story, not like this, oh Niles, not like this.

Niles lies on his back as the doctor thumps on his chest. And in those forty-five seconds, as her husband lies flatlined on the gurney Katherine thinks she sees her lover enter the room, hovering in space over the gurney holding out her phone to her saying why didn't you answer? I called. Where were you, Kathie? Why did you scream? I came to you, baby, I was the only one to come, I was here for you. I found you. But then the doctor finds the plug which has come out of its socket when Niles had his seizure, plugs it back in, and now his vital signs register again though he goes on bleeding, and now a nurse is comforting her, saying that was so scary, I'm so sorry, it was the plug! Just the plug! and Katherine is smiling, saying yes to all those assembled and to the ghosts who have entered the room, to all of them she is saying yes, I am so pleased, he is back, her mouth fixed in a half grin, her wet hair flat against her skull.

ONE MORE THING

The second thing Annie Riser did after receiving her diagnosis was to find a realtor in the Yellow Pages and put her house up for sale. It was a big house in the Connecticut suburbs with ugly casement windows that were difficult to clean, and Annie knew she wouldn't miss it. She understood that Ronald would disapprove but was ready to fight that battle too.

The first thing she did was book a flight to Colorado. It was mid-winter, and the western sunshine surprised her. In Denver she rented an all-wheel drive vehicle and drove west to Ouray. Her husband had died twenty years before when he got caught in a spectacular avalanche while skiing in the back country near Telluride and Annie had never been to Telluride or to Colorado. Annie chose Ouray for the big mineral springs pool, and for its proximity to the backcountry where Ronald, Sr. had met his death.

Now Annie stretches her body in the hottest section of the pool and watches the passing traffic, people who seem comically white. Steam rises from the hot water and hovers over the pool as over a tea cup, and to Annie, staring at her scissoring legs, it feels as if she is living in a cloud. But when she raises her head to see the spectacular red cliffs, and the mountains that ring the pool, bathed in late afternoon light, she sees a family of deer picking their way through the foot high snow just beyond the protective railing of the pool. The deer come at the same time each afternoon. Annie wonders where they go each night.

Her cell phone rings. Annie picks up the phone, to see who is calling, then lets it go to voicemail. Scrolling through the menu, she selects silent.

Annie lies in the water with her feet braced at the bottom of the pool and her arms behind her head. She pulls her upper body into a series of crunches. She doesn't feel sick. Neither had Rose at Stage 3, when both women had felt free to speak of hope. But Annie understands what is coming, what cannot be stopped. She understands also that it is the third thing she did after receiving her diagnosis that will set things in motion.

*

Annie is 72. She lost her youngest child three years ago to the same ravenous form of ovarian cancer. Rose struggled but succumbed at last, upstairs in the rambling Connecticut house, in her girlhood bedroom. Divorced and childless, Rose had wanted to go home to her mother's house to die. Together they had made the hospice arrangements.

An enormous man enters the hot water section. His big belly overhangs his fashionable trunks. He wears a beige hat with ear flaps that reminds Annie of Lawrence of Arabia. The fat man nods at Annie and collapses into the hot water like a descending hippo, one leg at a time, his enormous head and pink nostrils disappearing into the mist.

Annie glances at her phone. It lights with a silent call. She sighs and places the cold screen to her wet ear.

"Mom, what the fuck! You put the house up for sale? Why didn't you talk to me? Where the hell are you, anyway?"

"Are you at the house now, Ronald?"

"Mom, you understand that I am a realtor, right? You do understand that, correct? What'd you do, pick this idiot out of the phone book? What were you thinking? He couldn't even get his sign into the ground straight. Where the hell *are* you, mother?"

Annie snaps the phone off. The third thing she had done after getting her diagnosis was to call an auction service. She gave orders to set all her belongings on the snowy lawn of her house and to accept the highest bid. Proceeds will go to the Greenwich Ovarian Cancer Fund in Rose's name.

Annie looks at the dying light of Ouray, the last bit of sunshine on the highest peak, how many miles away? How cold would it get on that peak tonight, Annie wonders, in the harsh Colorado winter. How odd it was, to be warm in the cold, lying in the mineral springs pool. Contradictions. Like Rose, healthy and strong and dying, painlessly. Bit by bit our life slips away, Annie thinks. Better to go out strong than to fade molecule by poisoned molecule, to endure the body's cruel betrayal, or a son's callous disregard for his mother's wishes, his taunting of her politics, his criticism of hospice care, his mirthless rich life in a diseased community of the living.

The phone rings again. As compassionately as she can manage she explains things to her remaining child. Ronnie, she says, about tomorrow. One more thing, she says, and pauses. She lays it out, what is coming, what cannot be stopped.

Annie places the phone in her bag. Pulling herself up by the rails she steps out of the pool, her swim suit dripping water. Looking at the darkening mountains, she climbs over the protective railing. She places her bare feet carefully in the deer tracks. She walks out into the Colorado night.

WHAT IS IT?

Throw the emptiness out of your arms
to add to the spaces we breathe; maybe the birds
will feel the expansion of air, in more intimate flight.
~ ***Rainer Maria Rilke, Duino Elegies***

He woke before noon dreaming he had drank wine from ballet flats and milk from her breasts. Outside his apartment window a pigeon softly cooed. Another lay dead on the window sill, its shriveled legs retracted against its mottled gray body. Harris opened the window and pushed the dead bird to the street, six stories below.

He found a straight razor and slit the underside of his left arm above the elbow. Raising the bleeding arm to his mouth he sucked the slit but still there was no pain so he went into the kitchen and got salt and rubbed it into the flesh. He winced but continued rubbing. He tore a strip of rag and bandaged his arm.

He took the easy walk to the harbor. It was June and the fish were running well and the air stank of putrefaction up against the curb and outside the walls of the canneries where Harris walked, urine and decayed fruit in the streets.

His nostrils filled with the scent of bilge water from the tankers and rotting lumber and crude, and he imagined the oil poured into barrels and bound for distant places on the tide that carried all things off. The street held water from last night's rain, and the run-off was slimy and yellow and toxic.

The sun was higher in the sky and he walked north until he saw a white bridge. A tanker was unloading. Fishermen repairing their nets smoked and cursed and stretched an entire block, and Harris regarded the old rope and tug boats and the smell of scrap iron. Stevedores worked in their bare backs at low tide.

Harris made it to the Bronx. The sun was lowering in the sky and there was the faint light of a planet in orbit, he didn't know which one.

He stood in front of a corrugated iron building at the Bronx terminal market. The elevated train roared above his head. Steel girders thick with rust supported the track, each numbered with black paint on gray. There was little traffic. Workers had gone home for the day. Harris inspected his bandage, red with blood.

He picked the lock. Looking inside, he saw that the building was deserted. Dirty water dripped from the rafters. The heat of the day was trapped and Harris felt as though he had entered a dungeon.

Harris retreated to the door. Across the street at the girder marked 13 a woman stood with an umbrella. He stared at the woman until he pulled a look. The umbrella shadowed her face, which was angular and long and cruel at the mouth. The shadows carved her face into triangles.

He re-entered the building. Steel tables were scattered where workers had gutted mackerel and sea bass, and fish oil stained the green floor. Harris walked across the long room, feeling his way in the dark until his eyes adjusted. The walls were caked with old dust and grime. Immigrant women once bent over tables like these gutting mackerel with fish knives, he knew. The women he imagined in winter, clothed in heavy yellow oil-skins. Their hands were gloved, their feet cased in rubber boots. They stood ankle deep in fish guts wielding sharp knives, cutting the unessential.

Harris hesitated a moment. He was of medium height with well-formed features and gray fowl eyes, listless with disorder. Lowering his back to the wet green floor, he stretched out and waited.

The acrid stench from the floor burned his nostrils. Harris

sat up and removed his shirt. He used the shirt to cover his nose, and he breathed through his mouth. Still sitting up, he carefully removed his pants, his wristwatch, his wedding ring, and his underwear. The watch and the ring he placed in the pocket of his pants. He folded the pants neatly in thirds. His arm began to bleed. Ignoring his bleeding arm, he lay back down.

Harris heard a light knock at the door. He sat up and squinted into the darkness. It was the woman with the umbrella. The woman held the collapsed umbrella and a small flashlight in her right hand. He registered her appearance, then sank back into the floor, waiting. Through the dark room she walked slowly towards him, weaving her way through the cutting tables. Dropping the umbrella to the floor, she lowered her mouth to his cock. She propped the flashlight against his pants, which remained folded beside him on the filthy floor. The flashlight she positioned so that it shined on her eyes, which were green but now burst with white light. She sucked delicately around the tip of his cock, gripping the base of it with one hand.

The triangles had disappeared. Her hair was short in a blunt cut and the color of straw against the green floor. She wore an expensive raincoat and one white glove. One arm of the raincoat swung empty and loose in a lazy circle as she worked his cock with her gloved hand. She shrugged off the raincoat and backed her ass to his mouth. He ran his tongue around the rim of her ass then sucked greedily as she worked his cock with her one hand and mouth. He saw the pink stump of her arm, the flesh finely stitched to make a smooth flap. She let go of his cock and he watched her work her gloved index finger into her anus. Aroused, he lifted himself from the floor and knelt on his bare knees behind her, following her finger with his tongue. Then he mounted her roughly, reaching his hands around her to slap her breasts. When they were done he turned off the flashlight. He retrieved the bloody rag from the floor. She lay on the floor with her eyes averted. Standing over her, he dropped the rag beside her. Then she looked at him and he motioned for her to use the rag. She licked her one arm and hand like a cat. He left her in the dark to clean herself.

They walked together to the zoo. It was early evening and the sky had lightened. She dropped her umbrella into a trash barrel. A peacock walked across the graveled path, its tail feathers low to the ground. The head was absurdly small. It bobbed and darted in a comic way as it did its stately walk, like the city's mayor walking the ward.

They sat on a bench under a canopy of trees. The zoo was empty of people and would soon close. They'd met on his last tour in Fallujah. She covered the war for *Haaretz*. He'd been a surgeon.

Harris looked into the top of the trees and tried to recall what he had known of the language of love. It seemed to him that language was an old city, a maze of little streets and squares, of old and new houses, and houses recently renovated, the additions added over the years, and modern quarters with straight regular streets and uniform dwelling places. The language was incomplete but each person added the few words that he knew.

She sat beside him on the bench and leaned into him. He felt the nothingness of her arm, the armless sleeve of her raincoat, and wondered how she carried that emptiness, had carried it for years. She had lost the arm in Tel Aviv on a bus when a bomb burst from the seat opposite her. Her little boy, gone too. Harris held the empty sleeve against his wounded arm and then wrapped it around his shoulder on the bench. They sat there as darkness fell and then it was time to leave.

*

The subway car was empty except for them. Harris was hungry but had nothing to eat. She reached into the pocket of her raincoat to find something for him but there was nothing. The raincoat smelled of fish oil. His pants were filthy. Her hair held the scent of their sex.

The train rocked though the Bronx and down into Harlem where it suddenly stopped. The lights of the train went out.

They were alone in the blackened train.

Why do you want me this way, she asked. These places? She asked again, why is our apartment not good enough for you?

Harris turned toward her. He felt for her in the dark and lowered his head and spoke into her hair, feeding the ends into his mouth.

Because it makes me feel alive, he said.

Our lovemaking makes you feel alive? she asked.

No. Fucking.

What is it? What is the difference between lovemaking and fucking?

I don't know, he said.

The train lurched ahead, then settled. They both looked around. There was nothing to see. He played with the button on the armless sleeve of her ruined raincoat. A raincoat he had purchased for her in Paris at Printemps. She left it behind getting off the train one day at Gare de Lyon but when they retraced their steps they had been able to retrieve it. Harris thought of the women he had fucked before her, all of them missing something.

In Fallujah he'd been in surgery all night but in the morning there was no one else available and he stayed another shift. The nurses wheeled in another gurney with another soldier. Harris bent over him with a sharpened scalpel. But he cut too deep. The soldier whose nerve he had severed was nineteen, from a farm outside Ames, Iowa. Harris knew instantly that the kid would never walk again or take a shit by himself.

He took the hand that she offered. She was a thin colorless flame and her hand rested lightly in his.

Were you surprised that I wanted you to fuck me in the ass?

No, he said.

Did you do that with the other women? I mean, before me?

No, he said. Not often.

Did you ask them for it?

I didn't, he said. Not often, no.

Harris thought for a moment. Sometimes they offered, he said. Sometimes I asked, or didn't. But it was never my impression that women liked it.

I wanted to, she said.

Why did you?

She lifted herself in the seat beside him so that her head was above his, and pulled him into a long kiss with her one arm.

Because I want to feel you. I need your touch. Everywhere I am, I want you there with me. I wanted to feel you hurting me there and to know it was you where the pain came from, to know that the pain came from somewhere I could trust.

He thought about this. And you trust me, he asked.

I do.

Marital fucking is still fucking, he said. Does it make you feel like a whore?

I want to be where you are, she said.

I'm in the darkness.

She cried, then.

It was unbearable. Standing up suddenly, he reached down to remove her raincoat. He felt her breasts against his face. When her lips searched for his, he lifted the blonde wig from her head. Her hair was dark and close cropped. The air in the train was stagnant. He ran his dirty blunt fingers through her hot hair. Then he kissed, roughly. She bit his lip. He pulled away, then moved in and kissed her again, harder. She removed her shoes. Harris went to his knees and licked her dirty feet. He felt the dampness of his tongue between her toes, and a familiar ache rising not from his appendages, from arms and legs, hands or feet, but from his center, the place he trusted least.

The lights of the train came on. Her face was clouded with desire. An ugly scar ran from her scalp to her chin, and he wondered again about her child, about the pieces of him they had cleaned from the Tel Aviv bus. They placed the boy in a thin pine box that narrowed from head to toe. Heavily sedated from her own surgery, at her son's funeral she had worn a black suit with narrow lapels. The Orthodox rabbi had ripped the lapel over her heart. She sat Shiva for seven days in the ruined black suit.

Harris parted her cunt with his fingers and thrust his tongue inside her until she quivered and was still.

He held her in the circle of his arms and thought of the deadly third rail beneath them.

Then the train was moving. He placed the raincoat on her slender frame and sat back down beside her. She reached into his pocket and found his wedding ring. The ring he had received from her under the chuppah. He held out his hand to receive it. She placed the ring back on his outstretched finger.

He showed her his arm. The dark hairs on his forearm were matted with dried blood. He took a penknife from his pocket and reopened the cut. They watched as blood poured slowly down his forearm then dripped from his arm and fell silently to the floor of the train.

Slowly the train made its long slide into the dark caverns of Grand Central Terminal. The lights of the train flickered on and then blinked off as they rocked gently from side to side.

The train moved carefully through the cavernous hole in the heart of the city, the locomotive's powerful headlamp throwing light forward as they inched their way ahead.

They rode in silence.

Where shall we meet tomorrow, she finally asked.

At the Palm Court, Plaza Hotel.

What shall I wear?

A tiara.

She laughed lightly. Your Armani tux, she said.

Yes, he said.

Overhead the lights of the train flickered. For a brief moment the cabin was lit. With her one good arm she took her flashlight. She traced the length of his body with the small beam, locating the cut on his arm. When the light reached his eyes he looked away. She placed her mouth on the wound and took his blood.

SHOT

This happened in Saint Louis. I was a graduate student, and a regular at a half dozen bars. I managed to fail my language examination in German, then French, a language I had studied since seventh grade. By then I was meeting students after class in bars. The students were female, Catholic, and underage. I made $550 a month as a Teaching Assistant. Rent was $225. Jobs in my field were non-existent. What I did next is that I fucked one of my students, then fucked another.

The first girl was named Ann and the second one I don't remember.

Ann was trying to stop smoking. She sang along to the radio in my rusted Triumph Spitfire. It was winter and I had the top up and the heater blasting. She wore a tartan skirt with a kilt pin and red knee socks. The skirt rode high up her waist and she twitched and sang off key. She was drunk and I was well on the way. Her hair was dark and shiny and she wore one pink barrette, which kept slipping out of her hair.

In class, she tracked my movements. She sat in the second row, just to my right. I smoked in class, which was illegal even for the Jesuits, and came to class half lit after three beers and whiskey shots at Humphrey's bar. Ann liked that I smoked, and teased me about the way I held a cigarette like a joint. Word was out among the undergraduates about my teaching. Student evaluations were among the best in the department, and my classes always closed early. Ann told her parents that she was staying overnight with a friend in West County. From the SLU Library, she called a friend in Ballwin to make sure she had cover. Then she took my hand and walked me out of the library and into my car. She was nineteen with good ID. She set the radio to a station I never used.

We made our way to Rollo, Missouri, where we hooked up with a few of her friends who attended engineering school. Ann made me stop at a grocery store in town where she bought a toothbrush and toothpaste. She told me she hated brushing her teeth with her fingers after a night out. She pulled me into a long sloppy kiss when we stalled in the checkout line. Her small breasts pressed against my chest. She jammed her hand into the back pockets of my Levis and held on.

We got back in the Triumph and drove to a dive bar. Kicking aside some empty longnecks, I jumped the accelerator. Ann lit another cigarette.

Tom Petty and the Heartbreakers wailed "American Girl." Her friends looked at me, hard. Ann said, "He's a great teacher." I wanted to smile. She looked over and said, "You're a bad guy, you know that?"

We ended up at some guy's house. There was a single bed and we fell into it. I pawed at her. She pushed my hands away and said "Mmmm, later, I'm sleepy." Ann was too drunk to fuck so I watched her sleep for two hours. Her small chest rose and fell.

I lit a cigarette and checked my watch. The watch was a high school graduation present, with hands that glowed in the dark. Ann's eyes were shuttered black buttons. She hadn't removed her makeup or brushed her teeth. I parted her lips with my finger and ran it along her teeth until she sucked it. She moaned and turned over. Her pale arms sprawled behind her like a baby seal. Her body took little space on the bed. I felt like a giant. The kilt pin was still fastened to her pretty skirt. I peeled off her knee socks, one at a time and placed them carefully on the hardwood floor. The bed had a small patchwork quilt. I pulled the quilt up over her hips.

After the second hour I pulled the quilt off. I pushed her

skirt aside and looked at her plump white thigh. She was small but finely calibrated in that way petite women have, that can drive you crazy if you let it; everything made to scale but fully operational. Her thighs narrowed into runner's calves. I kissed the back of her knees, traced her tendons with my tongue and got as far as her feet, which had red lint between the warm toes.

Ann got up to pee. I watched her go and then she was back. She crisscrossed her arms to remove her sweater. Off came the black bra. The palest nipples, I could barely see them. Her doll's eyes were sightless. I liked how the black bra looked against her white skin, but then the bra was off and tossed to the floor with the socks. She left the skirt on, but reached down with two fingers and twisted her panties aside. "Have at it," she said.

The next night I was at Tom's Bar & Grill. Stephanie wasn't a student. She explained that she was an event coordinator. I bought cocaine from a guy I knew at the bar and told Stephanie. Her sweater smelled of cigarette smoke and White Shoulders perfume. She was working this event, she said, but we'd get together later. I nodded. Stephanie was five ten in strappy heels with long straight hair, a blonde, and her voice was whiskey and soda. Some guy saw the way she looked at me and said "Sure, her shit don't stink." I turned away toward the wall. Where I watched her in the big mirror Tom had mounted above the bar. The liquor bottles stood like soldiers. Stephanie caught me looking and smiled. Her teeth were white and even and she was tan under all that blonde. She was pretty and slightly used, and I mouthed at her into the mirror, "Sure, I'll see you later."

But I did the rest of my drugs and then poppers and my nerves were jangling and time sped and then slowed, and I nursed a pint and grew tired of waiting for her. Just before leaving I saw her come out of the bathroom, her heels off and slung over her shoulder. She still had a full eight inches over

Ann. I told her I couldn't wait for her anymore. She said, "You seem angry," and I said, "No, not angry, just tired of waiting." I left her there and went out to my car.

I went back a week later, and the week after that, and she wasn't there. I asked Tom whatever happened to Stephanie? The leggy blonde with the voice? Tom looked at me (I was a regular) and said, "Stephanie? I don't know any Stephanie, sorry."

Ann struggled to write an analytic paper on Descartes' *Meditations on First Philosophy*. She couldn't understand the Pakistani guy in the writing help room, so she climbed three flights to my dingy office. I sat with her under blinking florescent lights, diagramming sentences. Multiple choice threw her, too. Ditto Venn diagrams and Aristotelian logic. We took a cigarette break and walked into the weak Saint Louis sunlight down by the river. She told me she had had twelve years of Catholic school and attended mass until she was sixteen. Then one Sunday, standing in line for communion, she saw a girl her age wearing a T-shirt that said "I love my pussy." Then that was that.

Oh, I liked her.

These were years I counted as lost. Soon I would be married, though I couldn't have known it at the time. Waking up, married, I would think I heard someone crying, then rush through the house, remembering. Outside, bright moonlight on concrete.

I held on and finished my dissertation but there were still no jobs in my field. The teaching continued for a while. I gave up trying to find Stephanie. It was as if she never existed.

There were other students, none I liked as well as Ann. But she was right, I was a bad guy.

The day Reagan got shot I was at Tom's, drinking. The bar exploded in applause. Dan Rather was on the CBS news, remembering dead presidents. Dealy Plaza. This was a bar where guys handed over their paychecks, fifty cent beer. The TAs would huddle together and try not to make eye contact with the regulars. When Dan Rather announced that the president was going to be okay, the bar groaned. One guy threw beer at the TV. A fight broke out. I left the bar and called Ann at her parent's house in Ballwin, but she wasn't home.

Someone once told me, or maybe it was a poet, that marrying is like throwing a baby up in the air, the baby happy and gurgling, and then throwing it higher till it hits the ceiling, jarring the bulb loose, and it goes out as the baby starts down.

I tried to find Ann on the Internet, which led me to idiotic sites like "My Life," which is a joke in itself, right? All I could come up with was her name, her age, and her city. She hadn't moved. I could have paid money to discover more. She'd be twice as old as the girls I see now, in bars, and yeah, in class. More than twice as old.

It'd been late March, all those years ago, when I made that trip to Rollo with Ann in my Triumph. Now it's March again, the month I managed to finish my dissertation, the year after I had Ann in class. I received my doctoral hood the following May. I saw Ann walking to class one day, before I left St. Louis for good, and nodded to her, but she didn't know me, or pretended not to. I taught Maimonides in those days, *The Consolation of Philosophy*, but there didn't seem to be any. Women were my consolation, but even then, every day that passed seemed an assault on a flimsy castle.

There is a time that comes after one is young, and this is that time. There is a time after that, and I'm headed to it, unsteadily. You tell yourself it will get better, and that joy is aligning yourself with what is most real, and the moments of self-soothing arrive when you say *don't cry, I'll get you something better*. And you hope for whatever hope is for.

I gave Ann a "B" in my course and that's a pity, really, because she tried so hard.

LULU

On his tenth wedding anniversary Joe DeMarco parks in the driveway of his first girlfriend's house. His grandfather has turned up dead in Miami, a victim of a carjacking gone haywire; the body was shipped up to Peekskill for the funeral. Joe discouraged Liz from attending, pointing out that Abbey needed her, and besides, had she really known his grandfather? Though the gesture was appreciated, Joe told her he thought it better if he just went alone. Saddened by his grandfather's murder but happy for the time off work, where a new product launch had seen him writing source code for two weeks in a windowless room, he set out from Seattle on a non-stop flight. Liz agreed they would celebrate their anniversary upon his return from New York.

The girl lived in Waterbury Manor north of Peekskill, in a stone house with a sliding glass door that opened onto a breezeway with a small TV built into the paneled wall. At a dance on the last Friday night of ninth grade Joe stood with some basketball teammates near the free throw line at the north end of the high school gymnasium. Lulu came up and whispered in his ear. "I know you," she said. She was wearing a baby blue sleeveless shell that showed off her olive skin, with a matching blue and white checked skirt and saddle shoes. "From where?" Joe asked lamely. Lulu made him nervous. What he had said was senseless, and he knew that she knew it too. But she played along. "I've seen you around, on the basketball court and in English class. I'm a cheerleader." Lulu slipped her arm around Joe DeMarco's waist. Then she said, "Follow me, and relax for Christ's sake," and guided him to the dance floor. His buddies smirked and struggled to control their giggles. Joe went with her. They watched him go.

He was aware that she had a reputation, of course. For all her athleticism, she smoked in the woods out behind the school, drank like a fish, and was rumored to have stolen the boyfriends of several girls in the Junior class, offenses that had earned her a reprimand from the cheerleader advisor and a threat to be cut from the squad if she didn't shape up. At the start of seventh grade he'd seen her caught shoplifting records at Caldor with some girlfriends. Joe was in line with his mom buying new shirts when he saw the manager haul her by the arm into his office. She'd glared at Joe, and given him the finger.

They danced a slow dance to an old Beatles tune. Having never danced with a girl or even held one in his arms, Joe tried not to step on her shoes as they moved slowly in circles around the perimeter of the court where he had spent hours practicing free throws and running wind sprints.

Lulu leaned into him as they danced. She slid her arms down his back, clasping her hands around him. "You're mine," she said in her hoarse voice. "You're quiet but nice. I like the way you move on the court. I'll cheer for you when you make varsity next year." Joe lay his head against her cheek. They stayed in that position for a while, and then he felt her mouth find his. Relax, he told himself. He was conscious of his breathing, his racing heart.

Later, they leaned against the gymnasium wall and she turned again to kiss him She tasted of lip gloss and candy and cigarettes. When he opened his mouth to receive her greedy tongue he felt a tightness in his shoulders and neck. She pulled out her tongue, placed two fingers on his cheeks and turned his face to hers. "Relax," she said. And then the music was playing again, the Doors this time, "L.A. Woman," and Joe drank in her smoky sweetness, forgetting about the stolen boyfriends and the drinking and the gossip. Their bodies swayed together as the music crashed in waves around the polished wood floor and rattled the gymnasium windows high above them.

*

An open casket held the body of Joe's grandfather. He'd been shot in the stomach when he'd refused to get out of the car at a traffic light. His killer threw him under the car and ran over him as he sped away. He bled to death while bystanders debated what to do. Someone finally called the police but it was too late. His bloodied stomach was concealed beneath the smooth oak casket, and his blue eyes were stitched shut. At eighty-eight he still had the barrel chest and the gnarled hands of a New York longshoreman.

After the funeral Joe's extended family, minus Liz and Abbey, gathered for a meal at his parents' house. Asked about his wife and child, Joe gave brief, correct responses. He picked at his food, then asked to be excused, and headed upstairs to his old room. Bored, he entered the bathroom, closed the door and drew a bath.

Sitting in the bath always reminded him of the ocean. He and Lulu had liked going to the beach. Before he could afford his own car they would ride out to Jones Beach with older friends. Afterwards they would change clothes and go out dancing using fake IDs. Lulu enjoyed dressing up. Joe recalled her walk-in closet, with dresses, sashes and scarves half hung on hangers, and clothes strewn on the floor. Once, she found a skirt, a thrift shop flamenco with flowers and rick rack. She wore it to school two days in a row. When Joe tried to compliment her on it, she laughed and said, "It's heinous, but it swings in this certain way when I walk so that even when I am dog tired from cheering practice I feel playful."

*

Lulu never got to cheer for Joe. She broke her leg in a car accident, and by the time she healed in their junior year he was no longer on the team. He got cut from the squad on the same day they broke up. Theirs was a tempestuous relationship, with a half dozen prior breakups, but this time seemed different. Joe doubted that he had the energy to chase her down again. There was college to think about, and he was interested in schools out west. On the afternoon of the big scrimmage when the coach was making final decisions on the roster, Joe was so upset about the breakup that he couldn't do anything right. Every pass he made whistled out of bounds, every shot he took clanked off the rim, every teammate he attempted to guard spun right around him like his legs were nailed to the floor. Joe cursed the team's starting point guard, and tripped him after the guard stole the ball from him at mid-court. After the scrimmage, his coach found him in the locker room and said to him, “Son, I don't think I can use you this year, I'm sorry.” When the coach left Joe slammed his fist into his locker, breaking his wrist. He never saw Lulu cheer, and didn't pick up a basketball for the rest of high school.

After the breakup, Lulu dated a series of boys who misused her and then wouldn't call a second time. For a time Joe simmered with anger and regret. He sat two rows behind her in chemistry class. From this position he studied the line of her shoulders beneath her light sweater, the graceful curve of her neck. He watched as she kicked off her penny loafers. She crossed her bare feet under her desk, lifted her hair to inspect the ends, bent over her notebook to write, glanced at the clock over the classroom door. Her smallest gestures stabbed his heart. But he hadn’t put up a fight for her. He wasn’t sure if it was a lack of desire on his part, or a fear of failure (Lulu was a full time girl) or whether he was just being sensible, with college approaching.

Instead, Joe took up with a girl in his French class, a girl named Karen Tuttle that he picked for her plainness, and the next week he switched out of his chemistry class. Finally, he graduated and moved a continent away. A few times he drunk dialed Lulu from his dorm room far away in Seattle but always hung up before she could answer.

Joe was drawn to Liz's plainness, too. Pale straight hair, parted on the side, pencil skirts, oxford no iron shirts. When they first met, in college, she was girlish and shy, unsure of herself. Her mother had died when she was a young girl, and her father had abandoned his young family for the bottle. Joe and Liz's courtship was a series of tests to see if Joe would abandon her. He'd passed every one, and they married at twenty-three. They settled in Redmond, where Joe found work with a software company. Liz also worked for a time, as a receptionist, but when their daughter was born she quit to stay at home with the baby. Abbey was a beauty, with her mother's fair hair and delicate features. Liz grew more confident with Abbey's birth, and had entered deeply into babyhood, a world of diapers and formula and car seats and play dates, with secret rituals and routines. As Abbey grew to be a demanding toddler a weariness overtook Liz. When Joe was away from them for a few days he could hardly remember who he was. He didn't know why this was, and was unsure whether this was a bad or a good thing.

Lulu remained in New York State, a home girl after all. She attended Marist College in Poughkeepsie, where she was once again a cheerleader. She had begun attending mass again, it was said. And then one day speeding home from a beer run for her sorority she wrapped her red convertible around a tree. His mother clipped the short obituary from the newspaper and mailed it to him along with a note that said, "The girl that tied up our telephone for hours. A pity. I'm so sorry, Joey." With the note and the obituary was a palm sized copy of the Tibetan Book of the Dead. Joe stared at Lulu's black and white picture for a long time, holding it close to his face. She was in her cheerleader outfit. He threw out the note and the book but folded the obituary in half and placed it in his wallet.

Lulu's house has a realtor's sign out front on the lawn. The breezeway is empty of furniture. At four a.m. the neighborhood is forlorn. Joe cuts the engine but leaves the headlamps blazing into the house. The car's engine cools and begins to tick. The TV remains in its paneled wall, reflecting the light from the headlamps. As he sits in his parents' car in the driveway of his dead girlfriend, Joe remembers the week after the dance in the gymnasium. It was summer vacation, and he and Lulu were together at the far end of Robert Moses State Park on a cool windy day in mid-June. They had driven to Long Island with Temple Thompson, and Temple's girlfriend, who was on the cheerleading team with Lulu. Temple and the girlfriend remained in the car making out and listening to music. Other than their Mustang, the parking lot was empty.

Lulu had taken off her shirt and thrown it at him. It landed in the sand at his feet. Then she stripped off her cut offs, revealing a bright yellow one piece swim suit. She laughed at his astonished face and dashed toward the water. Joe hopped after her, trying to shed his clothes and run at the same time. She disappeared under a large greenish blue wave. He waited for her to reappear. She didn't. Then he dove after her but came up quickly, snorting and blowing and rubbing salt from his eyes. His skin was on fire, the North Atlantic a thousand needles jabbing him at once. He shivered and wrapped his arms around himself and turned slowly in a circle, looking for Lulu. He couldn't see her anywhere. He looked up and down the beach, then out to sea, and back to shore. Nothing. The early summer tide was strong and he could feel it pushing at the lower half of his body, wanting to carry him out to sea as he struggled to stand against it. A wave of fear rose all the way through him. He thought of running back to the car to get Temple, and of what Temple would think of that. He imagined himself explaining to Lulu's parents what had happened, with interrogations by grim faced New York State Troopers, holding their big hats in their hands.

He heard a faint noise but it was only a pelican, diving. He turned in the direction of where he imagined Portugal, thousands of miles away, and spotted Lulu in the middle distance swimming parallel to shore a hundred yards out. He screamed to her, but she kept on swimming, a slow steady crawl east in the direction of Montauk.

Now, as his eyes follow the narrow tunnels of light into what had been her house, where she had applied eye liner and mascara in her bedroom and they had spent hours watching TV in the breezeway or making out on the sofa or doing their homework or just quietly talking, Joe DeMarco feels again the shame of his fear that day at the ocean and the foursquare courage of the girl. His first experience of women and love had been disastrous, marked by panic and disorder. But the only disaster had been his pounding heart and the sound of his own fear. He feels certain that he will never again be kissed in the way she had kissed him.

A light goes on in the house next door. Joe waits to see if a curtain moves or a face appears at the window. But there is nothing. The light goes back out.

Reaching under the driver's seat, he pulls up a bottle of Southern Comfort and takes a long drink until his throat burns. Then he takes another. He glares into the dead space of time. And with the drink Joe DeMarco understands his path, and how he must travel to other driveways and houses that will bring him additional sorrow, torment and misery, driven by the memory of Lulu's smoky kisses. His eyes fill with tears, not for himself, nor for his dead grandfather, lying in the frozen ground on the first night of his new death, but for Liz and for Abbey, who deserve better. The best that he could do at love was in that empty house. He cuts the lights and sits in the black night with his faithless, cowardly heart.

WING MAN

When I wonder, as I sometimes do, what happened to all my guy friends, and why I prefer the company of women and would just as soon they leave their men at home, I think of my brief employment with Sam R.

Sam R was an eye surgeon and sometimes that gave him the right. I was an unemployed house painter. I met him at Naughties & Nighties in a lineup for lap dances, when we nearly came to blows over a girl named Steph Swift.

But he slipped me two bills and I stepped aside. Steph moved into his ample lap. I knew Steph from high school when she was Judy Rude. Sam R showed me two more bills for agreeing to watch, and laughed when I took them. His mouth was oversized and had seen a lot of orthodontics. I hated him. Steph didn't seem to mind.

He paid for everything that night, and the next, and the next. I made good money as his wingman. Clearing the way, listening to his commentaries, running to the dry cleaner, answering his phone, scheduling his female companionship. Enough to get my flat screen out of hock and a bracelet for Steph and an X-box for her kid.

I was with Sam R at his man-cave in Venice Beach sucking down a Heinie when he started up on what he called The Art of the BJ.

"Like I was saying," he said, "the woman has to sell it. The BJ is 90% mental, 10% proper form. Form you can teach, attitude you cannot. Cock craving, or at least simulated craving for cock, is essential, and communicated primarily through the eyes. A woman's chief barrier, attitudinally speaking, is the feeling of ick. Ick is deadly to the dick, is what I say."

That Saturday we were on a plane to Taos.

Sam R brought along a girl named Caly. I wanted to take Steph but she had to work. Caly was named for the state in a spelling of her own choosing. Her former name, she told me, was Astrid.

The trip to Taos was a disaster. The hotel had thin walls and noise from the main drag outside. Sam R said he preferred it seedy, and it was. The carpeting retained odors decades old. Dead deer were stuffed and mounted on the timbered walls of the breakfast room, a cheerless place where surly families bolted down carbs before setting out to ski.

Caly was albino. Her eyes let the color of her red blood cells show. One eye drooped, but the other followed your movements perfectly. It was creepy. She had taught special ed in Petaluma but was fired for reasons known only to God, she told me. She was pretty funny when she wanted to be, and not bad looking if you could get past the eyes. She also claimed to be part Native American, which I had trouble figuring, but she swore it was true on her father's side. She had talked Sam R into Taos because of the Pueblo. "I want to visit my people," she had told him, and Sam R agreed. I was the wingman. I just went along.

Caly slept in. After breakfast, the plan was to ski. It was to be a male bonding day, said Sam R.

Driving up to the ski resort, he explained in some detail Caly's proficiency in BJs. The key was knowing how to sell it. "If you love cock and can say it with your eyes, that's the hottest place on earth. Take your basic woman, your garden variety good girl. She's insecure with cock in her mouth."

I asked him what about gay men, figuring he had answers. I looked at my watch and figured Steph would be getting up about now and making eggs for her kid.

"I don't know how it is with our gay brethren. God love 'em. But a woman, she worries. She worries in general, but in the BJ department the worry tends toward, Oh God, am I doing this wrong? Why is he so hairy? So smelly down there? Is there something I'm forgetting, technique-wise? Am I being sufficiently slutty?

"And let's face it, for some of them the mother gets in there. As in, what would my mother think of this, or how can I ever call my mother after, or what if my mother is trying to call me and I am giving head to this man?"

I tried to nod in all the right places. I was feeling lightheaded from the altitude, having come up from the flats.

"I'm saying, a woman is about 120 pounds of worry already, without the mother's weight thrown in. What it all comes down to is attitude. Good attitude, and good personal hygiene."

The road looked deserted. The treetops were shrouded with fog. I calculated how long it was between cars headed back down the mountain. It was like counting waves at the beach, finding the seventh wave, the biggest, the one you could ride safely to shore.

"And watch out for braces," he said.

I grabbed the wheel and steered us into a grove of aspens. There was much noise and then none at all. The hood of the rental car crumpled, and I couldn't breathe for the airbags. Sam R was unconscious and blood dripped from his jaw. I thought about Caly and her red eye looking up from his cock and I boxed his face till the blood poured good and free. I took what I figured he owed me from his wallet and got out of the car. If I hustled, and traffic was favorable, I could make it home to watch Mad Men with Steph on Sunday night.

IN TELLURIDE

This bed is a wreck. I've been lying here all day watching CNN. Frankie shut down the vet office where she works part time and jumped in bed just in time for a special edition of Crossfire, a stinking screaming madcap mess of a show. Our two kids are somewhere in the house, doing God knows what. It's early December, the night of the Supreme Court's Florida recount decision in the case of Gore v. Bush. A decision is at hand, we are told.

I surf over a few channels and punch the contrast button on my new universal remote until Ashleigh Banfield's cheekbones have more definition. Ashleigh is all about eyewear. Her sleek frames look dramatic. She's the perfect combination of sex, faux intelligence, and unavailability. I like the shadowy way she looks in this new light, the upward thrust of her savage chin. When MSNBC goes to commercial I mute the TV, flip over to Fox, and follow the crawlers.

On her left hip Frankie sports an Animal Planet tattoo, her latest work. In bed with us are some red fruit roll ups Frankie filched from Charles' private lunch stock, a box of cheddar Goldfish, two half eaten strawberry Pop Tarts, an empty quart of Ben & Jerry's Chunky Monkey, Frankie's black Wonder Bra, my white boxers, and asleep at the foot of the bed, our miniature Schnauzer, Sadistic. We've got our legs tangled up on the bed, over, under, over, in that way that couples sometimes do to keep warm. The black and white sheets are long since gone, twisted and hanging from the sides of the bed like capsized pirate ship sails.

Frankie reaches over and grabs a bottle of Rolling Rock from the nightstand. She balances on her bare stomach a bowl of buttered popcorn, just above the diamond stud and silver hoop in her navel, gifts from our drop out daughter Jade. Jade is nineteen. She dropped out of the community college down the road—Harvard on the Hudson, she calls it—when she made some serious money setting up a web site last month for a band called Nappy Hair. She thinks I have too many opinions on her life, opinions I am not entitled to. This view is shared by her ten year old brother, Charles, for different reasons. Charles lives in the basement, in an unpainted room I made him last year next to the furnace, where he runs a neighborhood electronics boutique bigger than the one at the mall, from which he IMs me when he needs the latest computer upgrades. Lately I've stopped buying. Jade skipped my birthday, hasn't spoken to me for weeks, unless you count some flaming emails.

A reporter waves frantically, a copy of the Court's ruling in his hands.

"Did you know that all of our affairs have taken place during Republican administrations?" Frankie interrupts. "Yours and mine, Jake. Do the math since Reagan."

"I am not unaware of that."

"Capital T true. But no foreign affairs," she continues. "We behave ourselves overseas. Don't we, Jake? We walk the walk."

Technically true. But I'm watching the action ping pong between the reporter at the Supreme Court, and the anchor room. I flip over to CNN to see if they have a speedier legal analyst.

"Hey, leave it there," Frankie says. She bumps me with the beer bottle, catching me on the kneecap, then pours the rest of her beer into a Styrofoam cup. I flashback to MSNBC and rub my knee. We're in the homestretch now.

It all seems so wonderfully wacky. It's crucial and momentous and absurd all at the same time. But I dread what comes after the show is over, the old assurances that don't assure anyone, and the updated lies. Everything's been so confused and uncertain the past few weeks that it's made me feel better about my own life, like I'm not the only one who is lost. Before the election I had felt exhausted, like I'd been heaving around an entire evil empire of my own. But ever since Katherine Harris and her scare 'em makeup, the butterfly ballot, swinging chads, dueling lawyers, and the Bush brothers I've lightened up and been able to laugh again, letting things go at work and at home and not worrying about what comes next. If the big boys in Washington and Tallahassee were making it all up as they went along, I featured, that might work for the rest of us.

But now that the end is in sight, the balance is tipping away from the unknown back to the known and I don't like the known one damn bit. I'm tired of Frankie, tired of her increasingly manic ways of getting my attention. I'm tired of me being tired with Frankie. I'm tired of our kids never missing an opportunity to point out our parental failures. I'm tired of the smallness of our dreams, what we've settled for, tired of our house, our cars, our things, our safe little domestic nut, tired of the lies and the viciousness at work required to keep this sick enterprise going. I feel shot. Business as usual begins again on Monday, and business as usual is stupid no matter how you dress it up. My job on Wall Street is to make people money, and people with more money just get more stupid. I wanted something to distract me from the smallness and stupidity of my life and the election comedy had provided it.

When they finally figure out that it's Bush—and it's clear that he's really going to get the house, the cufflinks, the plane, the whole enchilada—Frankie goes jihad. She throws her beer at the TV, missing it by a foot and a half but waking Sadistic, who growls loudly at me, then jumps off the bed and laps at the beer where it has puddled on the floor. Frankie turns to me in bed and tells me the following three things: she's had enough with this country; she's thinking of doing the bag boy at the grocery; and maybe we should ice the marriage.

Before she beats me to it I volunteer to leave.

I quit my job at the brokerage and book a flight to Denver to see my friend Henry with the idea of staying out there until something, somewhere, begins to make sense. Things didn't go the way I had hoped at the brokerage, where I am regarded as an ex-college professor too smart to make any real money and a wise ass to boot—a pretty accurate assessment. Jade and Sam have been sending me hate filled emails for months, and I need some time away from them too. Seeing Henry is perhaps not the best idea in the world, since he's had problems of his own in the marital department, and pretty much every other department, enough to drive him to drink. But it's time for my annual early season Telluride ski trip with Henry and I like the idea of staying on schedule even as things are slipping their moorings. So I call Henry, pay the bills for Frankie, sell 5,000 shares of Cisco, and get a room in the city for the night. In the morning I take a taxi to LaGuardia.

The plane is packed. I have an aisle seat. My fellow citizens are stuffing bags, coats, hats, cameras, guitars, tennis racquets, books, briefcases, and backpacks into the overhead compartments. I get bumped on the shoulder three different times by late passengers on their way to the rear seats, even though I am leaning over as far to the right as I can. The woman next to me asks if I would mind if she puts her laptop on the floor under my seat, as she has no more room under hers. Just till we get airborne, she says. I oblige. A slim flight attendant whose name plate says Julian asks me to kindly put my legs under my seat. I place my feet carefully on top of the laptop. Just before takeoff another flight attendant, a large woman with flaming red hair and the voice of Ethel Merman slams the bin above my head, shoots me an aggressive smile, and asks me to fasten my seat belt, please. I take that opportunity to order four vodka tonics. It is nine o'clock in the morning.

An hour later, Ethel and Julian come rolling up the aisle with the beverage cart. My drink order apparently is the talk of the plane. I peel two fifty's off my clip and order up rounds for everyone who wants one. I get plenty of looks and one taker, the laptop lady next to me who's on her way to rescue her sister Georgia from a bad marriage.

"Married five times, my sister."

"What's her secret?" I ask.

"Oh, you're bad," Ethel sings. "You're soooo bad."

"I'm waiting for Mr. Right, too," Julian says. He breaks into song. "I'll know when my love comes along." Ethel harmonizing at the chorus, her voice low and supportive. There is scattered applause. Julian does a supermodel pout with his exquisitely tanned, elastic face.

"He'll come along, honey," Ethel says. "Soon as you ditch Mr. Wrong."

"I'd settle for Mr. Wrong," Georgia's sister says. "Long as I get the house and the dog."

"I got the dog, honey," Ethel says, "My husband Harry. Took me years to housebreak him, but I got him right where I want him now, believe you me."

"Oh, no," Julian says, but it's too late. She breaks into an impromptu and very un-Ethel Merman like rap, bobbing and weaving and using a can of diet Coke as a mic. "Yessiree, I said I'm over here and I'm fifty three, and since nineteen hundred and seventy three, he's chained there to the Tee-Vee, I said you know it's true, I'm free to be me, but my righteous bitch can't get up but to pee."

"Oops," Ethel says, suddenly self-conscious. "Sorry, got kind of carried away there, folks."

"That's a big amen," Georgia's sister says. "But I know what you mean. Mister Sofa, I had one of those units. Horizontal Jerry used to keep me in coins. He was more reliable than the Denver mint. That man lost a small fortune in coinage. He had all denominations. He was all the time wearing these Dockers, you know the ones made specifically for the big butted man?" Julian breaks up, starts braying uncontrollably, and then covers his mouth. Ethel reaches over to high five Julian. She clips a fifty to her name plate. I watch them roll down the aisle in tandem, a tag team on wheels.

"I'm serious. I used to fill a jar after every Monday Night football game. How do you think I raised this plane fare?"

I nod sympathetically to Georgia's sister, and mix her another drink.

The laptop lady's name is Lucinda. She has some advanced views on TV which she feels compelled to share. I'm only too willing to listen. It is a long flight, and Ethel is keeping us in tiny bottles of vodka.

Lucinda's favorite daytime TV is Jerry Springer, the one with Mini Me and the midget sluts.

"I don't watch it much," I say, "but I do like the way they put those captions at the bottom of the screen, you know how they do that? It's the new Tolstoy. 'Happy kids who eat dirt.' 'Says his brother's sister is a slut.' 'Slept with his mother's analyst.' Who writes those things, anyway? I love those. They're like little truth pistols."

"Truth pistols?"

"Well, cap guns."

"I know what you mean," Lucinda says. "Springer does the whole trailer trash encyclopedia, A to B. His staff must be filled with geniuses. I think that's where Tarentino got his start. Or maybe it was the cue ball headed guy who got Clinton elected and dissed Paula Jones."

"Uh huh. So, did you see that new cop show?"

"You mean the one with whatshismug? God, I love that show! Who would have thought that guy could act? I mean, I thought he was funny in that shitcom, what was it called?"

"Married But Slutty?"

Lucinda punches me. "Yeah, that's the one, the one with the baby sitter slut girl. Used to watch it all the time. But Jake, this guy is unbelievable in this new show, I swear. He's the Big Irish. He's making the old New York cop thing new all over again. The writing is perfect, and it's got this slick, tricked up editing, so fast your head is spinning, and if you blink you've missed the good lines, the throwaway asides, but they keep coming up with more, faster and faster. It's like roller coaster TV."

"It's the light. That's what makes the show. They've got this bleached out, blistered, flash bulb light with the deep shadows, it's light like we've never before seen on TV. I mean, in a previous life I used to make movies and I played around with light forever, out in Los Angeles where God created light. But this overexposed look they've got going in this show, it makes New York look like Miami Beach except with character, and when they do an inside shoot it makes it look like the characters crawl right off the screen into your room. It's just amazing."

"Did you see that scene he did with his sister's that's dying, and he arranges to take her to the museum?"

"The planetarium. Yeah, I saw that one, when he's telling the sister about how good and decent cops can be, how this one partner he rode with for just two weeks fourteen years ago set all this up at the planetarium, a special showing just for the sister, who's in a wheelchair, and they have the motorcade procession down Central Park West, and it's snowing, and the whole scene looks like it's taking place inside one of those snow globes that kids play with at Christmas."

Lucinda freshens her lipstick with a pocket mirror she digs out of her purse. Her hands are small and plump, like the rest of her, and seem friendly to me for some reason, like they're an extension of her brain, the visible part.

"NYPD's gotta love this show," she says. "If anyone's watching. Helps their image. Redeems New York's finest."

"Yeah, no broomsticks in rectums, no one shot forty-one times. Complete absolution for Rudy and the boys."

"Not quite. But the big Irish cop this guy plays is just astonishing," Lucinda says. "He looks dumber than his lunch pail, but he's cagey. He's about four steps ahead of the FBI and the street scum, the wacky Russian bad guys, everybody. But the most startling thing is his ability to feel, to be intimate. I mean, it's shocking for a guy who looks like that and who does his kind of work, and it catches you off guard. He's just a quivering mess of pure feeling. It's the way he connects with people. When this guy loves you, you know you've been loved."

"Exactly. That's why that scene with the dying sister is so powerful. It takes balls just to put a scene like that up there, it is so cliché after all the hospital shows, but this scene is truer and cleaner emotionally than all of them put together. It's just so weird to be able to use the words truth and honesty about a TV show, but it's all there. You can see that he's just raw with grief and sadness but he's willing himself to go on, to keep things in their place."

"Well, he wants to keep everything in place, maybe," Lucinda says. "He wants to keep the status quo like we all want, but he knows he's losing, it's all slipping away from him, and he's fighting for all he's worth. He's ferocious and dedicated to his sister and at the same time trying to deal with the raft of shit he knows this latest loss will bring."

When she says this I just look at her. I take the compact out of her hands and hold it up to my face. My eyes look red and I can see the lines of my face hardening around my mouth and eyes and chin, going deeper than I remember them. I hadn't looked for a while. I want to get up and use the airplane bathroom mirror. The mirrors in those places are always the best. The times in my life when I looked the best were always in airplane bathrooms. It's the light, soft and recessed behind the mirror. It almost seems like your face is lit from behind, an old trick of the movies, to show you what you want to see, a less distressed version of you. It must be the FAA's way of keeping everyone calm and centered.

Lucinda stirs her drink and looks carefully at me. She looks to be about 50. Someone has streaked blonde highlights in the front of her frizzy brown hair, which has short bristles in back, like a boy's crew cut. Angry hair.

"So, tell me Jake, what do you do? Do you live in New York?"

"Hard to say. I mean, I used to. I sort of checked out today."

"That a good thing?"

"Not sure. Feels good so far. It's only been about half a day."

"Are you married?"

"Who's asking?"

Lucinda does the Jim Carrey elastic face routine, then says, "Well, alrighty then! Bartend!" She goes sleepy eyed and bobbles her head back and forth, then raises her glass in mock Dean Martin style.

"No, I mean it in a good way. I have this thing where you have to tell me stuff first, then I figure out how much to tell you, okay?"

"Look, Jake, we can drop the subject if you want. How about that Warren Christopher, isn't he a hunk of burning manhood."

"Do not make fun of your elders, Luc."

"How'd you know I'm called Luc?"

"Wild guess. The thing about Warren Christopher is he moves well for a cadaver."

"His suits are well tailored but uninhabited."

"He got his clock cleaned by Jim Baker."

"They did a show on that."

"I saw it. I've been watching a lot of TV. I have this thing for Ashleigh Banfield."

"You and the entire middle aged male population. My ex-husband included."

"Wait, your ex-husband likes Ashleigh Banfield? Geez, now I'm getting worried."

"Of course he does. He's still breathing. You men are all alike. He says it's the way her mouth twists up when she's trying hard to pronounce something right, that high seriousness she has under all that fashion eyewear and capes and shit."

"It's the way the wind blows her hair on the live shoots. She's always got this wispy strand of hair perfectly escaping from her scalp, always brushing it back with her one hand while with the other she holds her notes and still maintains eye contact with the camera. She's the perfect blend of soft news and hard body."

"She's the Edward R. Murrow of our day."

"I'll drink to that," I say. Then we do.

"Ethel," we sing out together. Ethel is making the rounds picking up peanut wrappers, twenty feet in front of us. She walks up and wags her finger at us. Then leans over and whispers that we are officially cut off. We do a mock pout together, and then raise the peace sign. She slips us another mini bottle like it's a covert op.

"My husband had difficulty speaking. To me, I mean. He was okay on the phone with his clients and he did real well when addressing the idiot anchor people at Fox news, but there wasn't a lot left over. He cited some study that said that men have only 10,000 words a day to use, and women have 200,000, and he had already given at the office. For him it was a science thing. He was always watching the Discovery channel or Nova, remember when that was on? Poor Carl Sagan. He died of a full self. But my ex, Jerry, he liked the idea of empty space and black holes. He left me for a woman named Brenda at the office who is a deaf mute."

"Uh huh."

"Yep. That's one version of the story. I felt bad at first, but then I started to like it with him not around. I got a lawyer from the local firm of Dewey Cheatum & Howe who killed his lawyer, and for the past three years I've felt much better."

"Do you work?"

Lucinda nodded, and frowned. "I used to teach history at a community college. This one day I just walked out. It was not long after the settlement with Jerry, I remember, and I had just got sick of teaching, you know? I started to hate the dumb little fucks. I had some sweet kids, don't get me wrong, some that I knew were grateful to be there, and I knew that they tried. They looked so hopeful and so unbelievably young with their new skin still tight on their faces. It made me feel kind of sorry for them that they were there, that they couldn't do any better than us. We were failing them, it seemed to me. We had some major assholes in that department. Don't get me started. But the older students that we got were the worst. These adult learners, as they were called, would sit there defiantly, daring you to say something they didn't already know, like I was a jerk and a no account for being at this podunk school trying to teach them. I had this one guy who thought of himself as the king of all real estate, but he had never earned a college degree and it irked him. He thought he was the stuff. He had a buddy in the class and the two of them would get the tee hees whenever I tried to talk about anything I cared about, and it got so that I couldn't care either."

The woman across the aisle from me has a dog in her purse. It's a big straw purse with flowers on it, like the kind you see in Cancun or Aruba, one of those places, and a very small dog. This dog is stuck deep inside the purse so that all you can see is his little brown furless head. He looks like Dr. Evil's cat. She strokes the dog between his ears with her fingers and every so often feeds it from a zip lock bag she's got there in her lap. She introduces herself to us as Florence Best.

"How do you do, Florence," Lucinda says. "This here is Jake. Nice dog."

"His name is Ralph. I take him everywhere with me. He has stomach trouble occasionally, but if he lets one go, don't worry, I've got some cleaning stuff in here." She pats her bag proudly. "I got it under control. Listen, I couldn't help overhearing that you teach."

"That's right," Lucinda says. "Used to."

"Well, I used to teach too. But I gave away all my books. I boxed them all up and took them to the Goodwill."

"What'd you do that for?"

"Damned if I know. But I don't miss them. I don't have a goddamn book in the house now, it's a book free zone. At the time I remember thinking that it bothered me that I hadn't read some of them. They were just sitting there on the shelf unread, mocking me, and the ones I had read I couldn't even remember a damn thing in them. I figured, what's the point? I didn't like the look of those books on the shelves, looking down on my stupid life, making me feel guilty, so I got rid of them."

"That's the spirit."

"I think TV is the thing. I like TV. I don't know why we need books anymore. Teaching is dead. So is self improvement, it's way overrated, especially in New York. That's the worst place on earth for the self-improvement dildos. But back to books, see, this is where I think Oprah is jacked, and I love Oprah. But it's just so dumb, you ever see one of those shows?

It's just so precious, the way these women sit there in this phony living room and talk about these books as if we should give a flying fuck. The whole self-improvement thing, what's the point? Improve yourself for what, the milk man? The gynecologist? These women in the audience, their lives are as fucked up as anyone else's, but they sit there pretending that because they read this book with Oprah it's all going to be okay, they'll be model citizens tomorrow, they will have felt the correct things and said the correct things, and their husbands and boyfriends will in time come to say and feel the correct things. Get real. I wanna puke."

"Oprah does her best," I say.

"She's product."

"Well, yes, but she's billion dollar product," Lucinda says. "That makes her different."

"Give me Springer any day. Like I said, I couldn't help overhearing. It's a much more original show, Springer. Plus it's funny. It's your number one rated show. Oprah is not funny."

"She can be," Lucinda says. "But she has the furrowed brow syndrome. She inherited it maybe from Phil Donahoe, but she does it better. She cares for America and its denizens. And about the many fat people in our midst. She's the wounded healer. Whatever has been done to you, it was done to Oprah first, only more so, and she survived to help us on our journey."

"As if I care. Ralph hates her. He tosses one every time he sees her. And this Doctor Phil guy, where'd they scare him up, he's a freaking moron! That phony accent and the way he does his hands, chopping the air while women swoon. He's pathetic. He gets my panties all in a wad. I don't let Ralph watch." She tosses the dog another Bonz, which he catches midair, before it hits the handle of the purse.

"So, what's going to happen with you and Georgia when you get there?" Florence asks Lucinda.

"I'm going to take her out to a strip show."

"That ought to help," Florence says, nodding her head thoughtfully.

Lucinda rolls her eyes at me when Florence isn't looking and makes the universal sign for crazy, circling her pointer finger in the air around her ear.

Florence gets up from her seat and makes the long walk down the aisle to the bathroom, tucking Ralph into her bag and zipping it shut.

"But you, hon, I like you," she calls back to me. "We can work on you."

"I'm with her," I say, grabbing Lucinda by the shoulders and pulling her close.

We watch her walk down the aisle to the toilet, holding the flowered Ralph bag high as she twists out of the way of Julian, who's coming down the aisle with more pretzels.

"When we get to the gate we radio the asylum for help," Lucinda says.

"That's a big amen."

"So where did you meet your wife?"

"How do you know I have a wife?"

"Please, Jake. Be serious. It's obvious that you are a man who likes women. Not all men do, you know. Men who like women get married, sooner or later. Nine times out of ten. You can look it up. Besides, you're on the run, and men on the run are running from women, nine times out of ten."

"What's the tenth time?"

"The tenth time is you don't want to know. The tenth time is the witness protection program. So, what's her name?"

"Her name is Frankie."

"Frankie and Johnny! I love that song!"

"They made a movie out of it."

"Of course, they had to! Too good a song to pass up. Pacino, Pfeiffer, and the ode to the VCR."

"I met her in LA. I taught film there and she was a student

in the theater department."

"Naughty you."

"She wasn't in any of my classes."

"Who cares. But go on."

"She had the look. The first time I saw her she was slouched against a wall outside the dressing room of the university's theater, playing with the ends of her hair. She was in between scenes in a play that one of her friends had written, some experimental thing the students were doing as a class assignment. She was still in costume but you could tell she was bored. She had on a black halter top and a long black skirt that was slit on both sides. Her legs had makeup on them to catch the light on stage, and she had the middle panel of the skirt all bunched up in her lap, so all you saw were these long white legs curled out sideways under all that black. She'd kicked off her heels, which had long straps attached to them, and they were lying next to her, one on top of the other, like snakes."

Lucinda nods her head in an encouraging way. "Yep, you see that all the time nowadays," she says. "Mostly in the Hamptons, but sometimes in Prague. So then what happened?"

"I asked her what she was up to and she said about five nine. Then she said that she was bored beyond belief. I asked could I help and she said that depends. I said, 'Depends on what?' and she shot me. Right there, from the floor, she made her fingers into a pistol and pulled the trigger, then turned the gun on herself and pulled it again. Her tongue came out of her mouth and she lurched back in convulsions against the wall, smacking her head hard against the wall when she did that, and then she rubbed her head for about a minute. She wasn't dead, just wounded. I watched her for a while, and she watched the way I was looking at her, and then she said, 'Torment and misery.' I said, 'What did you say?' And then she said it again, 'Torment and misery, that's what I'm going to cause you. You might as well know. That's what I bring all my boyfriends. You can stop now if you want.' I said I'd take my chances and she said, 'Suit yourself. But don't say you weren't warned.'"

"Wow. She's a mindfreak."

"A real pisser."

*

I've known Henry Luce for twenty-three years. We met at a bible school in the Adirondack Mountains of New York. Graduating from high school we had both lacked direction and were made to believe by our concerned parents—his in North Dakota, mine in Vermont—that a year of bible school was just the ticket. He was a tall skinny kid with freckles, chiseled cheek-bones, blue-gray eyes, and hair darker than mine. The combination amused me. I liked him right off. Times have been better for both of us.

The rest of the year we're guys—we don't call or write or email. But once a year we meet in Colorado to ski and to get caught up.

I find Henry seated at a table in the rear of the hotel's restaurant. Beside him is his four year old daughter, Kylie. They sit against a floor to ceiling plate glass window, looking out over the mountain. The big cats are already crawling up the front side of the mountain, three at a time, grooming the intermediate trails. In the morning they'll look like white corrugated cardboard. The light from the cats bounces nervously into the trees on the sides of the slope. It is a cold, clear night, and the stars are shining.

The three of us hug, kiss, and order dinner.

A giant spider plant, menacing in its gigantic clay pot, sways above Henry's head. A long tendril from the spider is in orbit around Henry, propelled by a ceiling fan. Sometimes it lands directly in front of him, so that he looks like he's grown a third striped eye. Every few minutes it bats him in the head, and he swats it into a new orbit.

Ten minutes into our meal, Henry says he doesn't feel anything.

"Try to understand this, Jake," Henry says. "It's like trying to tickle yourself. Or jacking off with mittens. It doesn't work. You see what I'm saying here?"

"I hear what you're saying, Henry."

"I'm not sure you do. My so-called life, what is it, Jake? It's like the white queen stuck forever on the black square. It's like a search for the right word in a language you don't quite understand. That, plus forever."

"Modern times."

"Jake, my wife left me for another woman. The one before that took off with a traffic cop."

"I remember that guy. Basic bowling pin build? Head like a cue tip? Wasn't he the one out there doing Main and Broadway," I say, trying to lighten Henry up.

"He was the one doing Janice," Henry says.

"Another public service. To serve and protect, that's our men in blue."

I remembered Janice. She taught a course at the university called "The Future of Women." She had a wide, cruel mouth, turned down at the corners. She had that way of talking women sometimes get where everything is a question you don't know the answer to, and a slight stutter. Whenever I saw her she seemed to have a glisten of cold cream in the corner of her eye.

"Look Henry, maybe women are not your calling. Maybe you should join the other team?"

Henry takes my hand across the table, knocking over the salt. He flutters his eyes and puckers up.

"I thought you'd never ask," he says.

"Glad you're feeling better," I say, jerking my hand away and straightening the salt. "Look, Henry, I'm sorry, I wish I had better news. But you have to keep this all in context. I mean, the whole world has problems, right? We're not that special. Look at the U.N. lady. Excuse me, Secretary of State. Remember her? Oh, yeah, wait a minute, we dumped those guys, I forgot. Anyway, think about her daily shit. Arafat today. Whatshisface tomorrow, the killjoy guy in Jerusalem. All that, plus the French. You think you've got problems. And now the shrub, little Bush, a heartbeat away from the Presidency."

"Forget all that. Listen to me, to what I'm saying here. Do we actually know anyone with lives we admire, Jake? Whatever happened to Troy?"

Troy was another guy we knew from the bible school. Women adored him. He was from Australia. He had the accent, the deep tan, good bones. The whole time we were there he seemed above it all. He prayed to the trees, befriended small animals and children, improvised imitation Saint Francis prayers at dinner, was a cool dresser, and generally fit in wherever he went. This was not the case with us. The last I heard he was an investment banker living in New York.

"Troy is Standard Issue," I say. "He has an account with a prominent LA plastic surgeon. He's cheating on his mistress. His assets are frozen, like his smile. Forget Troy."

"Easy for you to say."

"He's Industrial Strength, an Infomercial. He's not real, Henry."

"So maybe I'm tired of real," he says.

"What are your choices here, Henry?"

"What's happened to us, Jake? I mean, we were these religious kids. We grew up loving Jesus. We were the original Honk If You Love Jesus kids."

"We skipped Woodstock for God."

"Exactly. We knew where we were headed. Now we don't know shit. How could this happen to us?"

"It's not so bad," I say. "We've just turned into the people we were praying for."

"So who prays for us now?"

"Mother Teresa and Princess Diana. The wrinkled and the dead. The never lovely and the newly dead. The scourge of the world. How the hell should I know? I don't do theology anymore."

"My point, exactly. Maybe we need to get back into it, Jake. Go into religious recovery. Get those sunbeams beaming back our way. Our lives were charmed back then."

"Come on, Henry, everyone's life seems charmed at eighteen. Youth is wasted on the young. This is widely known. Besides, what do you think, we drive up to Schroon Lake, sign back up with God, and everything is going to be restored to us? You get back your wife, I get my kids to stop hating me? Be serious. It doesn't work that way. Those people up there hate us now. We're traitors to the cause. They see us as the enemy. We'd scare the hell out of them, the way we are now. We're failures. They'd hold us up as examples. We'd make all the summer camp sermon illustrations, examples of what Jesus meant by a wasted life. We'd be fodder for the altar call. It's over, Henry. You can't go back again. We're on our own now. God's not interested in us. We killed all that, or they did, or someone did. No one's going to save us now, Henry. We have to save ourselves."

"Then we're in big trouble, pal."

"I know it."

Henry bats the spider plant again, harder this time, so that it swings out over the table, then says, "It's like we're a bad idea of God's, a dream of his that went south."

"Then how do you account for Kylie here?" I ask. Kylie is Henry's four year old daughter from his second marriage. Her ponytail has come loose, and her long brown hair dangles dangerously close to her uneaten soup. She sleeps in one of the restaurant's wooden high chairs, her food untouched on the plate next to her head. Kylie is with us this weekend because Fran changed her mind at the last minute and made Henry take her. Something about Nancy's parents coming in from Connecticut. Nancy is Fran's new love, a conceptual artist from the coast that specializes in Latino religious kitsch and butter.

"She's part of the dream before it went nuts. She's a reminder of what could have been. Jesus, Jake, how should I know? Every time I look at her I see Fran, and weep. One of God's cruel jests."

"I thought we agreed, no theology?"

I liked Fran the best of all Henry's women. A six footer and naturally athletic, she played first base in a fast pitch softball league. She liked to hang out with us on our ski trips. She was a brave liar, but Henry was mad for her. We broke the male-bonding rules for her, against Henry's better judgment. One year Henry couldn't get off work and Fran and I drove up to Vail for the day. There was a Billy Kidd-wear revival going on and we wore the big hats and told the big lies all day, getting high on grass in the lifts and doing lines of coke in the restaurant afterwards, with shots of Jack Daniels. We wound up on Fran's couch at her Denver apartment. This was before she and Henry were married. One of us came to our senses, I can't remember who, and a sort of boozy sanity broke out. We didn't officially do it. But it remained, the sexual tension between us, for four or five years after the two of them were married. It's a sore point with Henry, and each year we work harder at trying not to bring it up.

So I'm relieved when an argument breaks out at the table across from us. Two girls, still dressed in their ski board gear, are waving their arms a lot and slapping the table. One of them has a safety pin clipped to her right eyebrow and white pancake makeup that makes her look like she just walked off the page of Bram Stoker's Dracula. Her friend, a strawberry blonde with the chest and hoarse voice of a cheerleader, is a foot shorter but no less lovely. About seven other girls are watching these two, groaning or applauding as necessary. Every time the Dracula girl, who is seated closet to us, slaps the table, Kylie gives a soft moan and appears ready to wake up. Henry looks like he's getting pissed. The girl gets up from the table and comes over to us.

"I apologize for that. They're giving me shit over my choice in men."

"In that case, they're gonna love this," I say.

"Ignore them. They're twats. My mother has socks smarter than them. My name's Anna, by the way. That's me. Anna-the-moi. But you can call me Clarice."

"Well hello, Clarice," I purr, in my best Hannibal Lecter voice. "This is my friend Henry."

"How you do, Henry," Anna says, sticking out her long arm in front of my face and squeezing Henry's hand.

"So, what's the deal," Henry asks. "You girls going to mud wrestle next?"

"You wish," Anna says.

"What's with her," I say, nodding in the direction of the blonde, who shoots me a disgusting old geezer look.

"Well, it appears that Tiffany's in a snit today," she says. She looks at Tiffany, then at me, and starts twirling like a ballerina. Tiffany rolls her eyes.

"What's with the Clarice thing," I ask.

"I'm in love with her. I feel that I *am* her. That's the whole thing right there. They can't accept that I love Hannibal."

"The man or the movie," Henry asks.

Anna shoots Henry from point blank. Makes her fist into a gun and blows the barrel to cool it off.

"Both, silly," she says.

"Uh huh," Henry says.

"I knew someone who used to do that gun thing," I say. "She is no longer with us. I mean, she is, but not here."

"Whatever," Anna says.

"So what is it that does it for you in the movie," I ask.

"Dunno. I mean, I'm almost eighteen for God's sake, so I ought to know, but the movie just speaks to me on some inner, unexplainable level, and I adore it. I've seen it eight times already, once here, tonight. Before I hooked up with Frog-go." She leers at her friend, does the tongue, which I see now is studded. Around her shapely neck she's wearing a choker made from plastic yellow and black police tape. "It upsets me every time someone criticizes it!"

"They give you major shit, eh?" I ask.

"Exactly. They'll say, 'Oh, it's so gory!' Or, 'It makes no sense, Anna!' But I don't know, it makes perfect sense to me. I went to see “Silence of the Lambs” for the first time in the beginning of January, so I would be ready to see “Hannibal,” and I was just so immediately in love with him. With Lecter, I mean. Dr. Lecter. He's charming, chivalrous, and, at the same time, daring, precise, more or less evil."

"Sure, what's not to like," Henry says.

Anna frowns and gestures to her friends. "You wanna go join 'em pal, you're more than welcome."

She hooks her arm through mine.

"What's your name," she asks me.

"Jake," I say.

"Jake, when Dr. Lecter's letter to Clarice was read, you remember that part? Well, my hands were clasped right here in front of me, just like this."

She grabs my hands and holds them in hers so close to her chest that the hairs on the back of my hand brush her sweater. I do a good job pretending not to notice. Instead I let my eyes take in the jut of her mouth, the provocation in her clear blue eyes, her blooming and ghostly sexuality. Her fingers are long and tapered, with black and silver half-moon nail polish . She is creamy with depraved promise.

"I am just so in awe of him. In so many ways, you can tell he loves Starling. Even the way he speaks and writes to her, almost teasingly. In the museum, on the carousel, I was dazzled. It's startling, you know? I mean, the way he carries himself, the way he *knows* her, what's in her heart. And then she tries to pin his location, you know, to be the good FBI agent, and he brushed her hair, and then when he kissed her in the kitchen, and she slapped the handcuffs on, I cried with Clarice. At the end, she lost her love because of her stupid morals that were programmed into her by herself and her parents. I was in tears."

Kylie stirs herself awake, finally. Anna smiles widely at her, as Henry reaches to lift her out of the high chair. Kylie rests her head on her father's shoulder and closes her eyes again. Henry closes his eyes and hums a lullaby softly into her tiny ear. I want to lean in to listen, but Anna reels me back in.

"Jake? Earth to Jake! I mean, I comment constantly on how I adore this movie, how romantic it is, and how much I wish I could be Clarice Starling. And now all my friends think I either have serious issues, or think I'm weird. 'He's a cannibal! He's old!' They don't see the movie as it was meant to be seen, a romantic story. No, romance is too small a word. Whatever. The only part I found frightening was when they showed the tape of Hannibal attacking that nurse. His ferocity is terrifying."

"Yeah, that part got me too," I say. "Came out of nowhere."

"Yep," Anna says, getting up now and loosening her grip on my hand, finally. "That's love alright."

It's awkward with my hand still on her chest. I look at Henry still humming gently to Kylie, to take my mind off it. But then Anna pulls away, so suddenly that I fall forward into the table, spilling my wine.

"Sorry. Well, gotta go," she says, and sticks out her hand to shake. "See ya! Bye Henry!"

"So long," Henry says. Then he says, deadpan, "Hey, Anna? I'm giving serious thought to eating your friend."

But she's gone, off to the restroom. Henry looks at me with the look he meant for her. Then he gets up, throws some money on the table, and puts on his jacket and gloves.

"I'm going to an AA meeting," he says to me. "Will you get

Kylie to bed?"

*

The streets are filled with college kids out clubbing. Here and there couples walk arm in arm, talking in whispers. The town has changed since we first started coming here sixteen years ago, pre-Nicole and Tom, pre-Darryl Hannah, pre-everyone with money. It's not Aspen but it's in range. I saw Hannah on the back side of the mountain once, years ago. She carved her turns earnestly, a big girl all in white skiing alone on the left edge of one of the more difficult black diamond runs, blonde hair loose and streaming behind her in the wind. I waved, then whistled. She smiled and angled off into the trees, to a huge house hidden in the woods.

I ask Kylie what she wants to do. She shrugs her shoulders and lifts her palms to the sky. "OK, up you go," I say, stooping to lift her onto my shoulders. She squeals with delight, and hangs on to my head, knocking off my Knicks cap.

I'm thinking about Henry, wondering how he'll get us launched into the Fran discussion tonight, all the possible angles he could take into a talk I don't want to have. He's not getting his wife back, I'm thinking. And my kids are probably a lost cause, too. Jade can't forgive me for an affair I had eight years ago with an English teacher from her middle school. Ruined for life, she says.

On the edge of town we turn into one of the shops to get warm. I tell Kylie to duck so she doesn't hit her head, and she giggles as I swing her down and land her gently on the carpeted floor. It's a perfume and pottery store, called simply "Telluride." The woman at the counter smiles, and hands Kylie an oatmeal and raisin cookie. The shop is empty except for the three of us. Kylie looks at me, then at her, and takes the cookie with her tiny starfish hands, nibbling on it gracefully.

"She's lovely," the woman says.

"Wish I could take credit," I say. "I've already screwed up a pair of my own. This one belongs to my friend Henry. I'm just the babysitter."

"Henry is a lucky man."

"You'd have to tell him that. He's lost in grief for his many failures. But I'll tell him you said so."

"Are you looking for something in particular?" she asks. For some reason, her question startles me. I pick up a ceramic lamp from the counter, running my hands down its smooth cool surface.

"Did you make this?" I ask the woman.

"Yes," she says.

I lift Kylie back onto my shoulders. She giggles and grabs my head again, rocking back and forth like a cowgirl on her favorite horse.

"Would you like me to wrap this one," the woman says, reaching across the counter to take the lamp out of my hands. This is the second time a woman has touched my hands tonight, I realize. The wine at dinner is doing its work. I feel sleepy, and strangely calm. It is so quiet in the shop I can hear Kylie's breathing above me, can hear the fan creaking overhead. I don't know what I'm saying.

"Can you ever get them back," I ask.

She looks at me, this woman. She is all in black, a petite woman with streaked gray hair and very tan skin. I realize she doesn't know what I'm talking about.

"Kids, I mean. You know, when they grow up, become teenagers, they learn to hate you, and you figure that's normal, right? But I've done some stuff. I behaved badly. I look at Kylie here and I don't remember it ever being this easy. When my wife and I were together it was never easy. We ran out of things to say to each other. And the kids never forgave us."

The woman doesn't say anything. Kylie is reaching her hands for the fan, stretching out as far as her little body can reach. I feel her spine straighten, sense her muscles straining.

I watch her hands. She has wrapped the lamp in tissue paper, packed it into a box, and sealed the box with masking tape. Her hands are small and lined deeply, the nails clipped and clear.

"These lamps are re-creations of lamps from antiquity. It is a simple design. They have been burning ceaselessly somewhere in the world since before the days of Moses. You'll need some liquid paraffin, like this."

She takes another lamp from the counter and pours in the paraffin until it is three quarters full, then snakes the fiberglass wick around with a small wire, until it sticks out an inch from the top. The lamp is midnight blue. With a small whoosh she strikes a wooden match and the lamp lights. She dims the lights in the shop, sealing us in darkness. Kylie's warm damp breath is on my neck, her baby powder scent in the small space between us. The only sound we hear is the human noise we make, three accidental strangers. Outside, on the street, nothing moves. Silently, the three of us we watch the dancing flame for what appears like hours. My whole life seems to pass right through me into them, into this lamp which now lights our faces as at Halloween.

The woman takes my hand in hers and squeezes lightly. "There is always time," she says. "We are made of time."

We stop back at the restaurant to retrieve my keys. A waitress hands them to me with a smile for Kylie, still on my shoulders. On the way out the door Kylie whispers to me that she has to use the bathroom. We retrace our steps. I stop in the hallway, pondering my choices. It's been a while since I had to do this. Kylie points to the sign with a picture of a woman, and I push open the door.

Inside, facing the sink is Anna. She is hunched over, sobbing. I let Kylie down. Kylie looks over at Anna, who manages a weak smile. Kylie walks up to Anna and, reaching up to her waist, gives her a child's hug. Kylie walks to the last stall and pulls the door closed.

Anna looks straight ahead into the mirror above the sink, acknowledging me with a nod of her head. Standing close behind her now, I see the blonde roots of her jet black hair. She talks to the mirror.

"They left me here. Can you fuckin' believe that? Like I'm bad meat."

I rest my hand on her shoulder. "I'm sorry, Anna. Sometimes people are just cruel. It's pretty brutal, your age. I hated it. Anyway, I couldn't name you a person from high school whose name I even remember."

"Why am I like this," Anna says. She turns and faces me. She has wiped her lipstick off. Her eyes are filled with tears, streaking black lines into her makeup and tracking her lovely face. The yellow police tape lies in pieces on the floor next to her boots. She looks like a cross between a clown and Edward Scissorhands.

"Anna."

"What."

"You're worth three dozen of them. Trust me on this."

I open my arms, and she moves into them. We are the same height. Her forehead gently taps my own. She reaches down and squeezes my hands, gently at first, then harder. She lets go and pulls at the pockets of my jacket, hard. I feel her reaching through the pockets with her long fingers, trying to encircle my waist with the span of her hands. Kylie appears, reaching up her arms to me. Anna bends down to kiss her. We do a group hug.

*

When we reach the hotel Henry is already in bed, snoring. I reach down to turn him over onto his side. Carefully, I dress Kylie in her pajamas. Blue and yellow giraffes now cover her little body. I lift her to my lips and kiss her gently on the forehead. She sleeps on a cot next to her father.

I undress. Emptying the pockets of my jacket I find a small envelope from the hotel. Inside is a key card, identical to the one I received from the reception clerk when I checked in, but with a different room number scrawled at the bottom of the envelope. Anna's key. I carefully place the card back into its envelope, and toss it into the trash. Then I think better of it, retrieve it from the trash and place it on the nightstand next to my car keys.

I brush my teeth, pull on a T shirt and fall into the other double bed, exhausted.

In the morning what I will recall from my dream is this: A woman is standing in the corner of the room, watching. It is a woman I have never known but have seen frequently. She seems within reach of my outstretched hands, but does not move toward me. When she opens her mouth to speak, the words are captured by something dark in the room, and fail to reach my hands, groping for them blindly in the dim light. I watch her mouth for hours. Just before I wake, she is still rehearsing sentences.

MIREILLE

Her name was Mireille Bouchet and there is nothing much I can tell you. It's better to begin with Petal.

It seemed I was living another life inside my daily life when I went with Petal to the Whitney downtown and saw a strange art exhibit: water passing noisily through exposed PVC pipe, filling a large white plastic holding tank mounted overhead. Microphones amplified the humming water; graffiti covered the walls of the museum. Petal posed by the window; it was just before sunset. Below us, the Hudson River glimmered. I missed the shot. The sun had set. Her face was shadowed in the photo, her long pale neck invisible. I deleted the picture without showing her. We walked the Highline, above bars and restaurants long closed, unable to afford the rent, bookstores gobbled up by chains. Impossibly expensive Chanel handbags hung where poetry once sat dusty on a shelf. We passed places that held afterimages of former lovers, a party we attended, someone we owed money to. Returning to Gansevoort, we walked down Greenwich to Jane Street, crossed the West Side Highway and watched the lights of New Jersey blink on. We walked up Christopher Street, passing brownstones whose lit windows created a feeling of both presence and absence. Behind the glass pane the room of course is empty, but someone has left the light on. At night New York is a city of hidden intentions. It was pointless to pose a question to Petal. No one ever answers questions. There was too much between us, which meant there was nothing at all. I watched her enter the small door of a parking garage on Horatio. It is always the same life that is lost, I thought.

Days later I was in France, doing research on the Situationist International. I was interested in tracing the movements of Guy Debord, whom some believed responsible for the student uprising in May 1968 at the Sorbonne, and the wildcat strike that followed. He shunned publicity, and did his best to erase traces of his life. He spent most of his time in cafes, drinking. "Although I have read a lot," he said, "I have drunk even more. I have written much less than most people who write, but I have drunk much more than most people who drink." Debord made a film called "Howls for Sade." It concluded with these words: "Like lost children we live our unfinished lives." Perhaps it is more accurate to say that with these haunting words Debord *failed* to conclude his film, for what followed was twenty-four minutes of silence and a blindingly white screen. The film had vanished. In the most literal sense, "lost children" meant soldiers chosen for impossible missions, the kind no one returns from. But the term evokes an entire sphere of oblivion—what I have lost of myself, the time that has gone, the general evanescence of things. How is it possible to lose one's childhood, to turn one's back on it? Debord mentions nothing of the first twenty years of his life. Lost children come into the world disavowing the childhood they are given, yet one is never lost alone. There is a line in one of his books that fascinated me: *My method will be very simple; I will tell what I have loved.*

I rode a train into Paris. The train rushed too fast to read the name of the town. A woman entered my car and stood by the window, watching.

Mireille slouched beside the door of the train and asked my name. John, I lied. You're a writer, she said. How did you know that, I asked. You lied about your name, she said. We walked Rue Montparnasse, and turned into a side street. At the lower end of Rue d'Odessa a heavy rain began to fall. We took cover in the lobby of the Montparnasse cinema and found seats in the back. At intermission we had no idea what movie was playing. We returned to the street and walked past a Metro grate, the unmistakable whiff of ozone. We hurried to cross the street. At Rue Monge the pavement gave way to hard packed dirt. Puddles of rainwater splashed up, soiling our shoes. A black skyscraper, barely finished, rose menacingly higher as we walked toward it, diminished as we walked away. The headlamp of a car illumined Mireille's face. She was no more than a spot of light without relief, an overexposed photograph. Near the Val-de-Grâce hospital she had taken my arm. It was very late.

A hotel. Its glass door was open. Light came from the lobby. A large dog lay in the middle of the lobby, asleep. The dog's chin rested on its paws above the dirty tile floor. Behind the reception desk a man, quite bald, thumbed the pages of an architecture magazine. I don't remember who led the way. We stepped lightly over the dog, not waking it. Calmly, we walked upstairs. A room covered in shadows, partially lit by a flickering corner lamppost filtered through a filthy curtain. There was a small table lamp and I lit it. I drew the curtain. She asked me to undress and then she undressed herself. Her wrists were small and graceful. She confided in me, hesitating in places, but not stopping, the way the truest encounters can take place between two people who know nothing of each other. A clock in the room chimed each half hour. The dog barked once, below. I felt as if I were outside Paris. Before daybreak, the sound of horse hooves clip clopped on the dark street.

Many years later, walking near the Val-de-Grâce hospital, I tried to find the hotel. I hadn't written the name or even the address in my notebook, in that way we fail to record the most intimate details of our lives for fear that once recorded, fixed on paper, they will never be ours.

YOUTH

I ran away with a girl one summer. We stole money from our parents and stuffed our things into a large backpack. Jacqueline had two pairs of jeans, a thin leather jacket, bras, her pairs of red espadrilles, assorted oversized sweaters, and toiletries. I put some shirts, pants, and underwear in the backpack with a couple of first editions from my father's library that I hoped to sell.

We made it to London where it rained for two weeks. Our room was close to the train station. The room had a sickly sweet smell that clung to our clothes and seemed embedded in the pores of our skin. The smell must have come from the drain, or the nearby kitchen, or the rotting green carpet. Each morning we went for long walks in Hyde Park to escape the smell, but the rain would drive us into department stores or movie theatres, where we watched looping newsreels and the feature movie. It didn't matter that the same movie repeated night after night.

One afternoon in the London Underground, at the Charing Cross station we had our pictures taken in a PhotoMat. We posed with our faces close together. I kept the picture as a souvenir. Jacqueline's face is in the foreground, and mine is set back slightly, cut off by the edge of the photo, so that my right ear is missing.

The money we had stolen didn't go far and the first editions brought a pittance. At night we teamed up to pick the pockets of tourists in Trafalgar Square. Jacqueline got a job cleaning an office building. She went through the trash looking for anything that would help us make money. We were able to blackmail some poor bastard who had stupidly thrown into the trash a letter from his mistress.

In a public house not far from the international youth hostel on Oxford Street, a man sat down at our table without saying hello. He was of average height and quite fat, round face, bald in front and on top, and he wore tortoise shell glasses. His childlike hands contrasted with his substantial build. A cigarette dangled from his mouth and ash had dropped onto the lapels of his tweed jacket. He said his name was Renchfort. He had heard about our predicament and wanted to help. I knew he was lying, as we had no friends who would tell him such a thing. I told him to go to hell. He insisted that he meant no harm, and that he wanted only to be of service. He swallowed his smile when I called him a pervert and told him to try a different hostel. But Jacqueline pulled his unlit cigarette from his mouth and asked him for a light. He slid a thin blue envelope across the small table. Jacqueline took the envelope and excused herself. In the bathroom she opened the envelope and found a £100 bank note and an address, written in a shaky hand. Jacqueline returned from the loo. She swept the ash from Renchfort's lapels and slapped his face. No, she said. Not there. We would return to our hotel room which smelled of rotten carpet and filthy water, or not at all. I was paid an additional £100 to watch.

After the PhotoMat flashed our picture that afternoon in the London Underground we couldn't stop laughing, and Jacqueline wanted to stay seated on my knees for a long time. We kissed, long hungry kisses, and didn't feel like leaving. Much later, I found the picture in an old suitcase of letters, and I was struck by the innocence of our faces. We inspired trust in people. We had no real qualities, except for the one youth gives to everyone for a brief time, like a vague promise that will never come true.

ACKNOWLEDGEMENTS

Grateful acknowledgement is made to the following magazines, where these stories were first published: *Story Quarterly, Mississippi Review, Westchester Review, elimae, Word Riot, Red Fez, Wigleaf, Necessary Fiction, Bluestem, Fogged Clarity, Short Story America, Moon Milk Review, Houston Literary Review, Metazen, Lit n Image, Enterzone, Intertext, Corium, Twelve Stories, U City Review, FRiGG, Pure Slush Press, Maine Review,* and *The Good Men Project.*

I'm grateful to Frederick Barthelme, who published many of my early stories at *Mississippi Review*, then brought me on board as an associate editor, and to Robert Fogarty at *Antioch Review*, who recruited me to work for a time as an assistant fiction editor under the guidance of Nolan Miller. If Nolan taught me how to read and edit fiction, Barthelme taught me to write; I'm grateful for his friendship, and for the cover design of many of my books.

Sara Lippmann was first reader for many of these stories. Sara once told me that the relationship between a writer and a first reader is a particular and peculiar kind of love, one attentive to language in its every word, sentence, gestures, feints, and false starts. I want to thank Mary Grimm (in whose seminar I wrote the first sentences of the title story of this collection), as well as early readers of these stories and friends along the way, including Frederick Barthelme, James Robison, Ann Beattie, Meg Wolitzer, Sam Rasnake, Bill Yarrow, Kim Chinquee, James Thomas, Rick Moody, Morgan Harlowe, Kate Rutter, Meg Tuite, Pari Berk, Kimberlee Hynes Smith, Kerry

Langan, Heather Cox, Ellen Parker, Kathy Fish, Rae Bryant, Matt Potter, Kate Hill Cantrill, Jules Archer, Danielle Grilli, Sarah Herrington, Thom Butler (who designed my website), as well as all of my editors, whose reading and guidance and careful edits have been invaluable in my work through the years, and T.C. Boyle, whose brief teaching career at Lakeland High School taught me that another way was possible, and that it was permissible to write fiction. Special thanks to Joelle Fraser, and to Nick Courtright, Kyle McCord, and Ronaldo Alves, Evan Courtright, and Erin Larson at Atmosphere Press.

I'm grateful to my family: Giovanni and Rose, Flora and Federico, Arnold and Rosalie, Tommy, Jeanne, Bob, and Doug, Jae and Vinny, Resea and Ashton, Gavin and Zachary, and Søren, the philosopher poodle.

Years ago, I worked as an assistant fiction editor at *Antioch Review* in the village of Yellow Springs, Ohio. It was there that I received my education in "aesthetic preference." You cannot be an editor without acknowledging this thing called aesthetic preference, but no one seems able to slap a saddle on this rough beast. Maybe the best description is the one Veronica Geng cites from George Orwell: "Gut reaction rationalized afterward." Geng says that you might say "reasoned" or "tested" instead of "rationalized," but clearly the process seems to work in only one direction. As Geng puts it, "Reason first, gut reaction afterward is a recipe for a bar fight." As the philosopher David Hume once said, "the principles of art are grounded in experience, not in reason."

It was at Antioch that I learned to trust my gut reaction to stories that I read, and I read a lot of them. The best times were when I would read and discuss them with Gabrielle. She was, like me, an east coast Italian American with attitude, a bit lost in Ohio but writing her way through it. I recall Gabrielle in her Antioch commencement costume: an elegant black cocktail dress that showed off her hairy armpits to perfection, and her string of pearls. One night she surprised me by reading me pages from her journal, a journal she had showed no one else in this world, the entry she had written days before, the week she came out and the day she interviewed Ani DeFranco and knew she was in love.

I'd see Gabrielle once a week in the cramped office of the *Antioch Review*, which in those days was housed in a stale upper room in the library. The magazine had a good reputation. Thousands of hopeful writers sent their short stories to a post office box downtown. Gabrielle logged them in. The managing editor scanned the pile for names she recognized—writers we'd published previously, like T.C. Boyle, James Purdy, Gordon Lish—and for "agented work." The rest was slush. The slush was stood upright in two large boxes in the far corner of the magazine's one room office. There it would sit until one of the "readers" took home a pile. Gabrielle and I were readers.

One day I read a story that knocked me out. The author had no credits. Straight from the slush, wrapped in a plain brown envelope, the story was about two lonely and alienated teens who are surprised one morning to find each other. A story I'd heard a thousand times. But it was the way the story was told—full of feeling, accurate, without a trace of condescension, right as rain. It filled the heart. I called Gabrielle.

The office was closed. We met at the park. I read the story out loud. Toward the end, the boy and girl meet at the high school, at first light. There is the sound of a lawn mower in the middle distance, and the smell of fresh cut grass. They are seated in silence on the steps of the school. The girl raises her shirt.

I finished reading. There was silence for the space of a

minute. Then Gabrielle kissed me and told me she wanted to take off her shirt. Then she did. We laughed. "Shirt raising fiction," she said. She kissed me.

That was a gut reaction.

*

Around the same time, I was getting to know Nolan Miller. Nolan lived in the village and was a longtime editor of the *Antioch Review*. He was the author of four novels (*Sarah Belle Luella Mae; A Moth of Time; The Merry Innocents; Why I Am So Beat*) and in 1957 edited the widely circulated *New Campus Writing* which contained the best of creative writing from America's campuses. His 1959 short story "A New Life" was included in the O. Henry Prize Awards. He came to Antioch College in 1946 from a career as novelist and high school teacher to become a professor of literature in the English department. He taught many wonderful students in his years at Antioch, including the poet Mark Strand (who insisted that Nolan Miller was the best teacher that he ever had), and TV pioneer Rod Serling, of *Twilight Zone* fame. Once hailed as "the next Hemingway," by the time I knew him he was long retired. He lived quietly with his brother Richard, a wonderful painter and sculptor, in a house the brothers had designed for—well, two artists. Each brother had his own identical space: bedroom, office, workshop, library, bath, with a common living room and kitchen. The house was set back from the road and backed up against Glen Helen. It blended perfectly with its surroundings, a wooded retreat from the world.

Richard was deaf. He lost his hearing as a result of a childhood illness. Nolan was legally blind. So here they were in the woods of Yellow Springs: two bachelor brothers in their late eighties, taking care of each other and still practicing their craft. Visits to the Miller home were inspiring.

Nolan taught me to read. Specifically, he showed me how to read fiction, an ongoing tutorial, one story at a time. We used *Antioch Review* submissions as raw material. In his home laboratory, seated in his living room, he sat close by, nearly on top of me, as I read stories that I thought were possibilities for publication. He would listen quietly—no longer sighted, his ear was keenly attuned to the musicality of stories, the right words in the right order. Every now and then he would stop me. I then became a one-person recipient of the "Nolan School" of literary criticism. He disliked "talky" stories, which he called "reportage" rather than stories. "Show don't tell," he advised the invisible authors, at home somewhere in the world, awaiting our literary evaluation of the merits of these manuscripts they had posted in all those manila envelopes, long weeks ago. It felt like an awesome responsibility, to read these stories to Nolan, and he gave each one the weight they deserved. There was no hurry.

What did he want in a story? He wanted something made up. He wanted to be surprised, and infused with a sense of wonder. He wanted dramatic pace, for we as readers to be involuntarily asking "And then? And then?" He admired stories that were told confidently, with authorial precision and lack of pretense. He disliked "show offs." (He bolted John Updike to the wall with this category.) He once wrote, "The writer must work with a mind ever open, ever free, ever alert." His favorite authors were Wordsworth, Proust, Joyce and D.H. Lawrence. Chekov and Carver, sure. I introduced him to Mary Grimm at the Winds Café in Yellow Springs, and he fell in love (with her work, too). Experimental writing? Nonsense, he said, every story is an experiment. Most of all, he liked a story that engaged his imagination, treated its characters fairly, no matter how unlikable, and required that a story be honest. No tricks, please. He preached the truth in fiction.

Soon enough he was listening to my stories. He helped me immeasurably. When he was disappointed, my heart sank.

When he was delighted, I felt as if I'd lifted off the earth. "You Look Different" (which I had originally published with the title, "The Way You Live Now") was the first of my stories to win Nolan's approval and support. The rest followed from there.

Nolan died a few months shy of his one hundredth birthday. His obituary included these words: "Miller was an engaging and provocative conversationalist who could turn heads in a restaurant with a comment and who challenged students to shape their own education for their own ends, to write for their own pleasure and the discerning few rather than for commercial gain and to expand their taste for music, art and fine literature."

Richard continued to live for a time in the house by the glen in Yellow Springs. When Nolan died, Richard wrote:

"None among my brother's many students during his years of teaching could have been more enriched by his knowledge and understanding than I was throughout our lives together. His patience and care in helping me to understand the world around me followed and reinforced the moral and intellectual learning I owe to my mother and father. He has bequeathed me a gift of beautiful memories. I will miss him."

I never intended to write fiction, or poetry either, for that matter. What I wanted to do was teach philosophy. I got to do that for a number of years (and still do), but in the early 1990s I began to feel restless. I wanted to write without footnotes. I wanted to make stuff up. What I discovered was that "making stuff up" did not happen in a world devoid of history. And that this includes the long history of writers. Because at the time I was an avid reader of *The New Yorker* magazine, as a baby writer I began to try to mimic writers whom I admired. For me, these were easy to identify. Donald Barthelme and his younger brother Frederick, Ann Beattie, Mary Robison, Andrea Lee, James Salter, John Ashbery, Mark Strand, Elizabeth Bishop, Joy Williams, Raymond Carver, Richard Ford, James Robison, Mavis Gallant, Tobias Wolff, Mary Karr, Joan Didion, William Trever, Amy Hempel, Mary Grimm, John Updike, and of course, John Cheever.

As children, we mimic. It is the way we learn. As we grow older, we learn to differentiate from those we consider "models." As a philosophy professor I can tell you to go read René Girard and Jacques Lacan to explain the theories of "mimetic desire" and "mirroring," but it's easiest to say that the writers listed above had a profound effect on me, and reading through these collected stories, I can trace the many ways they influenced me, and continue to do so.

Much later, I read the French writer Patrick Modiano. I discovered Modiano had something of an obsession with a shadowy figure in post-war France, Guy Debord, an obsession I shared. In his book, *La Societe´ du Spectacle*, Debord observes that where modern conditions of production prevail, life is presented as an immense accumulation of spectacles. The "integrated spectacle" has spread itself to the point where it now permeates all reality, and has five defining features: incessant technological renewal, integration of state and economy, generalized secrecy, unanswerable lies, and the illusion of being "an eternal present," leading to a world without memory, where images flow and merge, like reflections on the water. When I read Modiano, after reading Debord, I came to understand that living in the integrated spectacle is like living inside a Modiano novel, take your pick: *In the Café of Lost Youth* (inspired in part by the photographs of Debord's circle taken by Ed van der Elksen), *The Black Notebook, Sundays in August, Sleep of Memory*. Entering Modiano, as Ann Beattie says, "we are adrift in a world of cosmic mystery which does not exist to be solved, only compounded." As Debord puts it, "With consummate skill the spectacle organises ignorance of what is about to happen and, immediately afterwards, the forgetting of whatever has nevertheless been understood."

The spectacle is a system of domination so total that in order to critique it is necessary to use the spectacle's own language against it in a general refusal. This requires not only skill but a keen sense of the ironic, and a fondness for play. Like Isadore Ducasse, whose *Maldoror* was published under the name Lautréamont, Debord is self-invented. His writing mixes genres, delights in parody and paradox, makes sudden transitions, and defies conventional notions of authorship and plagiarism. Like Lautréamont, Debord cannibalized his own writing as well as that of others. Lautréamont appropriated entire sections of Chenu's *Encyclopedia of Natural History*, borrowing and reworking passages from sources as various as Homer, the Bible, Dante, Shakespeare, and Baudelaire. Debord made no attempt to hide the "traces" of those whose work he reinscribed, refusing to deploy extensive quotations to "lend authority" to a particular argument. Like Lautréamont, he writes from the standpoint of himself. As his says in *Panegyric*:

> Quotations are useful in periods of ignorance or obscurantist beliefs. Allusions, without quotation marks, to other texts known to be very famous, as in classical Chinese poetry, Shakespeare, or Lautréamont, should be reserved for times richer in minds capable of reorganizing the original phrase and the distance its new application has introduced.

My obsession with Debord and Modiano led me to write "Styoppa," "Mireille," and "Youth," three late stories in this collection. Like Debord and Modiano, I have not troubled to hide influences or "traces" of their work. The ending of "Youth"—itself a story about theft, is lifted entirely from a

Modiano novel; parts of “Mireille” draw on stories from Debord’s life and writing; and Styoppa is actually a character in a Modiano story, about a man without an identity.

Now that I am back living in Westchester County, New York, within thirteen miles of where I was born, in Yonkers, overlooking the Hudson River, it seems important to thank John Cheever, who for many years lived just up Route 9A on Cedar Lane, and maybe Westchester itself, where the story really begins.

ABOUT ATMOSPHERE PRESS

Atmosphere Press is an independent, full-service publisher for excellent books in all genres and for all audiences. Learn more about what we do at atmospherepress.com.

We encourage you to check out some of Atmosphere's latest releases, which are available at Amazon.com and via order from your local bookstore:

Twisted Silver Spoons, a novel by Karen M. Wicks
Queen of Crows, a novel by S.L. Wilton
The Summer Festival is Murder, a novel by Jill M. Lyon
The Past We Step Into, stories by Richard Scharine
The Museum of an Extinct Race, a novel by Jonathan Hale Rosen
Swimming with the Angels, a novel by Colin Kersey
Island of Dead Gods, a novel by Verena Mahlow
Cloakers, a novel by Alexandra Lapointe
Twins Daze, a novel by Jerry Petersen
Embargo on Hope, a novel by Justin Doyle
Abaddon Illusion, a novel by Lindsey Bakken
Blackland: A Utopian Novel, by Richard A. Jones
The Jesus Nut, a novel by John Prather
The Embers of Tradition, a novel by Chukwudum Okeke
Saints and Martyrs: A Novel, by Aaron Roe
When I Am Ashes, a novel by Amber Rose

ABOUT THE AUTHOR

Gary Percesepe is the author of eleven books, including *Gaslight Opera* and *Light Turnout*, two poetry collections published in 2021. He is Associate Editor at *New World Writing*. Prior to that, he was an assistant fiction editor at *Antioch Review*. He resides in White Plains, New York, and teaches philosophy at Fordham University in the Bronx.

CPSIA information can be obtained
at www.ICGtesting.com
Printed in the USA
LVHW052347021021
699331LV00005B/10